ONE

THE BEST THING about the rain was that it blended with Rachael LeBlanc's grieving tears. Today was shaping up to be one of the most difficult days of her life. But it also would be the day she was to meet Aunt Mary Opal.

That morning, she had left her mother's bedside in Charlotte and driven home to Atlanta, a trip that took longer than normal because sporadic torrential downpours required her to stop every thirty to forty-five minutes. Caring for her mother over the previous six months had taken a toll, she thought, as she sat in her car that was stopped alongside the road and being drenched by rain. Rachael's hope that the cancer would go into remission had faded, and she had stopped wishing for anything other than for the pain to stop. She played her mother's words over and over again in her head: "Go on home, honey. You need some time to be with Jake, and I'll be just fine."

She knew that wasn't true. Her mother would never be just fine. The only things Rachael needed right then were to feel Jake's arms around her and to be in a safe place to let her tears flow. As she rounded the corner onto Rosedale Road, the rain had stopped, and the anticipation of being home and seeing Jake poured relief into the empty space in her heart, which had been occupied by a repetitive pattern of grief and numbness for the past six months. But the relief vanished when she turned into the driveway, which was empty. Jake's car was not there.

Knowing that she was only going to be home for a couple of nights, Rachael only had a small overnight bag with her. She picked up the bag, closed the top of her orange Mini Cooper convertible, and made her way through the wooden gate toward the front door. What was normally a carefully manicured lawn was overgrown with weeds.

A yellow sticky note jutted out from the refrigerator door. *Had to go do a show in Augusta. See ya when I get back. Teri's having a dinner party and wants you to join them . . . have fun.*

"Damn it, Jake." All of the times that Rachael wanted Jake to be there and he hadn't been rushed through her like wind in a tunnel. She walked through the house and saw everything that was left for her to take care of—dirty dishes, overflowing trash cans, an unmade bed, and filthy bathrooms. Rachael's need to cry was gone, and she was filled with anger. "Fuck you, Jake." She opened the wine cooler to find it empty. That explained all the empty bottles on the kitchen counter, right next to two wine glasses.

Jake's gold and platinum records lined the center hall all the way to the ceiling. As she walked down the hallway, she stopped and stared at his latest platinum record and remembered that she had not been with Jake at the celebration.

"I wonder if the pool is empty like the wine rack?" She left her clothes trailing down the hallway, dropping one piece at a time. Washing the doubt, mistrust, and her mother's illness off of her was the only thing on her mind. She dove headfirst into the pool, feeling the cool water rush over her long, slender, tattoo-covered body. "Thank God something's right." She swam one lap after another until her stomach told her it was time to eat and her mind said it was time for a drink. The water had done exactly what Rachael was hoping for—it washed all her grief and anger away. A dinner party would be the perfect boost she desperately needed.

Rachael and Jake had met Teri, a studio musician and singer from Australia, in New Orleans when Jake performed at the House of Blues. Rachael helped Teri get a lease for the house across the street while their neighbor was out of the country. The arrangement had been perfect for Jake. He had needed a studio musician and singer for his next album.

"Teri, I'm coming over," Rachael said over the phone. "Can I bring anything?"

"Just a smile."

That was the perfect response, because that was all Rachael was wearing at the moment. After slipping into oversized sweatpants and a tank top that failed to cover much of the tattoos on her torso, she made her way across the street, wine glass in hand. As she entered the dining room, everyone turned to say hello. Teri hugged her and ran her finger down Rachael's right arm. "New tattoo?"

"Mmm, it's about three months old."

"Nice." Teri flipped her dark hair over her right shoulder as she turned to her guests. "Hey everyone, this is Rachael, Jake LeBlanc's wife. They live across the street." Her voice clearly emphasized *Jake LeBlanc*. At that, all but one of six guests began singing Jake's latest hit, "Get To It."

Just to be polite, Rachael joined them in singing a few words. The only person who didn't sing had stepped back from the high-energy environment, wine glass in hand, and had leaned against the dark rosewood cabinets. A giggle curled up and out of the white-haired woman's smile. Rachael moved across the room to stand next to the older woman as the others continued to sing the entire first verse. She needed to stand next to the only person in the room who wasn't singing. Rachael leaned in to whisper in the older woman's ear. "Hi, I'm Rachael."

"Call me Aunt Mary Opal. That's what all the young people call me." Rachael noticed the older woman's eyes briefly land on her trail of tattoos and short bleached hair. The woman surprised Rachael by wrinkling up her nose and winking at her.

"I assume you don't know who my husband is," said Rachael.

"He must be a singer, but his songs are not on my record player, unless he sang with Frank Sinatra," Aunt Mary Opal laughed. "Your glass is empty, Rachael. Let's fix that."

Rachael wrapped her arm around Aunt Mary Opal and pulled her closer. "I like the way you think. A delicious cabernet is the best offer I've had all day. I think we're going to be fast friends."

Rachael breathed in the rich scent of spices coming from the kitchen and remembered that she had forgotten to eat so far that day. She reached out and touched a deep-orange glass vase filled with long-stemmed yellow roses. Thoughts of missing Jake filled her for a brief moment. He brought her a yellow rose on every date, a gesture that stopped after they were married.

"Oh my, that dinner smells delicious," Aunt Mary Opal said, breaking into Rachael's memory. Rachael was sure the older woman had noticed her shift from smiling to sadness. "I'm so hungry I could eat a horse."

Rachael smiled as her attention moved back to Aunt Mary Opal. "I think I could eat a pig, and I don't even eat pork."

WHEN DINNER WAS SERVED, Rachael and Aunt Mary Opal took two seats at the end of the table. Aunt Mary Opal was seated directly under a light that highlighted her stark, white hair, as well as a slight bald spot on the top of her head. Ignoring the bald spot, Rachael leaned down and whispered, "Your hair is beautiful."

Aunt Mary Opal seemed delighted. "It's the same color as yours, Rachael."

"Yes, but mine is bleached and from a bottle."

Aunt Mary Opal laughed out loud and whispered back, "I get mine washed and back-combed every Thursday morning at nine. Have for as long as I can remember." She then reached out and placed her hand on Rachael's forearm, shifting the conversation. "Do you have a story for each of your tattoos?"

Rachael nearly choked as she sipped on her wine. "As a matter of fact, I do. I look forward to sharing them with you."

The dining room filled with the aroma of red curry

and seafood as Teri placed each of the dishes on the table. Rachael knew that with Teri's cooking, there would no shortage of flavor and spices. Even the sautéed bok choy was laced with bright red peppers. Rachael ate around the peppers and noticed that Aunt Mary Opal didn't hesitate to eat all of the spicy food. "I don't know how you can eat those peppers," she said.

Aunt Mary Opal wiped her upper lip with a napkin. "The hotter, the better."

After clearing the table, Teri placed a homemade chocolate cake and bottles of wine in the center. Then she leaned back, letting her long hair drape over the back of the chair as she coated her lips with dark red lipstick. They smiled at each other, and Rachael noticed a frown on Aunt Mary Opal's face. Teri's guests were getting louder and more intoxicated.

"Let's go sit on the porch swing," Rachael said abruptly. She moved the dessert plates aside and picked up the bottle of Mile Post Trio that Teri had placed right in front of her.

"Good idea," Aunt Mary Opal said with a grin and a wrinkle of her nose. "Let's sneak out."

Rachael tucked the Malbec under her arm and made her way to the wraparound front porch. Aunt Mary Opal was trying not to attract attention as she hung her purse on her arm and followed. "Whew!" she said in a high-pitched voice as soon as the door closed behind them. We made it! I thought for sure one of those people would spot us and try to come out here too."

They sat on the wooden swing, rocking back and forth, letting their laughter fill the humid night.

"How do you know Teri?" Rachael poured the wine,

careful not to spill any on Aunt Mary Opal's white linen pants.

"I met Teri at the grocery store about five months ago." Aunt Mary Opal's feet couldn't reach the floor.

Rachael pushed the swing back and forth with her bare feet. "That was right after she moved here."

"Yes, I think that's right. I was hoping to meet her boyfriend tonight, but he had to go out of town."

"Out of town?" Rachael's radar of mistrust came up for her. "I didn't know she had a boyfriend. Who is he?"

"Oh, I don't know, but I'm sure he's handsome. If I find out, I'll let you know." Aunt Mary Opal gently jabbed Rachael in the side with her elbow and wrinkled her nose again.

Rachael pushed her suspicions aside. "Enough about Teri's boyfriend. Tell me about you. Are you married?"

"Not anymore. I met Harold in DC at a dinner for my father in 1951. He was so handsome, and so was his identical twin brother." Aunt Mary Opal shrugged her shoulders and laughed. "Once we were married, it was like I had two husbands. They looked exactly alike. Most people couldn't tell them apart, but I could. Wayne was so gentle and gay. And Harold, my husband, well, he wasn't gentle or gay." Aunt Mary Opal's smile faded.

"Is Harold still living?" Rachael slapped her thigh, missing the mosquito that had landed.

Aunt Mary Opal fanned her face with a piece of paper she had pulled out of her purse. "No, he died just over two years ago. Cancer."

As they continued swinging back and forth, the sounds from inside the house increased. When the music was turned up, Rachael and Aunt Mary Opal had to increase their volume of conversation just to hear each other, although they were sitting side by side.

Aunt Mary Opal went on to describe her life with Harold and their three daughters. "My favorite places were Rome and New York. Oh my, how I loved the beautiful flowers in Rome. It was as if everywhere you went there were gardens full of color. We had an apartment just around the corner from our favorite florist. I bought fresh flowers almost every day."

Rachael looked back over her shoulder to her own front yard, noticing that there were no flowers in the garden. She sensed that Aunt Mary Opal was once again taking note of her sadness.

"Every morning, I walked out my door to find bright, crimson-red flowers surrounded by ivy," Aunt Mary Opal continued. "Sometimes pink chrysanthemums and brilliant orange poppies were there too."

Rachael snapped out of focusing on her dismal yard and brought her attention back to the conversation. "You must have loved that time in Rome. Do you have a garden at your home here in Atlanta?"

Giggling, Aunt Mary Opal waved her hand in the air and changed the subject. "Tell me about you, Rachael. Teri tells me you're an interior designer."

"Yes, but I haven't worked much this year." Rachael's faced flushed as she tucked her head down. "I've been with my mother for the past six months. She has ovarian cancer, and I've been taking care of her. It doesn't look good." She started to say something else but stopped when her voice cracked.

"I'm a cancer survivor." Aunt Mary Opal took both of Rachael's hands in hers. "She can be too."

They shared a long, quiet moment, and then Rachael

changed the subject. "My dad was a general in the Air Force, and we stayed in Rome for a while. I was young, so I don't remember much about it. Was Harold in the Air Force?"

Aunt Mary Opal waved her hands in the air. "Oh, no, no, no. Harold was in the CIA. Even I had my own alias and CIA number. But I can't tell you more, or I might have to kill you." She laughed out loud, and Rachael joined in. "You know, back then everyone did what they had to do to help out. It's just not that way now. I think the Vietnam debacle killed the trust of the people. Not me. If they call me to help, I'll jump right in. And no one would ever expect top secret CIA documents being passed by a white-haired old woman. Plus, I can keep a secret." She leaned forward, wrinkled her nose, and winked, as she had done numerous times earlier in the evening.

Rachael brushed aside the CIA comments, thinking that it seemed outlandish. "I hope your garden is loaded with flowers."

"I wish it were. I try to keep up with it, but these old hands are so arthritic that I don't even plant flowers in my planters near my door. And my girls would never think of bringing flowers for those old pots." Aunt Mary Opal shook her head.

"Where do you live?"

"I live in Maple Hills. Do you know where that is?" Aunt Mary Opal pointed northwest.

"I sure do. In fact, my mother and I had dinner there about a year ago with a retired general who knew my dad—General Johnston, do you know him?"

"Of course I do. He built a house right next to my home."

"Which house are you in?" Rachael was surprised at the coincidence.

"The one right behind his. I've been there for thirty-five years." Her pride came through as she held her shoulders up and pushed her chin just a little further forward.

Rachael took Aunt Mary Opal's hand in hers. "Well then, maybe I'll have to drop off some flowers to go in your planters."

"Oh, you don't have to do that. I just close my eyes when I walk by them so I don't notice. But now, if you're in the neighborhood, you'll need to stop by and have a cup of coffee with me. Or something a little stronger." Aunt Mary Opal patted Rachael's leg. "Some people don't like drop-in guests, but I do. If I don't want to answer the door, I don't have to. Sometimes I sneak to the door and look through the peephole to see if I want company. Where do you live, Rachael?"

Rachael swatted another mosquito from her face and pointed directly across the street to the small cottage-style bungalow with the bright red door. "Right there. Jake and I have been there for almost four years. And, speaking of home, I'm exhausted. Could I have your phone number, so if I'm in the neighborhood, I can at least call before I knock on your door?"

After exchanging numbers, they both walked to the street without telling Teri good night. Judging by the sounds coming from the house, no one would remember much the next day. Just as Rachael opened her front door, she turned to see Aunt Mary Opal still standing in the street, staring back at her. From their vantage points, the sound of Teri's guests had faded, and the only sound was the hum of the MARTA train as it moved down the track, a block from where Aunt Mary Opal stood. They both smiled and waved to each other.

NORMALLY, after that much wine at dinner, Rachael would have slept in, but that morning, she woke up excited to surprise her new friend by planting purple, orange, and red flowers outside her door. Rachael made a mental note, from their conversation on the porch, that every Thursday at nine o'clock in the morning, Aunt Mary Opal had her hair washed and back-combed, and that day was Thursday. If she hurried, she could get the flowers, plant them, and be on her way before Aunt Mary Opal got home.

The morning air was less humid, and the wind rushed through Rachael's hair as she raced in her Mini Cooper to Pike's Nursery, where she found red-orange geraniums and miniature red roses.

Arriving at Aunt Mary Opal's house, she noticed large black urns next to the side door. They were full of drooping, dead leaves, and there was no sign of any living plant. The soil was hard, and it took some effort with her hand shovel just to get it ready to plant new flowers. Rachael had planted the last of the flowers in cast-iron pots and was squatted down to pick up all the soil that had overflowed onto the concrete drive when she became aware that a large SUV had turned into the driveway. Still squatting, she peeked around the front of her car. "Who was that in such a large SUV?" She stood up in a protective stance, towering over her car.

With caution, Aunt Mary Opal stopped her Ford Explorer when she saw the orange convertible in the driveway. Rachael realized she was bent over and not visible to Aunt Mary Opal. Slowly she stood, and the Sun fell on her hair and tattoos. Aunt Mary Opal, wearing Nike walking shoes and bright pink sweatpants and with a black purse hung over her arm, burst into laughter and hopped down to the driveway. "Well, good morning! What a wonderful surprise! And what beautiful flowers!"

They both laughed as they saw the humor in the moment, Rachael towering over the Mini and Aunt Mary Opal having to hop down from her SUV.

"Good morning! I was trying to finish before you got home."

Aunt Mary Opal grabbed Rachael's hand and burst into a giggle. "My, what have I done to deserve this?"

"Last night, when you were describing the flowers in Rome, you sounded so happy. I wanted you to have some color at your door. So, there they are!" She stretched out her arm to present the filled urns.

"Oh my, you shouldn't have! Come in and have a cup of coffee," said Aunt Mary Opal as she unlocked the door.

"I don't want to impose, I really just wanted to surprise you." Rachael had been taught that a drop-in guest could quickly become an unwelcome one, even though Aunt Mary Opal had mentioned she liked people to stop by.

"Don't be silly, please come in. I was just going to put on a pot of coffee. I like mine strong, blonde, and sweet." Aunt Mary Opal threw her head back and, in a high-pitched voice, said "Whew!" as she danced in a circle, tickled at herself for making what she considered a risqué joke about coffee.

As they stepped inside, Rachael gasped, then quickly recovered. Almost every inch of Aunt Mary Opal's home was covered with richly appointed antiques and art. The floors, tabletops, and walls were stacked with beautiful paintings, vases, rugs, and dishes. "Damn, I'm glad I didn't get her a vase of flowers," she thought.

"Aunt Mary Opal, your home is beautiful. You have such a nice collection of . . ." she hesitated.

"I know. I have thirty-five years of collecting in here," Aunt Mary Opal said, laughing. "My husband loved buying me things. I have an antique shop in downtown Ellijay that's just full of antiques. But it seems like it's just a storage place, because I've quit going there to open the store."

After the stainless percolator was filled with water and the steam rose, the aroma of coffee filled the kitchen. Rachael rubbed her hand across the white marble top on the small kitchen table where it was worn at each place setting. "I bet you have a thousand stories to tell from around this table."

"You bet I do. *Some* of them I can tell you." Aunt Mary Opal pulled her shoulders up and winked at Rachael as if to suggest that her stories were secrets.

"Well, when you're ready to tell me those stories, I'm ready to listen." In a few minutes, their cups were filled with strong, blonde, sweet coffee.

Aunt Mary Opal walked across the kitchen to the sideboard, where she picked up a magazine and placed it in front of Rachael. "After I met you last night, I remembered an article in *Atlanta* magazine about you and that beautiful renovation you did next door to the governor's mansion."

Rachael shrugged off the compliment and turned the

magazine facedown. "I couldn't believe they did that article. It was nothing, really."

"Rachael, I want to know how you decided to become an interior designer." Aunt Mary Opal sat in a petite wooden chair with wicker backing.

"I guess it just sort of chose me. It was always an easy thing for me. I think of it more as getting inside people's heads and learning about what makes them happy. Once I know what makes people happy, designing is easy." Rachael shrugged her shoulders and looked out through the adjoining room at all of the collections.

"After seeing my house, you must think it's a mess inside my head." Aunt Mary Opal laughed.

"No, I wouldn't say it's a mess. I'd just say it shows a lot of experience." Rachael shared in the laughter.

They chatted about flowers and antiques. Rachael knew it wasn't polite to stay too long, so as soon as her coffee was finished, she said goodbye and left to start her day. "Maybe next time you can come to my house for coffee. Or something stronger?"

"Yes, and yes. Jack Daniel's is my drink of choice," Aunt Mary Opal winked.

As Rachael backed out of the driveway, Aunt Mary Opal stood in the doorway watching, just as she had stood in the street the night before. She danced in a circle, waved goodbye in a back-and-forth motion, and repeated her burst of expression, "Whew!"

AFTER HER VISIT with Aunt Mary Opal, Rachael's anger at Jake for not having been there when she needed him had all but disappeared. Then her phone rang, and

Jake's name showed up on the caller ID. She jerked the steering wheel and pulled into a Starbucks parking lot. Anger filled her to the point of tears. When she didn't answer, the phone dinged again, indicating a text: "Home about 6. I love you." The familiar emotional roller coaster of the past few months was still in control of her. As soon as she read Jake's words, her tears that began in anger morphed into a mixture of tears and laughter. A glimpse of the hope she felt on her drive back from Charlotte rose up. She returned the text: "I love you too, Jake."

Rachael's entire afternoon was transformed into a vibration of anticipation to see Jake. At around 5:30 p.m., Rachael had the house stocked with groceries and wine. The house was clean, and she checked in with her mother to make sure everything was okay.

When Rachael heard the sound of a car, she ran to the kitchen, where she had opened another one of Jake's favorite red wines, Mile 71, a pinot noir from Oregon. As the front door opened, Rachael greeted Jake while wearing only a white apron and holding a wine-filled glass in each hand. Jake dropped his bag and carefully placed his guitar case just inside the front door. Without hesitation, he shut and locked the front door and reached out to Rachael. His hands slid past the glasses of wine to wind up around her waist, and he embraced her gently but with a confident intent of taking away any stress he knew he had caused her in his absence. While Rachael towered over most people, she and Jake looked eye to eye. She had not been aware of the tension in her body until her anticipation of a quick hug turned into a long and increasingly intense embrace. Jake did not release her until he felt all the tension from her body melt away and she had rested her head on his shoulder.

Only then did he whisper in her ear, "I'm sorry I wasn't here."

"You are now." Rachael held his gaze as she handed him his wine glass. "Welcome home." They quietly tapped their glasses together and walked to their bedroom without speaking.

White candles lit the room, and R & B music played quietly. They made love, moving their bodies together and in and out of letting go pent-up emotional pain and physical passion. Only in the still quiet, as Jake held Rachael, did they speak. "How long are you home?" Rachael reached over and filled their wine glasses.

"I have to be in Nashville in a couple of days." In an effort to change the subject and keep Rachael engaged, Jake said, "How was Teri's party? Did you go?"

She stood up and walked toward the door. "Yeah, I did. I met someone. Meet me in the pool, and I'll tell you about it." Her tone was emotionless, cool.

Jake's interest had clearly been piqued at the generic announcement of Rachael's having met someone. He jumped from the bed and rushed to her without getting dressed. "Who did you meet?"

Rachael, ignoring his question, walked down the hallway and into the backyard. She dove into the pool. Jake followed closely. As she stood with water dripping from her hair, a flirtatious smile had replaced her cool demeanor. "Let's just say I think we'll be in each other's lives a long time." Before Jake could ask anything, she dove under the water, swam to the end of the pool next to him, and kicked off the wall. As she turned under the water, Jake pushed off the wall and swam alongside her. Moonlight shone through the water, lighting up their bodies and the matching wings that were tattooed on their backs. Jake wore the left wing and Rachael the right. While they both wore tattoos of every color, the wings were shades of white with dark gray accents.

When they reached the end of the pool, Jake jumped up and sat on one of the corner seats. "So what are you trying to tell me? Who is he?"

By then, Rachael's grin had turned into a laugh. "It's a she, and I think you'll like her."

Confused, Jake continued to question. "What's her name and what's her story?"

"I'm not telling. But how about I have her over for dinner tomorrow night? She loves Jack Daniel's." Rachael dove backward into the deep end, and Jake watched with intrigue.

"You're not going to tell me, are you?"

"Nope, but make sure you get home from the studio early. I'm going to cut my gallery installation short too. I want to get an early start because she likes to pour at five."

JUST AFTER SUNRISE, Rachael threw on her running tights and shoes for her usual morning run through Candler Park. She returned about an hour later to see that Jake's car was not in the driveway. The yellow sticky note on the refrigerator told her that he was looking forward to meeting her new female friend and that he would pick up the Jack Daniel's. The note ended with *Maybe you and I can sing to her?*

The words took her mind back to a year earlier when Jake talked her into singing a song with him on stage. For Jake, her singing was a victory. For Rachael, it was an embarrassment, as well as a wakeup call. It showed another side of her husband. After she had agreed to sing on stage, they practiced for days to make sure that the harmony and timing were perfect. The idea of singing on stage frightened Rachael, even though she had a well-trained voice. Jake had promised her he wouldn't change anything about their practiced song, so no improvising. On the night of the performance, the audience got quiet as Jake introduced Rachael not as his wife, but as his mainstay. He had introduced her that way before, and he had explained to her that some of his fans like the idea that he could possibly be available. "It's just a musician thing," he had said. As the band started playing, just as practiced, Jake and Rachael filled the room with a melodic version of "Crimson and Clover." Even though the applause erupted and Rachael's voice was perfect, it was the last couple of verses that put a smile on Jake's face and embarrassment inside Rachael. Jake changed the tempo, and Rachael's voice went flat. The change had to have been practiced because the band went right along with Jake. The applause turned to laughter and sneers. She had always feared singing on stage, and the smile on Jake's face when he changed the tempo and she was not able to follow imprisoned her voice forever.

Jake's suggestion that they would sing to Aunt Mary Opal seemed like another setup. It would never happen again. The sticky notes were placed in the trash can.

In Rachael's studio, Jake met Aunt Mary Opal, and he was clearly surprised to learn that their guest was a tiny white-haired woman. "Are you telling me you are the woman driving the huge SUV out front?" he asked. When Aunt Mary Opal laughed with him, shaking her head up and down in agreement, Jake grabbed her with both arms and hugged her. "I can't believe it. Can you even reach the pedals?"

Aunt Mary Opal pushed back, looked up at Jake, grabbed his forearm, and winked. "I push on the accelerator a whole lot more than I do the brake."

Laughter filled the room, and Jake put his arms around Rachael and kissed her on the cheek. "I see what you were talking about. She's great."

The entire evening was filled with question after question between Jake and Aunt Mary Opal. "Why do people call you 'aunt'?"

"You know, aunts are a lot more fun than moms, and I don't want there to be any mistake in how people think of me."

Jake was still intrigued. "What if you don't seem like a mom or an aunt to me? Can I just call you Mary Opal?"

"Of course you can. Just don't call me after the bar closes." Rachael could see that Aunt Mary Opal's wink and wrinkled nose had captured Jake's heart. She watched Jake's charm light up Aunt Mary Opal's eyes for the entire evening, the same way he did hers when they first met. At the end of the evening, Jake walked Aunt Mary Opal to her car, an action that sealed her admiration.

Just before they dozed off to sleep, Jake reached over and took Rachael's hand in his. "I think you're right."

"About what?"

"Aunt Mary Opal. I think she's going to be in your life for a really long time."

TWO

THE NEXT DAY, after Jake left for Nashville, Rachael was driving north on Briarcliff Road toward Whole Foods when her phone rang. It was a 704 area code, Charlotte, but it wasn't her mother's number. She held her breath as she answered the call.

"Rachael, this is John Campbell, and you need to come back to Charlotte. Mildred's in a coma." John Campbell was not just her mother's doctor. He and his wife, Sarah, were her mother's closest friends.

When Rachael hung up the phone, she called the first person she thought of. "Aunt Mary Opal, this is Rachael. I know we said we were going to get together for a drink this week . . ." She stopped and began to cry.

"What is it, honey?"

"It's my mom. I have to go to Charlotte today. I wanted you to know. It doesn't sound good." Rachael stopped talking and cried.

"Oh honey, I'm so sorry."

"It was Dr. Campbell, my mom's doctor. He said Mom's in a coma, and that I need to get there as soon as possible." Rachael wasn't sure why she had called Aunt Mary Opal instead of Jake. She just needed to tell her. "I told him I'd be there by three."

Aunt Mary Opal encouraged her to leave soon. "Is there anything I can do to help you get going?"

"No, but thank you. I'm so happy to know you, Aunt Mary Opal." Rachael's voice was clearer.

"You too, dear. Now you get on the road and be careful. The rain probably won't let up. I'll pray for you and your mom." Aunt Mary Opal was reminded of the words all those years ago when she was told she had cancer. "Is Jake going to be with you?"

"No, he left for Nashville this morning. I can't stand him right now. Nothing ever gets in the way of his performing. Not even me." Rachael was angry.

"You don't think about that now, just get on the road, okay? Will you call me when you get there?"

Rachael didn't even go home to pack a bag. She headed north on Interstate 85. The rain started just north of the Atlanta Perimeter Highway and continued in a steady, strong downpour until she reached Lake Hartwell, where it slowed to a mist. She pulled into a rest stop, where people were rushing from their cars to the travel center as if the rain would somehow melt them. She walked slowly, allowing the raindrops to cover her hair and face. Once back in the car, she picked up the phone, for the third time, to try to get Jake on the line. That time he answered. "Mom's in a coma," she said.

Jake listened quietly. "Rachael, take a plane there. I don't want you to drive alone."

"It'll be okay, Jake. I need the quiet time. This way I'll have my own car." Rachael hadn't told him she was almost halfway there.

"Is there anyone to go with you?"

Rachael raised her voice. "No, Jake." She was not able to hide her revived anger and hurt that Jake had not been there when she arrived in Atlanta. She had all but given up hope that she would be more important than his career, but occasionally the hope would creep back into her mind, and when it did, she was let down all over again. "I really don't want to talk to anyone. I'll call you again when I get there. Jake, I knew I shouldn't have come to Atlanta. I knew it. If she dies alone, I'll never forgive myself." She softened her tone as she shared her fear with Jake.

"It'll be okay, Rachael. She'll hold on until you get there. And if she doesn't, it means she didn't want you to be there at the end. I love you, Rachael." Jake's sincerity was clear.

Rachael drove straight to the hospital. As she entered the lobby, the familiar sterile odor took her back to the many times she had had to rush her mom to the hospital so she could get relief from the pain.

Even though she was only going to the fourth floor, it seemed like the dinging of the elevator floors would never stop. Once she was off the elevator, she slowly pushed open the door to Room 432, where she found Dr. Campbell and his wife, Sarah, sitting next to her mom. Sarah had played in a bridge club with Rachael's mom for more than fifteen years.

"How is she?" Rachael's voice was empty of emotion.

Dr. Campbell reached out to hug Rachael. "Still in a coma." Rachael tucked her head and moved away from Dr. Campbell and toward her mother.

Sarah glanced over Rachael's shoulder to her

husband and stepped back so Rachael could get close to the side of the bed. "How was the drive, Rachael?"

"Long." Rachael's eyes still never left her mother.

"Have you heard from your sisters? When will they be here?" Dr. Campbell had a sense of urgency in his voice.

Rachael stared at her mom. "Yes, they'll be here in a bit."

"Would you like some time alone?"

Rachael said nothing. She sat in a cold metal chair, lowered her head to her mom's shoulder, and began weeping. Sarah and her husband quietly left the room. Rachael held her head there for what seemed like an eternity, wishing that each sound meant that her mom would somehow wake up and talk to her. But the only sounds were the rhythmic beeping that was proof of an irregular heartbeat and the swishing sound of the pump that pushed air in and out of her lungs.

Her sisters arrived at the hospital together. They had stopped at a bar around the corner to have a drink before they went to see their mom. It wasn't unusual for Sharon and Kathleen to have at least one drink before dealing with emotional issues. It was a habit they started in their teens.

Sharon, the middle sister, now with salt-and-pepper hair, began wailing as soon as she entered the room. She had always been emotionally expressive, and even a slight amount of alcohol multiplied the intensity of her outbursts. Sharon had learned early in life to exaggerate her expressions. She was the only one of the three girls who could distract their dad away from verbally or physically combating their mother. In some ways, Sharon was their mom's defender.

Kathleen was the oldest sister and still dyed her hair strawberry blonde, telling anyone who asked that it was her natural color. She shed no tears as she patted her mom's hand, and she quietly told her that she needed to hang on. "There are so many things you need to get done." Kathleen had lived life disconnected from her emotions, so Rachael was not surprised that it was easy for her sister not to sense that their mom was actually dying. Kathleen took a sip out of her stainless steel flask and passed it to Sharon.

Rachael was the youngest. She was also the only one of the three who had spent any time with their mom in the past six months, and she was angry about her sisters' distance. However, even with her anger, it seemed easier to be at the hospital with them in the room. Just as in other parts of Rachael's life, she was really good at pushing aside other people's poor behavior. She felt a sense of great gratitude as she sat looking across her dying mom at her sisters, who were huddled together on the sofa.

It suddenly occurred to Rachael that it was getting late and that she had forgotten to call Aunt Mary Opal to let her know she had arrived. She jumped out of her chair and whispered what she was thinking. "Shit, I forgot to call Aunt Mary Opal."

Kathleen and Sharon looked at each other with confusion. "Who is Aunt Mary Opal?" Kathleen asked.

"I'll tell you later," Rachael responded, as she rushed out of the room.

Rachael walked to the waiting room and dialed Aunt Mary Opal's number. She only got voice mail. "Aunt Mary Opal, I am so sorry I didn't call earlier. I'm here, and Mom is still in a coma. My sisters finally showed up, not drunk but getting there. Anyway, I'm okay, just sad. Thank you so much for caring."

While Rachael was out of the room, Kathleen and Sharon continued to pass the flask and talk about who Aunt Mary Opal might be. They came to a consensus that she must be a distant relative who showed up to try to get some of their mom's inheritance.

By the time Rachael returned to the room, the flask was empty, and her sisters were full of a story they were trying to get control of. "Let me tell you something about whoever this Aunt Mary Opal is, Rachael . . ." Kathleen stood up as she began. Then Rachael's phone interrupted.

Rachael gave Kathleen a look of confusion at her aggressive approach. "It's Aunt Mary Opal. I'll be right back." As she opened the door to leave, Rachael looked back. "You need to stop drinking. Hi, Aunt Mary Opal."

"I was worried about you. Thank you for letting me know you arrived safely." Aunt Mary Opal explained that she had fallen asleep in her chair and had not heard the phone ring.

Rachael filled her in on her mom's condition and about her sisters. They both shared a laugh about how Kathleen started to grill her on who she and her sister thought Aunt Mary Opal was. "I have no idea where she was going with that attitude."

"Well, if it's about me, it must be interesting," said Aunt Mary Opal, joining in the sarcasm.

Rachael ended the call quickly when she saw a doctor walking toward her mom's room. She followed right behind him as he entered. "You must be the daughters," he said. "I'm Dr. Blevins, John Campbell's associate. He asked that I step in, considering his friendship with your mother." They all three nodded quietly and waited for more. "Your mom is in a coma and is being held in that state. We can keep her here forever if that's what you want," he continued.

Sharon burst into tears with her face in her hands as Kathleen stood up to face the doctor. "Isn't there something you can do?"

"We have done all that we can do. Now it's in your hands. We need the three of you to talk about what you think is best for your mother." The doctor looked at Rachael for a reaction.

Still standing between him and the doorway, Rachael responded. "We will. Can you give us a few minutes to talk?"

"Take the time you need." Dr. Blevins started toward the door, stopped, and turned slightly back toward the three daughters. "I'm sorry. I know how difficult this is." Then he turned and left the room.

Rachael wished that the room were quiet, but the beeping and swishing seemed louder than before. "We need to let her go, y'all," she said softly. "It's time."

Kathleen and Sharon walked to Rachael, and they all held each other in silence while listening to the machines. *Beep swish, beep swish.*

FOR THE FUNERAL, Jake flew from Washington, DC, to be at Rachael's side. But that morning, when he walked into her mother's house, Rachael noticed no rise of hope in her heart, not like usual. It was missing. She was empty of emotion toward Jake.

"Thanks for coming, Jake," she said, looking him in the eye.

Jake stretched out his long, colorful, tattoo-covered arms, and held her. "I don't have to be back for a few days."

Her mother's home was a classic colonial revival with white columns and dark green shutters. The day before the funeral, the house was filled with the smell of casseroles. It was a tradition for the ladies from church to deliver casseroles before a memorial so there would not be a delay for people who were hungry after the service.

The funeral was held at the First Congregational Methodist Church, which their mom had attended since their dad's death. It was a large church, and the entire building was filled, standing room only. It seemed, from the number of pink flowers, that everyone had known her mother well enough to know that pink was her favorite color.

Just as Rachael and Jake began walking with the family to the front of the church, she saw Aunt Mary Opal. She was stunned to see her, and she broke away from the family to reach across the others in the pew and hold her hand for a brief moment. Aunt Mary Opal was quiet.

As Rachael rejoined the family, Sharon asked, "Who is that?"

"Aunt Mary Opal. I'll fill you in later." Rachael smiled as she said her name.

Kathleen and Sharon, walking just behind Rachael and Jake, quickly turned to get an inquisitive look at their new "aunt."

THREE

WITHIN A COUPLE WEEKS of the funeral, Aunt Mary Opal and Rachael settled into a weekly routine of long conversations filled with laughter and, sometimes, tears. The conversations were often shared in Aunt Mary Opal's garden or Rachael's front yard while cleaning the fallen leaves and planting fall flowers and vegetables.

Aunt Mary Opal planned every week around her Tuesday morning therapy session, Wednesday morning aerobics, and Thursday morning appointment at the hair salon. She considered all three appointments important for maintaining a healthy body and mind, although only aerobics and getting her hair back-combed were anyone else's business. Therapy was a secret.

Aunt Mary Opal shared details of her past with Rachael, details that seemed to change a little with each new telling. *Artistic privilege* was what Aunt Mary Opal called it.

"Just when I thought I couldn't take any more of that awful man's lies, he would lie again. It was never about anything important. But that last lie pushed me over the edge." Aunt Mary Opal sat on the edge of her rocker. Her eyes were wide open, and her body leaned forward for emphasis. "That's when I slapped him."

Rachael screeched. "No, you didn't!"

"Yes, I did. I just slapped him." The room filled with their laughter, and Rachael remembered the last telling of the story, in which Aunt Mary Opal said she had just walked off the job, no slap. But the slap was a lot more interesting.

Rachael enjoyed the freedom of Aunt Mary Opal's storytelling so much that she began incorporating that same artistic privilege into stories she shared with Jake.

". . . that's when the store manager slapped the guy," Rachael said, exaggerating.

Laughing out loud, Jake said, "That's bullshit. You made that up."

"Yeah, but it sure sounds better, doesn't it?" Rachael said, laughing with Jake.

Rachael never stopped Aunt Mary Opal's stories to say she had heard them before, because the new versions seemed to be more interesting than the old ones.

Part of the money from Rachael's mom's estate was put into an account for the three daughters to take a vacation together to Spain. Their ancestors were from Seville, and Mildred's intent was to help create a closer bond between her daughters. Rachael had no intention of going anywhere with her sisters. "Aunt Mary Opal, what am I going to do? I'm supposed to take a vacation with my sisters, and I just can't. I love them, but that's the last thing in the world I want to do. Help me get out of this."

"I know exactly how you get out of it," Aunt Mary

Opal interjected confidently. "Didn't you say that neither of them could go a day without a drink?"

"That's an understatement!" Rachael said.

"Tell them that your mom said she wanted you all to go to a convent in Spain to brush up on your Christianity," Aunt Mary Opal said. "Tell them you already made the reservations and that it would be a week of healthy food and no alcohol."

"Oh, you are good! I'll say that they only serve a vegan diet. And I can say it's a vow of silence for the whole week," Rachael said, expanding on the story.

They both laughed out loud. "Tell them that when they get there, they'll be in lockdown the entire time," Aunt Mary Opal continued. "I think you should call them right now."

"I think I need a drink to do that," Rachael said, nervously.

Aunt Mary Opal slowly stood up from her chair, careful not to knock her book off the antique table that sat a little too close. She had added a few more items to her living room, making every inch a little tight. "I'll join you. It's five o'clock somewhere in the world. Jack for you?"

"A Jack is perfect, but not too much. I need to be able to handle this conversation," Rachael said.

"You'll do just fine. There's no way they'll want to go with you when you tell them that story." Aunt Mary Opal lined up two rocks glasses, pouring just enough to make them one-finger drinks, holding her right pointer finger to the etched glass to make certain it was the right pour.

Rachael didn't sip her drink like she usually did. This time, she downed it like a shot.

Once she had both Kathleen and Sharon on the phone, she explained what their mom had supposedly asked them to do, but she added artistic privilege that she wouldn't have been able to muster up were it not for the Jack Daniel's and Aunt Mary Opal's encouragement. "We have to shave our heads before we are allowed to enter the monastery."

Aunt Mary Opal clasped both her hands to her mouth to hold in her laughter. Rachael saw her run to the hall bathroom, fairly certain that if Aunt Mary Opal didn't get there quickly, the laughter would cause her to wet more than her face. After a couple moments, she walked back into the room just as Rachael went in for the kill.

"Doesn't that sound like an amazing time for us to share? I bet Mom's spirit will visit us while we're there, too." Rachael knew she was pushing her sisters.

Aunt Mary Opal remained between her and the hall bathroom, noticed Rachael, who surmised that if the older woman couldn't hold in her laughter, she could dash back into the bathroom again.

Kathleen and Sharon remained silent throughout Rachael's description of the trip. When they finally did respond, Kathleen spoke first, with her usual condescending tone. "Rachael, I think that you and Mom shared a special connection and that it would be really good if you could spend that time without me. You know, just you and her spirit, in silence. I can't speak for Sharon."

Sharon was quick to follow. "I couldn't agree more. You're always so wise, Kathleen, I guess because you're the oldest. Rachael, just take our money too. Maybe you'll want to stay more than a week. I really think you'd get more out of the time without us there. I hope we aren't hurting your feelings. And I hope that Mom's spirit will understand when she visits you there."

The plan was working. Kathleen and Sharon were mortified at the entire idea. "But Mom and I will miss you both," Rachael pushed harder.

By then, Sharon started into full-fledged sarcasm. "Oh no, Rachael, Mom came and visited me just last night. She'll be just fine with it. You just let us know if there's anything that you need from us to make sure you and Mom enjoy that time. Okay?"

"Well, if you both insist. But I don't want your money. You keep it. If I want to stay another week, I'll pay for it. We'll miss you, Mom and me." Rachael had been pacing back and forth from the living room to the sunroom, having to step over a small footstool each time in order to get past all of the newly acquired items that had been placed there. On her third pass, Aunt Mary Opal moved the footstool into the front bedroom to create a clear pacing area.

After the conversation came to an end and Rachael hung up, she mimicked Aunt Mary Opal. "Whew!" she said, waving her right hand in the air, lifting her knees, and twisting her hips as she danced in a circle. Rachael was learning more than artistic privilege from her new friend.

Aunt Mary Opal was already standing over the white marble tabletop in the kitchen with two more Jacks on the rocks, two fingers instead of one. That would not be the last victory Aunt Mary Opal and Rachael would concoct. It was just a beginning.

∿

ONE MONTH LATER, Rachael called Aunt Mary Opal before she left for the airport to fly to Spain. "This is your last chance to go with me."

Aunt Mary Opal giggled. "Oh, no, no, no, I'm too old. All I would do is slow you down. You go and have a fun time. It's the best thing to have, you know."

"What is?" Rachael felt confused.

"Fun. Fun is *always* the best thing to have," Aunt Mary Opal replied.

Her decision to go to Spain alone had been easy. The last year had been about taking care of her mom and wishing that her relationship with Jake were different. She was still his biggest fan, but she realized that living in his shadow was lonelier than she thought it would be. Traveling by herself would give her a chance to spend ten days with no one to answer to or wait on. She didn't care if she just got a hotel in Seville and spent the whole day watching television. She just needed to have no responsibility for another person.

Rachael could hear concern in Aunt Mary Opal's tone. "Are you sure you feel safe traveling to Spain by yourself?"

Rachael took in a deep breath. "Yes. I'm sorry, I'll be fine. I just ask because I know I'll miss our visits. Do you remember how to text me if you need me?"

"Well, if I forget, I'll ask a young person," Aunt Mary Opal joked. "Be safe, and don't do anything I wouldn't do."

FOUR

As the train stopped at the station in Seville, Jesi Viscuso fumbled with her bag that was stashed in the overhead compartment, only to have it drop squarely on the lap of a woman passenger. "Fuck, I am so sorry!" Jesi yelled out, in a panic.

Rachael laughed out loud. "It's okay, it didn't hurt. Where are you from?"

Jesi was surprised that the person who had been sitting next to her was obviously American. "Agrigento, Sicily, originally. Are you an American?"

"Yes, I'm Rachael. I'm sorry I didn't speak to you earlier. I thought you were Spanish and didn't want to have another conversation with someone when I can't understand a word."

"I'm Jesi Viscuso. Can you believe it? An American right next to me and I didn't even know it!" Jesi lifted her shoulders slightly and smiled in a slightly flirtatious manner. "My family lives in the United States now. Where are you from?"

"Atlanta," Rachael replied.

"You're kidding me!" Jesi said. "My parents and Noni live off Collier Road." She sized up her fellow passenger. "Listen, I'm on my way to get a glass of wine. Would you like to join me?"

Rachael smiled. "I'd love it. There's a bar right around the corner." On her previous trip to Spain, Rachael and her mom had used the bar as their home base in case they got separated.

The two new friends made their way through the cool November air until they reached a tiny bar. Because it was dark already, the lights of Seville reflected off of the damp streets, turning their experience into the kind of charm one sees in travel books. Jesi looked around to make certain they had not become targets for gypsies. The bar wasn't full, so they made their way to a table by the front window.

Just as the server was making his way to their table, Jesi reached across the table and leaned in, touching Rachael's tattoo-covered forearm. "Red wine?"

"Yes, that's perfect."

"*Dos vinos tintos, por favor,*" Jesi said, flashing a smile at the waiter.

Rachael's eyes widened as she watched the shared glances between them. Jesi noticed that Rachael seemed to love the spark of energy. "So Jesi," she began. "How is it that you're traveling in Spain alone?"

"I decided if I didn't go now, I might never get another chance. You?" Jesi studied the tattoos on Rachael's arms. "Why is this woman alone?" she wondered to herself. "She even looks alone in her eyes."

Rachael sunk slightly in her chair, her shoulders curled forward. "When my mom died, she left some money for me to go on a vacation with my sisters."

Jesi sat up straighter. "Where are they? Are you meeting them?"

"No, I really don't have anything in common with them," Rachael said. "My friend, Aunt Mary Opal, helped me make up this story about how to get out of traveling with them."

"What did you say?" Jesi inquired, intrigued.

Rachael laughed. "Aunt Mary Opal told me to tell them that Mom wanted us to stay at a convent and that we couldn't drink alcohol the whole time. And both of my sisters are alcoholics."

Jesi also began to laugh. "Is she your mom's sister?"

"Who? Aunt Mary Opal?"

"Yes." Jesi nodded her head, thinking that her question should have been obvious.

"Oh, no, she just likes to be called aunt so her younger friends don't confuse her with their mom. She thinks aunts are a lot more fun than moms."

"She's right. I think I like her, and I don't even know her."

Suddenly, Rachael grabbed her phone and started dialing. "I'm sorry. I need to make a quick call."

Jesi flirted with the waiter while she also listened in on Rachael's phone call, curious to know who she was calling with such urgency.

"Aunt Mary Opal, I made it. I'll try to call you tomorrow." Rachael hung up and put the phone back into her bag.

Jesi noticed her stomach growling. She hadn't eaten since early that morning. Should she ask Rachael to join her for dinner? "Where are you staying?"

Rachael's chuckle turned into such a loud laugh that Jesi couldn't help but join in, even though she wasn't sure why they were both laughing. They laughed until they became the center of attention at the bar. Finally, Rachael shared the truth. "Actually, I don't have a clue where I'm staying. I just had to get out of town."

"Well, you sure got out of town," Jesi said, a little shocked. "You're all the way on the other side of the Atlantic." After their burst of shared laughter, Jesi knew spending time with her new friend would likely add spice to her trip. "Why don't you stay with me for the night? We can get some dinner. Michael, my travel agent, told me about this great restaurant. Then if we feel like it, we can go dancing at a disco he said has mostly men. He said I would love the music. Besides, he said the men wouldn't bother me, they're gay." They laughed as if they shared a secret. "I'd love to have the company." Jesi eyed her new friend, wondering if Rachael would be secure enough in herself to let go and live. Or would she truly need alone time to grieve the loss of her mom?

"Aunt Mary Opal tells me to have fun. It's the best thing to have."

"I like Aunt Mary Opal even more." Jesi wondered what Rachael's story was. What kind of fun was she into?

Looking around the restaurant, she said, "Let's get out of here. I hear there are a lot of gypsies hanging out in this area, and the last thing we need is to lose our passports to a thief."

After they checked into the NH Sevilla Plaza de Armas, they took a cab to La Tagliatella for dinner and more wine. Jesi and Rachael split a carafe and spent three hours enjoying dinner, drinks, dessert, and the company of the all-male wait staff, who seemed to want time at their table. Jesi shared the history of the Bella

Artes Museum with Rachael. "I'm planning on going to the museum in the morning if you'd like to join me. At one time it was a convent, so it won't be a total lie if you tell your sisters you stayed at a convent."

Aware of the ring on Rachael's left hand, Jesi asked, "Are you married?"

"Yes. Jake and I have been together for about five years."

Jesi was curious. "Why isn't he here?" she asked.

"His work."

"Such a short answer," she thought. "What kind of work does he do?"

"He's in the music industry." Rachael offered as little as possible and looked away, appearing as if she were bored with the conversation.

Jesi, deciding that she would get the details tomorrow, accepted that Rachael didn't want to talk about her husband. "Okay, enough about him. Tell me what you do."

Rachael took in a deep breath. "I'm a designer. Mostly houses, but really anything. I love photography."

"Why didn't you get Aunt Mary Opal to come with you to Spain?"

"She would never just pack up and go. She's very planned and very proper, exactly the way you would picture a strong Southern woman. Besides, I needed to be free from any responsibilities."

"What about Jake? Is he okay with you traveling alone?"

"I didn't ask him," Rachael replied quickly and shifted the focus. "Tell me about you?"

Jesi was selective with what she shared about her life. She knew she lived a charmed life and that other people were jealous of her freedom. The story she shared was about her education, her Sicilian heritage, and her Noni's support for her to travel. What she didn't share was anything about her intimate life.

~

JESI WAS free to do what she wanted in life and was excited about living. She was happy to be born into a family who believed in sharing their wealth while they were living, not at death. It was her grandmother, Noni, who loved to give Jesi the opportunity to travel. They shared a special connection. Noni pushed Jesi to be independent and free-spirited, something that Noni never allowed in her own life. Jesi tried for years to get her Noni to travel with her, but it wasn't possible. Noni had no interest in traveling. She believed that it was her duty to stay and tend to Jesi's parents, her daughter, and her son-in-law, even though they didn't need tending to. Jesi no longer made an attempt to take Noni with her and no longer carried any guilt about her fortunate life. She just lived each moment as if there were no worries. Most women her age were married with children, working sixty hours a week, or both.

Jesi worked only when she chose to, for her father's business. She had three degrees in computer science, and she knew that her skills would be her safety net if her Noni ever decided to stop supplying her with the means to travel. Even though Noni was ninety-one years old, her mind was still sharp, but her body was slowly curling inward from arthritis. With each trip, Jesi sent more cards and made more and more phone calls, always fearing that it might be the last time she would have to

share the excitement of roads not seen by her sweet
Noni.

Jesi's friends referred to her as a trust-fund baby.
Unfortunately, most people who referred to her with this
term were jealous. That's why she liked traveling alone.
This, and her dating habits, something she kept a secret
from almost everyone she knew. At first, Jesi had
thought she was a lesbian: She loved dating women. But
she also liked to date men. It seemed like people always
wanted her to choose: lesbian or straight. But she didn't
want to choose. The one thing she never told anyone in
her life anymore was that she really liked dating couples.
Jesi liked sex with two people at a time. Two women,
two men, a man and a woman — it all worked for her. She
had tried telling a college friend and was chastised for
weeks until she told her friend that she went to confes-
sion and that God had forgiven her. "If God can forgive
and forget, then you need to let it go." Her friend said
she forgave her, but Jesi never confided in anyone else.
It was her little secret, and traveling alone made it an
easy secret to keep.

So there she was, in Seville, sitting across the table
from Rachael. Noni was going to love to see the
photographs and hear the stories about Rachael. Her
Noni was supportive of Jesi dating women, and Jesi
wondered if her Noni didn't have regrets of not doing
more in her intimate life after her husband died. It wasn't
a subject she would ever be able to discuss with her
Noni, so she made sure that she always shared a little
spice from her own life. Noni always seemed to be just a
little more alive when Jesi shared about some of her intimate escapades with women. But she didn't go further in

her sharing with Noni, as she worried that if she told the whole story, the funds might come to a screeching halt.

≈

AS THE EVENING WORE ON, Jesi noticed what whenever Rachael spoke about Jake, she heard anger. "I have an idea," she said, deciding to dig in a little further. "Let's travel around Spain together for the week. Would Jake mind?"

"No, Jake wouldn't mind," Rachael laughed. "He'd love to know that I'm not traveling alone. I do need to try to see my family."

"Did you come to see your family, or are you just trying to forget everything in your life for a week?" Jesi considered that perhaps she was pushing Rachael a little too hard, a trait she had always had to curtail. She also wondered if Rachael would be okay that she was staying in the same room with a woman who was bisexual. That is, if Jesi decided to share her real-life story.

Rachael seemed to think for a minute. "Let's do this. I'll call my cousins and find out if they're even home. If they are, go with me. If not, let's go see Spain. Deal?"

"Deal!" Jesi crossed her fingers that Rachael's cousins would not answer the phone.

Time slipped by as the conversation was filled with laughter. The thought of anything or anyone except that evening faded from consciousness for Jesi—she suspected that the same was true for Rachael. Jesi was aware of Rachael's shift from tense to relaxed as they moved further away from conversations about her husband.

~

THE NEXT MORNING, Jesi jolted out of a deep sleep. She sat up and looked down at Rachael, who was lying half-dressed on the floor with an embarrassed and shocked look on her face. Jesi laughed with a sound that came from deep within her. "What are you doing?" Her laughter didn't stop—it continued, louder and higher-pitched.

Rachael buried her face in her hands and laughed so hard that tears flowed down her face. She had not laughed that hard in over a year. She stopped laughing long enough to interject, "Actually, I was trying not to wake you up. Guess I missed that one."

"I guess so. Where are you sneaking off to?"

"Well, I guess I had so much to drink last night that I forgot I have a life back home. I forgot to call Jake, and my phone is dead. I was just going down to use the hotel phone."

"Don't be silly. Use my cell phone. Noni insists that I always get an international account when I travel. She's a dear. But you know it's only about two in the morning there?"

"Shit, you're right. I hope Jake's not upset. I told him I'd call when I got here."

"Don't worry," Jesi laughed mischievously. "Just tell him you got kidnapped by a band of gypsies and you just got loose."

"Oh right, that would go over really great. You're crazy." Rachael threw a pillow at Jesi.

"Call your cousins and get a game plan, then let's go grab some breakfast. I'm starving." Again, Jesi freely pushed her own will onto Rachael. Jesi was always in charge of herself and usually the others around her. The way she felt about it was that most people didn't really know what they wanted to do anyway, so she might as well help them. Plus, when people followed her plan, they had a great time and usually walked away hoping for more time with her.

As Jesi showered, she found herself hoping that Rachael's cousins were not available and that she and Rachael would be free to enjoy the trip without the confines of family. The thought of arriving at Rachael's cousin's home and having to sit through a dinner with old, boring Spaniards was not her idea of a vacation. In fact, Jesi had the perfect plan. She would check out the situation, and if it didn't look like a great scene for her, she'd just give Rachael her phone number and excuse herself. Besides, the last thing she wanted to sit through again was the heart-wrenching story of Rachael's mother dying. Jesi was very clear about one thing in her life. Her Noni was right—life is too short to waste on doing things that you don't want to do. At least that held true for Jesi. But Noni never did anything for herself. As a matter of fact, everything Noni did was for other people.

Jesi stepped out of the shower just in time to over-hear Rachael's voice, the same depressed voice she heard the day before. "I know she's not suffering anymore. I'm just sorry that she wasn't able to see you again before she died."

"Oh no," Jesi thought. "Here we go back to sadness. I may have to excuse myself now and skip the trip to see her family." But then she overheard Rachael's voice.

"I'm sorry I won't be able to see you this trip. It was great to hear your voice, and I'll write you when I get back to the States."

Jesi walked out of the bathroom just in time to see Rachael leap to her feet and yell, "Come on. Let's start a vacation!" They both screamed and giggled like college freshmen.

～

AT LUNCH, Jesi watched as Rachael sketched out the rest of the trip on a cocktail napkin. She connected the dots between Seville, Gibraltar, Granada, Barcelona, and Madrid. The plan was in place, and the one who rode shotgun was the tour guide for the day. First stop, Gibraltar.

The next seven days felt like twenty-four hours. The only down time either had was when they were sleeping. The trip was full of conversation, delicious food, and lots of wine. By the time they arrived in Madrid, they were exhausted, in a good way. The small shops that surrounded the Al Hombre were their favorite stops. Rachael purchased a colorful vase for Aunt Mary Opal, and Jesi found a hand-laced table runner for her Noni.

"So Jesi," Rachael said. "I know you have a lot of traveling to do, but why don't you go back to Atlanta with me for a few days? I think you'd really love Aunt Mary Opal and Jake. And maybe I could meet Noni and your parents."

Jesi hesitated and changed the subject. Most of her life had been spent alone. At fourteen, right after her younger brother died, she had been sent to a boarding school in Boston. She had seen her family only on school breaks and had learned to adapt to whatever the circumstances were so she could create a plan to get on the road, a road to anywhere except where she felt trapped by another person's needs.

For an entire week, conflict roiled inside Jesi. She had not wanted to rock the boat with Rachael, but she couldn't help but wonder if Rachael and Jake had ever brought another woman into their relationship. After a week had elapsed, Jesi still didn't have the nerve to ask. Every time Rachael talked about Jake, she seemed a little detached, sometimes completely detached. "Why did Rachael give Jake so much power?" she wondered.

Although Jesi would normally push any subject without concern of how someone else might feel, for some reason she didn't do this with Rachael. It was only after a few drinks that Jesi worked up the nerve to ask Rachael about a possible ménage à trois. Then, if Rachael got upset, she would blame it on the wine. Her fingers were crossed.

Over dinner, Rachael started them off with a toast. "Here is a toast to our last night on our trip, may we spill the beans, pop the top, you know, tell all. For there may be no tomorrow."

Had Rachael known what Jesi had wanted to talk about this whole time—a three-way with her and Jake? "Was she fishing?" she wondered. "How do I tell Rachael?"

"I was just wondering if maybe you could come to Atlanta for a while and stay with me and Jake," Rachael continued. "But there's one thing. Jake and I like . . ." Rachael tucked her head, and her face blushed.

"Oh my God! Me too!" Jesi laughed and reached out, touching Rachael on her forearm.

"We have an agreement with each other not to unless we're together," Rachael said. "We both feel it could be a bad habit, and I'd never want to break an agreement we have."

Jesi quickly pulled her hand back from Rachael's arm, hoping that it didn't look like she was trying to hit on her. She thought that it seemed healthy for them to be so open to bringing in another person and making sure they don't go out on each other. "Oh, I understand," Jesi said. "Personally, I like it so much better when there are three people. You know, the energy just flows, and it's so exciting. How long have you been into that?"

Rachael threw her a puzzled look, but continued. "Forever. I started in high school. But Jake . . ." Rachael said with a chuckle. "I turned him onto it. Now, he's hooked. He gets really creative."

Jesi could hardly believe it. She was ready to go to Atlanta. "Did you ask Jake about me?"

"No, I don't have to. I know he'll love you being there with us," Rachael said. "We don't invite many people to stay with us. You know, not everyone can be okay with it."

Jesi wanted more details on Rachael and Jake's sexual escapades. "Do you always include women? Or do you bring in a man sometimes?"

Now Rachael looked even more confused. "What do you mean? We don't care. It's really more about who can keep a secret. The last thing we need, with Jake's career, is that hitting the newspapers. Jake has always said he's clean."

"Wait. What do you mean clean? What are you talking about? Are you talking about a ménage à trois?" Now she felt as confused as Rachael seemed.

"What? No. I'm talking about smoking pot. What are

you talking about?" Rachael gasped and covered her mouth with her hands.

Jesi didn't say a word, and they stared at each other in silence. Finally, Rachael understood what Jesi had been holding back the entire time. "Are you hitting on me? I mean, on me and Jake?"

Jesi sat in silence.

"Oh my God. I am so sorry, Jesi," Rachael said. "I am so stupid sometimes. No. I mean thank you. What I mean is you're adorable but that's just not . . ." She stopped talking.

"Are you going to hold that against me?" Jesi asked, after a long silence and gulping down the rest of her glass of wine.

Rachael burst into laughter. "Are you kidding me? Against you? I love that you would think of me that way, I mean us that way. But we're not into three-ways. I don't think I can share. And Jake gets really jealous. So you figured out who Jake is, right?"

"What are you talking about? Who is Jake? I am so confused." Jesi shook her head and fell back in her chair as if she was giving up on the whole conversation.

"You didn't figure out who Jake is? Jake LeBlanc?"

"Your husband is Jake LeBlanc? *The* Jake LeBlanc?" Jesi could not have been more surprised.

Rachael nodded her head yes, and Jesi burst into laughter that turned every head in the restaurant. "Fuck. No wonder it seemed like you were keeping a secret. I'm really sensitive to people who keep secrets, and I knew there was something up." Jesi had a strong internal intuition her whole life, and most of the time when she felt energy, she was exactly right. The problem was that many times, while she knew there were secrets, if she couldn't figure out what was going on, her Sicilian temper would flare up and explode. Sometimes, Jesi jumped to the wrong conclusions.

Rachael and Jesi laughed for a few minutes, ordered another carafe of wine, and for the next two hours, they shared everything. Rachael opened up about Jake and all the issues about being a rock star's wife. Jesi shared about her three-way sexual escapades and how she loved the feeling of freedom it gave her.

In the end, Jesi decided to go to Atlanta for a bit, and they agreed to share their story of the hilarious and confusing conversation with Jake over a joint and a bottle of Spanish wine.

"And I promise I won't hit on you and Jake," Jesi said.

In the same spirit, Rachael replied, "Remember not to tell Aunt Mary Opal about any of this. Like she always says, 'It's our little secret.'"

As soon as their plane touched U.S. soil, Rachael picked up the phone. "Aunt Mary Opal, I'm back, and I can hardly wait to see you. I have a surprise. Call me."

When Jesi and Rachael arrived at the home Rachael shared with her rock-star husband, the part of the driveway where Jake's car would normally be and something that Rachael noticed made her bristle. Newspapers were piled up at the front door, which made it obvious that this rock-star husband of hers had not been home in a while. But Rachael walked past the newspapers as if she hadn't seen them, even though the porch light spotlighted them through the approaching evening darkness.

They were impossible to miss. Jesi noticed how detached Rachael had become, and she was reminded that you never really know what happens in someone's home until you see if for yourself. Trouble was brewing.

The historic bungalow, set back from the street, was beautifully landscaped and well-kept, making it obvious that the landscaper had been there. Inside, the house was a typical 1915 center-hall design with high ceilings and simple dark trim that had never been painted. Jesi was intrigued at the conservative interior décor. She had expected to see a mid-century modern or some type of colorful contemporary display. Instead, all the furniture seemed to be directly from the Arts and Crafts period, matching the design of the home. "Wow, Rachael, what's up with your house? It's beautiful, but I thought it was going to be contemporary."

"Yeah, most people do. But I don't think you can improve on the Arts and Crafts style, so I don't try. Come with me. Your room is in the back."

As they walked down the hallway and toward the back door, Jesi hesitated when she saw a baby grand piano in the parlor to the right. She noticed the gold and platinum records that covered the walls. "Damn, Rachael, that's a lot of energy. Is this where he writes his music?"

"Most of it." Rachael sighed as her shoulders dropped. She stood in the doorway and stared into the room. "This is his life."

Jesi hesitated and reached for the door to Jake's studio. She closed the door right in Rachael's face. "Enough about him. Where's my room?"

She followed out of the house, past the black lagoon pool to a cabana that looked like a miniature of their house. "I built this as my art studio, but it seems to have turned into the guest room more than my studio."

When Jesi walked into the studio, she threw her hands in the air and screamed out loud. "Now you're showing off!"

Rachael giggled, and her face turned bright red. Each of the studio walls was a different color—red, orange, blue, and gold. The color had been glazed, giving the walls a sort of textured appearance. The trim work was dark green, and the artwork covering the walls provided even more color. There was only one black-and-white piece of art, a close-up photograph of a white flower with a black background. The frame consisted of a shadow box with a simple black exterior and an ornate golden frame inside the glass surrounding the photograph. Jesi stopped in front of the photo, which hung above a cow skull that had what appeared to be a rosary hanging from one of the horns. "Did you take this picture?"

"You like it?" Rachael asked.

"I think it's a self-portrait of you. It's stunning." Jesi studied the image.

"Are you flirting with me, Jesi?" Rachael reached over with her elbow and nudged her, knocking her a little off balance. They laughed as Jesi's face blushed with embarrassment. They were exhausted from the long flight, so Rachael got Jesi settled in and announced that she needed to call Jake. Jesi heard her leaving a message, asking him to call her the next day.

FIVE

ON THURSDAY MORNING, Aunt Mary Opal stopped at the grocery store after her hair appointment. When she arrived back home, she set her grocery bags on the kitchen counter and, still wearing her winter white wool coat, she walked to the answering machine and pushed the flashing red light. It was Rachael, and she was thrilled to hear her voice on the recording. "I can hardly wait to hear about your trip and find out what the surprise is," she said in her message reply.

In anticipation of Rachael's return, Aunt Mary Opal had picked up the ingredients to make pimento cheese, a favorite snack for their visits. The cheese grater was old and well-worn from years of use. Once the cheese was grated, she added a small dollop of mayonnaise, two small jars of drained pimentos, and freshly diced jalapeño peppers. She never knew if the peppers would be hot or mild, but that morning the peppers were especially hot. "We'll need extra crackers for this batch," she thought.

Aunt Mary Opal had no idea that she was about to meet Jesi. Rachael had filled her in on her newly found traveling partner, but she was not aware that her new friend was the surprise. Thrilled to see Rachael but still not knowing what the surprise would be, Aunt Mary Opal waited in the driveway and, with her right hand twirling above her head, danced a jig as the orange Mini pulled into the drive. Just as Rachael had hinted, the two women loved each other instantly. Even though it was chilly, the three of them strolled arm-in-arm through the garden as Aunt Mary Opal asked Jesi one question after another. She asked about her family, where she grew up, where she had traveled, and last, she asked Jesi the question that would seal their friendship. "Jesi, tell me what it's like to be a lesbian."

Rachael and Jesi laughed so hard that Jesi started crying, Aunt Mary Opal wet her pants, and Rachael tripped on a stone and fell flat into a pile of wet leaves. Once they made their way into the house, Jesi cleaned the mascara that had run down her cheeks, Aunt Mary Opal changed clothes, and Rachael removed the leaves that had partially filled her panties. The grandfather clock in the hallway rang out five loud bells, indicating that it was time for a cocktail. Two fingers measured each of their glasses with Jack Daniel's.

The kitchen had always been the gathering place for Aunt Mary Opal's family and friends. The marble-topped table that sat in the middle of the kitchen was worn down in front of each chair where someone's arms had rested while visiting or eating. Over drinks and pimento-cheese appetizers, the women took turns telling stories of travel and family.

"The worst trip I ever took was to Sicily," Aunt Mary Opal began. "I will never go anywhere near there again. The airlines lost my luggage, and I didn't get my suitcases back until five days into my trip. It made me so angry." She was vaguely aware that this was not the first time Rachael had heard this story. When she said "It made me so angry," she looked across the table at Rachael, who held the story between them, seeming to share the subtext that Aunt Mary Opal hadn't quite spoken.

But Jesi pushed. "Oh, come on, Aunt Mary Opal. It was just the airlines. Maybe you need to give Sicily another try."

"No, no. I won't ever go to Sicily again. I just had such a bad experience."

Rachael, always the peacekeeper, offered a diversion. "Okay now, tell us about the time you went to New Orleans." She knew it had been a fun trip for Aunt Mary Opal and that telling it would lift her out of her anger.

"Oh my, Jesi, I need to know you a little better before I tell you that story!" Aunt Mary Opal winked and flashed a mischievous grin.

After two hours of cocktails and pimento cheese with jalapeños that were hot enough for everyone to need Kleenex, Jesi proclaimed, "Now I know exactly why Rachael loves you. You are everything I wish my Noni could be, full of life and laughter."

Aunt Mary Opal watched Jesi look around her kitchen, and she knew Jesi felt a sense of belonging. Maybe one day her Noni could come here.

∾

OVER THE NEXT FEW WEEKS, the three women began to refer to their gatherings as "ladies light luncheons," which entailed creating a menu, going to the grocery store, and preparing food together. While grocery shopping one day, Aunt Mary Opal shared with Jesi how to play a game called What's Her Story?

"Sometimes, it's a lot more fun to make up someone's story," she said.

Rachael joined in. "I don't know, Aunt Mary Opal. I think the truth about Jesi may be juicier than what I could make up." At that, Jesi poked Rachael in the arm to get her to be quiet.

On one of their first trips together to the Harris Teeter grocery store, Jesi noticed a woman reading the ingredients on all of the canned vegetables. "Okay, what's her story?"

Aunt Mary Opal jumped in and made up a story faster than either of them. "She's a spy from Whole Foods. It's her job to find anything she can against Harris Teeter so they can use it against them." She continued as Rachael and Jesi listened and laughed. "Last week, she discovered too much salt in the green beans."

Rachael tried to hold back her laughter. "No, I think she's a diabetic and can't eat anything with sugar, so she is obsessed with reading the cans."

"Hmmm," said Jesi. "I think she's competing in a scavenger hunt and has to find a can that only has 460 milligrams of salt per serving." Jesi waved them down the aisle past the woman who was obviously obsessed with something—of what, they would never know.

Their ladies light luncheons continued weekly. It was as if the three women had created a family of their own. Jesi started referring to them as "the terrific trio."

SIX

DURING THIS TIME, Aunt Mary Opal had become aware of increased pain in her body. It was more difficult to get moving in the mornings, and it was certainly more difficult to stand up after sitting for more than a few minutes at a time. She suspected that her pain was more than just old age. The red rash on the scar where her left breast used to be had grown to about the size of a quarter, and a lump had started to form under the rash.

"Mrs. Shook, we need to schedule your appointments as soon as possible." Dr. Baker leaned in and touched her on the shoulder for emphasis. As much as she liked her doctor, she thought there was nothing that felt so cold as an examination room. It was empty of warmth and compassion, no matter how much the handsome doctor tried to comfort her.

Although fairly certain of the appointments he meant, still she asked, "What appointments?"

Dr. Baker answered solemnly and confidently. "We'll start with radiation and then move to chemotherapy."

"Well, you'll have to do all of that without me, Dr.

Baker. I'm not going through any of that again." Her confidence was greater than the doctor's effort. While Dr. Baker attempted to convince Aunt Mary Opal that his recommendation was the best one, it was to no avail. She gently smiled and thanked him for sharing the news.

Aunt Mary Opal gathered her raincoat and umbrella, and she placed her purse across her right arm as she held her head higher than what her spirit was feeling. She walked out of the office and down to the building's entrance. The rain had slowed to a soft mist. She removed a plastic rain cap from her purse, carefully placed it on her hair, and started to open her umbrella. That's when Aunt Mary Opal did something she had never done before. She lowered the umbrella, attaching the Velcro to ensure that it would remain closed, and removed the rain cap from her head, placing it in her purse. The chilly mist coated her white, back-combed hair as she stepped out into the parking lot. She walked past her car and continued to a coffeehouse next to the storefronts she had frequented for the past thirty-five years. By the time she reached the coffeehouse, her hair was sagging with moisture and her face glistened with the reflection of light from the stores. She felt numb and empty, just like the exam room.

Aunt Mary Opal always ordered a regular coffee with light cream and one sugar. To her, it had always seemed silly to spend money on expensive drinks like cappuccino. She stepped to the rounded glass counter that held muffins and doughnuts. "I'd like a cappuccino with extra froth and two sugars. And would you please give me one of those sugar-coated doughnuts as well? Actually, make it two."

She chose a corner table set apart from the others.

The light above the table was not lit, which made the corner darker. Bookcases, filled with books from all genres, lined each wall. It seemed odd for the corner to be so dark next to all those books, but it was perfect for Aunt Mary Opal. "Is this what I've been missing out on all those years?" she thought, after taking her first sip of the cappuccino. "What a shame. That won't happen again." She was in her own world, unaware of an argument that had broken out between a customer and an employee until lightning and the loud banging of thunder startled her out of her thoughts. The customer's aggression took her back to a time when she was living in New York.

It had been in Manhattan, in 1958. Mary Opal Shook had been sitting at a table in a dark corner of The Gaslight Café, which had just opened in the basement of a building around the corner from where she and her husband lived with their two young children. A third daughter would come later. Young poets gathered around a table across the room, and they bantered with each other to see who would step up and perform for the patrons. She had been hearing about this coffeehouse from a friend, but this was her first time to step into the dark basement. It had seemed to be a good place to hide from her world. She could feel the heat and swelling in her jaw where her husband had hit her just thirty minutes earlier. A dark corner seemed to be a good place to hide the bruising and her shame. She began to imagine that she had no husband, no children, that she was single and completely isolated from anyone in her life. That was how she escaped the reality of her real life, by pretending she was somewhere else, living someone else's life.

She had only been there for about ten minutes when

a handsome, dark-haired man slid into the chair across from her. "So, what brings you here? I've seen you in the neighborhood, but I think this is your first time here." It was John Mitchell, owner of the café. He was so confident, so open.

"Oh, I just wanted to see what all the talk was about." Mary Opal normally would have been shaken by the intrusion of a stranger, but that day, she had been shaken so hard by the reality of her life that a stranger showing up so abruptly was to be a welcome event.

"Looks like you could use something in that coffee." He motioned to the waiter and whispered in his ear. Almost immediately, the waiter returned with a bottle of whiskey. John, without asking, reached over and poured some of the whiskey into Mary Opal's coffee cup. "I don't know what's going on in your life, but I own this place, and I want you to know that from now on, this is your table. You'll always be safe here."

She sat up straight, pushed her chin out, and, with a small tear in her eye, thanked John. For the next three years, Mary Opal frequented the café and sat alone unless John joined her. The staff knew that if Mary Opal arrived, whoever might be sitting at her table would need to move to another place. At first, she asked them not to move the people, but John let her know that it was his café, his rules. The table belonged to her.

After a couple of months, John had a local artist carve a wooden block with the letters *M* and *O* and install it on the wall next to the table. If anyone asked, John would simply say that it was no one else's business. They never spoke about her outside world. John knew how important it was for Mary Opal to have a place to go where she could put everything behind her, and Mary

Opal needed to know that this was a place of safety. When John sold the café in 1961, Mary Opal stopped going to the café, and her friendship with John drifted into her memory. For all those years, Mary Opal held a special place in her heart for John. While they were never lovers, she loved him deeply.

She moved with her husband and children to Vinci, Italy, where they lived until they moved to Atlanta in 1964. Her husband had always been seen by others to be a gentle man, and he was exactly that—except behind closed doors. In their younger years, he would hit her with his fist. Eventually, he learned not to hit her because it caused bruising and people would know that he had been violent with his wife. Instead of hitting her, his wrath would explode, and he would put his hands around her neck and squeeze until Mary Opal blacked out. She didn't know how to escape. By the time they moved to Atlanta, they had three children, and she knew that she and her girls would live in poverty if she left him.

Very few people knew that her husband had fathered a son before she married him. When he was asked to help with the child, he ran. At no time did he provide any assistance to the mother or to his son. Mary Opal was certain that if she left her marriage, he would leave her to raise the children without any help, just as he had done with his first child, and she was not willing to live like that. The occasional violence would be her price to pay for keeping a roof over her head and a father for her children. Mary Opal could never put into words how it felt to be treated with such violence while being expected to look and act like everything was perfect while in public. Only after her husband's death had she dared to read books on the shame that comes with abuse. It had been an odd existence, the way she had lived then, never doubting her husband's love, but fearing his internal demons.

Filled with this recollection, Aunt Mary Opal looked out from the coffeehouse, sipped her cappuccino and doughnuts, and decided that she would never again sit in that dark corner. Instead, she would keep young, vibrant women like Rachael and Jesi close to her. The rest of her life would be about living, not hiding.

It was Thursday, and she was almost late to her hair appointment. Late was something Aunt Mary Opal didn't ever do, so she rushed back to her car and arrived at the small salon just as the clock turned nine. Never in all her years of going to the salon had Aunt Mary Opal shown up with her hair sagging from rain. When she walked into the front door, a wave of laughter started with the receptionist and rolled all the way to the back of the salon until her stylist joined in. They were laughing at her white hair that had no sign of the previous week's back-comb. Aunt Mary Opal couldn't help but think of how perfect that moment was. "Out of my darkest moment and into total and complete joy." She joined in the laughter. "Ladies, let's fix this mess."

SEVEN

THE WAITING room outside Sandra Hanson's office was everything Dr. Baker's office was not. It was Tuesday, and Aunt Mary Opal always arrived early for her therapy appointment with Sandra. The room was split into two areas, one with small sofas piled up with pillows and the other with individual chairs that reclined. The scent of patchouli and the sound of a rather loud water feature filled the soft lavender-painted room—this was a sound barrier that protected the other clients' privacy.

As Aunt Mary Opal did before each appointment, she unplugged the water feature and sat close to the door of Sandra's office with her ear close to the door so that she could hear the conversation taking place on the other side. She usually had to strain to hear the other clients' conversations with Sandra, but that day it was easy to hear. A female client was yelling.

Aunt Mary Opal's eyes flew wide open.

"I don't think I can take it anymore!" the woman screamed. "She lied to me from the start. She started telling everyone in my life that it was me who lied. And now this. Now she came to see you."

Shocked, Aunt Mary Opal covered her mouth with her hand. Sandra seemed to try to calm the woman. "I know it seems like it won't be all right, Nicole, but I assure you it will."

"What did she want? What did she say to you? Tell me!" The woman's voice rose.

"You know I can't tell you that," Sandra said. "What I can tell you is that I saw right through her story. I wouldn't let her stay, and I told her that I would not work with her."

Aunt Mary Opal had never heard Sandra sound so nervous. She had always been calm and collected.

Then the woman's voice shifted and was almost too soft for Aunt Mary Opal to hear, so she cupped her hands around her ear and moved closer to the edge of the doorway. "It's never going to stop, is it?" The woman no longer sounded emotional. She sounded cold, like a person who was giving up. Aunt Mary Opal was shocked to hear the shift in her voice. "I must have done something to deserve this. But I won't live like this anymore."

Now Sandra sounded anxious. "You don't have to live like this, Nicole. Please sit down, and let's talk about a plan."

The woman's lack of emotion was eerie to Aunt Mary Opal. "No. I'm done," she woman said. "I'm done with all of it. It'll never end until either she's gone or I'm gone."

"Nicole, it's not going to stay the same. It will get better. Please sit down. Don't leave." Sandra was pleading now.

Suddenly, the door opened. Aunt Mary Opal quickly sat up and barely moved her head out of the way of the woman who pushed her way to the outside door. As Sandra touched the doorknob, she glanced at Aunt Mary Opal.

"Nicole, please come back inside," Sandra pleaded.

Aunt Mary Opal caught the reflection of the woman's face in the glass. She was dressed in a black business suit and had well-groomed red, wavy hair and strong hands that wore expensive bands of jewelry.

"Send me a bill, Sandra," the woman said as she pushed the door open and walked to her car, an old white Cadillac with a tag that read *68DIVA*. She drove away, never looking back.

The waiting area was completely quiet. Sandra stood in the doorway with her hands on the glass for a long moment before she turned and walked over to the water feature and plugged it back in. The room immediately filled with the sound of trickling water again. Aunt Mary Opal, still in shock at what she had overheard, watched Sandra walk back into her office. "Come on in, Mary Opal."

"Do you need a moment? I know that was not easy." Aunt Mary Opal felt sorry for Sandra. She had never seen anyone leave her office like that before, and she wondered what the woman meant when she said it wouldn't stop unless she was gone.

"You have no idea," Sandra replied.

"Do you think she's going to be okay?" Aunt Mary Opal asked. "She seemed like she meant it when she said she was done."

"I don't know. You know I can't discuss that. Come on in and have a seat." Sandra motioned to the usual chair and closed the door behind them. She poured two cups of tea and set one on the table next to Aunt Mary Opal before she sat in the adjacent chair. "Mary Opal, tell me something good."

Aunt Mary Opal held her breath for a moment. "Well, I feel like I'm stuck in that joke about the guy who shows up with a telegram. You know, the one where the woman always wanted a singing telegram and made the guy sing it?"

At that, Sandra placed her tea on the table and leaned in. "What are you talking about?"

"I can't sing it." Aunt Mary Opal's eyes filled with tears. "My cancer is back." She didn't know what to expect when she shared her news with Sandra, but she didn't expect what followed. Sandra stood up and took her hand. Aunt Mary Opal also stood, Sandra wrapped her arms around her, and they both wept.

Over the years, their relationship had become a friendship. While they never met outside of the scheduled appointments, their times together were more relaxed and less formal than with Sandra's other clients.

Over the next hour, Aunt Mary Opal explained to Sandra that she was not interested in treatment. "I refuse to live my last days in a doctor's office. I'm going to fill my days with young people so that when I go, I will at least be surrounded with joy."

Sandra didn't try to talk her into a different plan. "What can I do for you?"

"Just keep your calendar open for me like always. And I was wondering if maybe you would help me figure out how to finish everything I haven't finished and close every chapter I need to close, just a little quicker." Aunt

Mary Opal had been thinking about who would help her, and she knew that Sandra had to keep everything confidential, so it would be safe to talk to her about her plan.

"Of course I will," Sandra said, upon hearing the plan. "How do you want to do this? Should we make a list of things? Or do you already have what you need?"

"I was thinking that we could start by figuring out how I can end my life before it gets too painful." She watched Sandra closely for a reaction.

Sandra took in a sharp breath. "Mary Opal, you know I can't help you with that."

"I know, but you can't talk to anyone about what I say. Right?"

"Right," Sandra responded.

"Well, I just need to know where to find out how to die with the least amount of mess and pain." Her mind was set. "Then, once I figure that out, I need some help figuring out how to leave my estate."

"Mary Opal, you need an estate attorney for that, not me." Sandra's face was flush.

"I have an attorney, but I need to trust you to help me know if I'm being stupid or if what I am doing is okay." Aunt Mary Opal noticed that she was softly pleading.

"Can I think it over this week? It's been a really hard day, and now this. I'm going to really miss you, Mary Opal." Sandra's tears returned.

"Oh dear. I am so sorry. How can I be so selfish? Let's talk next week." Aunt Mary Opal slowly raised herself out of the chair and patted Sandra on her back to comfort her, reversing a move that was usually reserved for Sandra.

At the next meeting, Sandra agreed to the part where she would help Mary Opal complete unfinished business and find closure to relationships. The rest—what Mary Opal would have to do on her own or with someone else's help—was about finding a way to take her own life, preferably ahead of the pain.

EIGHT

RACHAEL, Aunt Mary Opal, and Jesi were shopping for their ladies light luncheon when Jesi spotted an attractive redhead studying wines. The woman wore earbuds and was moving her hips slowly from side to side. Jesi thought the music she was hearing through her earbuds must have been a smooth, sexy sound, because her movements were certainly sexy. "What is her story?" Jesi wondered.

With those hips, it didn't take much for the three women to get caught up in creating a story about her. Jesi picked up a box of crackers and pretended to read the label, while Aunt Mary Opal and Rachael stood back, exchanging smiles, as they watched Jesi move her gaze up and down the woman's body.

"Look, she's moving to the groove. Who do you think she's listening to?" Jesi pointed toward the woman, whose back was toward them, obviously in her own world.

"Dean Martin," Aunt Mary Opal interjected.

Jesi rolled her eyes. "No way!"

"I think she's getting ready for a hot date," Rachael said.

"Except she only has one of everything," Aunt Mary Opal said. "One prime rib, one lobster, one potato, and one bundle of asparagus."

As usual, Aunt Mary Opal had seen the details, with the exception of the woman's face. Jesi noticed that Aunt Mary Opal seemed to find something familiar about the woman, but she dismissed it. Maybe Aunt Mary Opal had just seen her in the store before.

"Oh, you're right," said Rachael, always the sympathetic one. "Do you think she's lonely?"

"Doesn't look lonely to me," Jesi said. "I think she looks hot." In true Jesi fashion, she continued looking the redheaded woman up and down.

The three women all watched carefully so as not to be seen spying on the unsuspecting woman. Getting caught spying on was quite awkward when their chosen subject saw them playing What's Her Story? Unbeknownst to Jesi, as the woman perused the wine label, Aunt Mary Opal finally got a glimpse of her face. It was the "I'm done!" woman at Sandra's office! But all that Jesi noticed was Aunt Mary Opal taking a frightened step back and tucking her head down as if she didn't want to be recognized.

As the woman studied the wines, she apparently failed to notice a box of wine placed in the middle of the aisle. She tripped on the box and fell sideways. Her chosen bottle of wine flew out of her hands and tumbled through the air. She fell into Aunt Mary Opal's arms and knocked her backwards into Rachael. Jesi watched as her friends tumbled to the floor like dominoes. All three women landed squarely on the floor in the center of the aisle, and Jesi caught the wine just before it hit the floor. No one had broken a bone. They were all a little startled, but they were okay. Jesi cackled so loud that everyone within a few aisles joined in. She scrambled to the floor to help everyone up.

Somehow, in that instant, the music the redheaded woman had been playing on her earbuds, "Sexual Healing" by Marvin Gaye, synched to the store speakers. The woman's face turned as red as her hair. "Oh my God, I am so sorry," the woman exclaimed. "This is so embarrassing. Are you hurt? I am so sorry."

Jesi gathered up the woman's phone and handed it to her, along with the bottle of amarone wine. "Nice combination," she said, flashing her a grin. The woman blushed even brighter.

Jesi was aware that the flirtation wasn't going unnoticed by Aunt Mary Opal and Rachael, but she didn't mind. Aunt Mary Opal poked Rachael in her side and gave her that slight "we're-sharing-a-secret" grin.

Once off the floor, they stood in silence as they watched the woman briskly walk away while pushing up her red mane to straighten it from the fall. Rachael, in her comforting manner, rushed forward and stopped her in her tracks. "My husband and I live in Candler Park..." she began.

Seeing what Rachael was up to but also seeing that she was botching it, Jesi turned to Aunt Mary Opal. "What's she saying?"

"I don't know," Aunt Mary Opal whispered back. "But I bet it'll be fine. I think the woman could use someone nice like Rachael to talk to."

Jesi settled back with Aunt Mary Opal and watched as Rachael accompanied the woman toward the registers.

By the time the woman checked out, Rachael had not only found out her name, but had invited her to join them the next day for their ladies light luncheon. Both women exchanged numbers, and Rachael wrote down the address, making sure that Nicole had Aunt Mary Opal's number as well.

"Oh my, this could get complicated," was the look on Aunt Mary Opal's face, Jesi thought.

"Is she going to join us?" Aunt Mary Opal asked.

Rachael stood up tall and smiled. "She said she would." She poked Jesi in her side. "Her name's Nicole."

Jesi slapped Rachael's hand. "Stop it. She won't come."

"She might." Rachael tried to poke Jesi again, but Jesi was too quick and moved away.

Aunt Mary Opal remained quiet. Jesi turned to see her wearing a look that said "Let's hope not."

WHAT JESI WOULDN'T KNOW until later was the effect this incident had on Nicole. Still shaken from embarrassment, Nicole returned home and started to prepare dinner. She looked around her expansive kitchen with dark, European-style cabinets. The sunset cast a beam of light on the white marble countertops and highlighted a manila legal-sized folder labeled *Last Will and Testament.*

Nicole was one to plan her evenings, but the incident at the store had shifted something in her. "That older woman looked so familiar. Who was she?" she wondered. "And was that other woman flirting with me? It sure did feel like it."

She rolled the potato in foil and placed it in the oven.

She then methodically lit all of the white votive candles throughout her condominium. Nicole was determined to work through all the emotions that had stirred up since her last appointment with Sandra. The problem was that all of the preparations made to be emotionally ready to take her own life seemed to be lost. "Why do I feel so sad?" she wondered. She told herself that she would only go through with it if she could be at total peace. Since her fall in the store, she was far from peaceful. Something had shaken her to her core. She flipped on the stereo, hoping the music would help her reach her prior emotional state when she had been ready. Her mind returned to the fall. Then the song changed to "Sexual Healing." "Jesi, that had been her name," she thought. "She was flirting, and it felt good."

With the last bite of prime rib, Nicole stared at the container of helium in the corner of the living room. The peacefulness she desired was nowhere to be found. The cold numbness had been replaced with a deep sense of grief. She couldn't do it. She left the dishes on the dining room table and lay in bed, sobbing. Her tears flowed until she fell into a deep sleep.

As the sun came up, she walked into the kitchen, still wearing her clothes from the night before. She walked by the helium tank that stood untouched in the corner. The coffee seemed to taste stronger than it had in months. As she poured her second cup, she noticed the white paper on the counter with the address of where to meet the women from the store.

Ladies Light Luncheon, noon Friday, 2221 Maple Avenue. Be there or be square. This is Aunt Mary Opal's number if you're running late.

NINE

IN HONOR of their new friend, Aunt Mary Opal announced that she would make her famous Italian sausage lasagna instead of her usual pimento-cheese sandwiches. She also changed the sheets on her three guest beds in case the luncheon turned into dinner and none of the ladies were able to drive home. She was ready for guests. If so, it wouldn't be the first time, and she hoped not the last time, that the ladies light luncheon turned into breakfast the next morning.

She stored her sheets in a locked room, not because of the sheets, but because of all the documents from her past and her plans for the future. She felt it was best that her secrets were kept secret. No one knew everything about Aunt Mary Opal, not even Rachael and Jesi. The files from her husband's days in the CIA were stored there. She was slowly shredding all the files, but until they were shredded, the room would stay locked. She felt that this was just one of the many patriotic acts that was her responsibility to carry out. As she gathered the sheets, the phone rang. She grabbed the sheets and rushed out of the storeroom, locking it behind her. She ran to the phone just in time to hear the answering machine pick up. "Hello, this is Nicole from the grocery store yesterday. You are so kind to invite me but . . ."

Aunt Mary Opal grabbed the phone. "Oh, Nicole, I am so glad you called." She never gave Nicole a chance to refuse the invitation. "Will you please stop by and pick up a bottle of red wine for me?" She didn't wait for an answer. "My goodness, I forgot to turn off the stove. See you in a bit." At that, she hung up the phone.

While Nicole literally had no idea of what she had stumbled into, according to Aunt Mary Opal, the trio had grown to be a quartet. She strutted her little dance and high-fived the mirror as she checked to make sure her back-combed hair was perfectly in place.

At around 11:30 a.m., Rachael, Jesi, and Nicole all arrived, filling the driveway with cars. Next to the door were Aunt Mary Opal's SUV and Rachael's orange Mini. Next in line was Jesi's convertible Mercedes, and last was Nicole's 1968 Cadillac convertible. Aunt Mary Opal laughed out loud at the three convertibles in her driveway. "There are no mistakes in this world," she whispered to Rachael as she motioned at Jesi and Nicole's cars. They both hugged each other a little longer than normal, which sent energy to Jesi and Nicole. Rachael quietly sang into Aunt Mary Opal's ear "Matchmaker, matchmaker, make me a match."

It started to rain, so Aunt Mary Opal's garden tour and planned interrogation of a new friend did not take place. She knew that she would have to move the questioning inside, but she thought it best not to rush into her questions of Nicole until they all had at least one cocktail. Outside in the garden, people seemed to feel more open. She guessed that being inside and surrounded by so much "stuff," as Rachael had so accurately described, would cause people to feel a little claustrophobic when she started asking them questions. "A cocktail should calm Nicole's nerves," she thought. A cocktail would also calm Jesi, who seemed to be wound tighter than a top.

Four glasses had already been placed on the counter, ready for whatever libation was desired, but Aunt Mary Opal had her rules, and when they all agreed to pretend that noon was five o'clock somewhere, that didn't mean 11:45 a.m. While they waited for the clock to strike noon, Aunt Mary Opal set the latest issue of *Atlanta* magazine on the table. On the cover was Jake, standing in front of the studio in their backyard. "Rachael, you never told me Jake's talents stretched into interior design, too," Aunt Mary Opal said. "You must be so proud of him." Rachael's face turned red, but she smiled. She seemed to go along with how proud Aunt Mary Opal was of her husband.

Jesi flipped through the pages of the magazine. "Not only is Jake LeBlanc a talent on stage, his talent extends to the colors of interior design and renovation. His Cabana-style studio is just one of his creations." There was a picture of Jake standing in the studio, surrounded by the colorful walls and photography that had been Rachael's work, not his own. Jesi set down the magazine. "What the fuck, Rachael? He didn't do anything. That's your work."

~

NICOLE, new to the group, sat and quietly watched the emotional exchange. Aunt Mary Opal wondered what

Nicole knew about someone else taking credit for her work.

"Jesi, it's okay. I know the truth, and that's all that matters." Rachael slumped in her chair and looked to Aunt Mary Opal for support.

Aunt Mary Opal clasped Jesi's forearm to the table in a way that told her to calm down. "Did you ask Jake about that?" she asked Rachael.

Rachael's voice was soft, the kind of soft when a person has given up. "Yes. He told me that the writer just assumed he did it. I can't worry about it."

Jesi slammed the magazine shut. "That's bullshit and you know it."

Aunt Mary Opal strongly squeezed Jesi's arm. The room was quiet for a long moment.

Nicole broke the silence. "I look forward to seeing your work, Rachael." Then she shifted the conversation. "I thought you asked me over here to have a drink? I think the clock already struck twelve." Following Nicole's lead, Aunt Mary Opal poured their drinks.

They drank Jack Daniel's, all except Nicole, who preferred vodka. "She'll learn," Aunt Mary Opal thought. "I'll give her some time. It's vodka from May through August and bourbon from September till May." That was just another one of Aunt Mary Opal's rules. Her life was governed by structure. When and what to drink was just one form of control that brought her happiness.

The need to control was one of the main reasons Aunt Mary Opal's daughters moved across the country and only visited a couple of times a year. One of her daughters hadn't been home in over two years. She said it was because of work, but Aunt Mary Opal knew the truth. She knew she'd paid the price for keeping her home and family in perfect order for all those years by deciding that was the easiest way to ensure that her husband and their father would stay calm. Their father had never had the ability to deal with chaos, and anything out of order represented chaos to him. Even though he had been dead for more than two years, Aunt Mary Opal still pushed control on her daughters and, apparently, on her friends as well. Old habits die hard, and there was no reason to let go of her need to control her entire environment. Because of her bad memories of her husband, whenever she saw something or someone out of proper order, she still got a knot in her stomach. In some ways, she still felt like his rage was going to show up and strike out at one of her girls or at her. So it was simply more pleasant to stay in complete control. At least that way, she could focus on more important things, like her new friends.

Jesi had planned the luncheon activities, which included a game she said she had learned at boarding school in Boston—Fictionary Dictionary. Balderdash, a new game that was sold in stores, was actually the same game, but Jesi said she didn't see any reason to buy a game when all that was needed was to buy a dictionary. She explained that she'd learned the game by using the dictionary on her computer, but she knew that Aunt Mary Opal would not like using a computer. They would use Aunt Mary Opal's huge dictionary that was kept next to the chair where she sat to read every day.

After only one hour into the luncheon, it was as if Nicole had been a part of their group forever. Not once did any of the women quiz her or say anything that made her uncomfortable. For Nicole, Aunt Mary Opal observed, being with these women was like putting on a favorite old sweater. It was as if nothing outside the walls of the house existed, not even her past.

"Okay, Nicole, you get to pick the first word because you were the last one in the driveway," Aunt Mary Opal announced, wanting to make sure that Nicole was included from the outset. She pretended as if there were an actual rule about who went first.

"Great!" Nicole took the worn dictionary and opened it to a random page. She closed her eyes and placed her finger on the word *quidnunc*.

Aunt Mary Opal, Rachael, and Jesi wrote down definitions that they individually made up for the word, while Nicole wrote down the actual definition: *One who always wants to know what is going on.* After Nicole read each of the four definitions aloud, Rachael burst out, "One who always wants to know what is going on. I think that's the definition of Jesi." The next few hours were filled with laughter and competition. Nicole fit in perfectly.

After their first drink, they took a break from the game and brought out the pimento-cheese finger sandwiches that Aunt Mary Opal had made earlier that day. Rachael said that it was the best batch she'd ever made, but she said that every time. Once they finished the sandwiches, it was time for another drink and another round of the game.

"Nicole, I am so glad you're here," Aunt Mary Opal said. "Now someone besides Jesi may be able to win at a game." She winked at Jesi.

"I don't think I can have another liquor drink, wine is next for me," Rachael said.

"Hard liquor for me," Jesi said. "I'm certain I'm

spending the night." Then she turned to Aunt Mary Opal. "I have a surprise. Aunt Mary Opal, you can put the lasagna in the freezer, because I brought everything to make dinner."

"Whew!" Aunt Mary Opal let out her cheer and danced a jig around her chair, with Rachael and Jesi following. Nicole wasn't quite sure what to think about their dance moves, so she stayed seated and watched how sweet they all were, dancing around their chairs.

"What did you bring, Jesi?" Rachael asked.

"Pork tenderloin, Idaho potatoes, asparagus, and a salad. And for dessert, Mick's chocolate pie." They screamed out loud, and Nicole joined in. "I'll get the cooler out of the car. Rachael, will you start the grill? And Aunt Mary Opal, would you set the oven on four hundred?" Jesi headed out the side door.

"What can I do?" Nicole jumped up from her chair.

"Open some red wine, Nicole," Jesi yelled back to the house.

Through the easy laughter, Aunt Mary Opal noted that this was the first time Jesi had brought dinner—just one more level of her flirting with Nicole.

After dinner, Aunt Mary Opal tried to talk Nicole into staying the night, along with the others. That was a little too much for Nicole. It was one thing to spend a day and evening with new friends; it was another thing to wake up and have coffee with them the next day. She moved her car to the street and summoned a Lyft.

As Aunt Mary Opal and Rachael stood in the driveway and waved goodnight to Nicole, Jesi stood alone, close to the door of the house. Aunt Mary Opal sensed that Jesi was confused about her feelings. The alcohol must have left her feeling anxious about Nicole's departure. It was the same feeling she got when there was a secret someone was keeping, uneasy and a little queasy. After Nicole left, Aunt Mary Opal and Rachael tried to have a conversation with Jesi about her flirtation, but she would have none of it and quickly climbed into bed.

"We probably need to give her a little time, but I think today was progress." Aunt Mary Opal winked at Rachael as she turned off all the lights except the kitchen light, a habit she always kept.

TEN

THE NEXT MORNING, Nicole arrived to pick up her car just as Aunt Mary Opal was getting home from her aerobics class. Aunt Mary Opal had been going to aerobics classes three times a week for the past fifteen years, ever since she had been declared cancer-free. "Nicole, I'm so happy to see you. Please come in and help me with something." She didn't give Nicole a chance to respond before she walked into the house with the expectation that she would be followed. "Come on in, I need another cup of coffee. Have a seat. How do you like your coffee?" She was giving no opening. She patted the back of the chair that Nicole had sat in the night before.

"Cream and sugar," Nicole said.

"Oh, me too. Blonde and sweet," Aunt Mary Opal said, smiling at Nicole as she sensed an uneasiness in her. "I've been in the same aerobics class for almost fifteen years. Can you believe it? Fifteen years."

"No, I can't even imagine it. I wish I exercised more, but I just don't make the time for it." Nicole had an hourglass figure and was slightly overweight, but her shape added to her appeal, especially for Jesi, Aunt Mary Opal noted.

"If I didn't go to aerobics, my backside would be bigger than a barn," Aunt Mary Opal said, which made Nicole visibly relax.

The two women visited over coffee. When they were almost finished with their cups, Aunt Mary Opal asked Nicole to walk through the garden with her.

"Nicole, look at how beautiful those lilies are, those purple ones," she said, as they strolled the garden and stopped at each plant. She described how each flower grew.

"I love flowers, but I've never had a garden," Nicole said. "Sometimes I think about learning to garden—it just seems like as soon as I have a little time, I fill it with either work or travel." Nicole was more relaxed walking with Aunt Mary Opal in the garden than she had been in the house. As Aunt Mary Opal talked about the garden, she sensed that Nicole was intrigued with her.

"Well, let's pick some flowers for you to take home," Aunt Mary Opal said.

"Oh, no," Nicole said. "You don't have to do that." She stepped back.

"That's why I grow them, dear, to share." Aunt Mary Opal picked up a pair of scissors that she kept in the garden for times just like this and began cutting some flowers. Then she turned to Nicole. "Here, you can cut some that you like. Take any of them, they're all going to die out here, so take as many as you like."

Nicole took the scissors, and as she cut a few more of the flowers, she hid her face from Aunt Mary Opal. She was deeply moved by this new friendship, and her eyes filled with tears. So that she didn't embarrass Nicole,

Aunt Mary Opal pretended not to see the tears in her eyes, even though they both knew she was well aware of Nicole's emotion. They walked through the garden in silence for a few minutes, until Aunt Mary Opal was certain that Nicole had been able to regain her composure. "Nicole, tell me about yourself. Do you have a partner?" She knew the answer but didn't want to remind her of where they first saw each other.

"No. Luckily, I'm single." Nicole smiled at Aunt Mary Opal. "I left her about two years ago, and it's probably the best thing I have ever done for myself."

"Well, she lost out."

Nicole laughed at Aunt Mary Opal's response. "My only regret is that I stayed so long. I don't want to bore you with the details, but it turns out that all the confusion I had about her was because from the very beginning, she lied about her past. I felt so stupid when her friends started telling me the truth, and it's taken me a long time to forgive myself for staying in such an abusive relationship for so long." Nicole took a deep breath and changed the tone. "But that was then, and I'm in a better place right now than I have been in seventeen years."

"How long were you married to her?"

"Fifteen messed-up years."

Aunt Mary Opal wrapped her arm around Nicole and walked her to another part of the garden. "You see that section right there?" She pointed to an area of the garden that had just been tilled. "That's going to be called Nicole's garden. Let's plant that lavender and rosemary together. It's God's miracle garden right there, proof that there's always a chance for new life." That was when Nicole's tears came back. But that time she didn't hide them from Aunt Mary Opal. They planted Nicole's garden in silence, Nicole watched every move that Aunt Mary Opal made, and she repeated them. Having never planted a garden meant that it was a whole new experience for her, as were her new relationships with her new friends.

When they finished planting, Nicole hugged Aunt Mary Opal and thanked her. As she was leaving, Aunt Mary Opal leaned in and grabbed her arm. "Let's keep all this as our little secret, okay?" She winked at Nicole and gave her a mischievous grin.

"You got it, Aunt Mary Opal."

She watched as Nicole drove off with the colorful flowers on the dash of her Cadillac, waving and, as always, dancing a jig.

ELEVEN

As THE MONTHS FLEW BY, all of their lives got so busy that they kept their ladies light luncheon dates to Saturdays, when none of them had any obligation the next morning, except Aunt Mary Opal, who agreed that she didn't have to go to church on Sunday mornings. "I'll pray for you Saturday morning before the cocktails flow," she had announced.

The next ladies light luncheon was delayed an hour because, as Rachael would learn later, Jesi got home late after a one-night stand that had left her wanting another shower. Rachael knew that Jesi had told Aunt Mary Opal and Nicole that she is a lesbian, but she also knew that Jesi would not be comfortable telling them that her favorite dates were actually when she was with two people, like her date the night before. Rachael had agreed to protect Jesi's secret, and Jesi had let her know she was grateful. Jesi had confided in Rachael that she'd spent a lot of time trying to understand why she loved a ménage à trois, and she had come to the conclusion that it was because she could stay emotionally disconnected and still have a thrilling sex life. For her whole life, she had felt that the best relationship for her was with two people, and at age thirty-three, she had come to the conclusion that she probably would never find one person who could keep her attention.

When Jesi finally reached Aunt Mary Opal's, Rachael deflected any possible tension stemming from Jesi's tardy arrival by asking Jesi and Nicole to help her bring the card table and chairs up from the basement. It was Rachael's day to plan the events for the luncheon, and she announced that she had decided that Aunt Mary Opal needed to teach them all how to play bridge. "Bridge helps people maintain their mental capacity as they age," Rachael explained.

Jesi reached out and jiggled the locked basement door. "Why do you think this door is locked?"

Nicole smiled. "I think it's where she hides her moon-shine." The three women giggled quietly to make sure that Aunt Mary Opal didn't hear them.

"No," Jesi chimed in. "I think it's where she takes her boyfriends for a little S/M. She hangs them from her handcuffs."

At that, all three laughed so hard that they had to cover their mouths. "Stop it!" Rachael squeaked out a plea between the laughter. That's when they heard a loud thump on the ceiling of the basement. Rachael quickly recovered from her laughter and rushed back upstairs to see if everything was all right. Just before she started up the stairs, she stopped and turned to Jesi and Nicole. "Don't do anything I wouldn't do."

Jesi put her arms around Nicole and yelled back to Rachael. "Is there anything you wouldn't do?" She then kissed Nicole on the cheek. They shared a brief moment of eye contact.

When Rachael reached the top step and turned the corner into the living room, she saw Aunt Mary Opal lying faceup in the middle of the floor. She wore an embarrassed expression, and her hair was a little messed up. Rachael ran to her just as Aunt Mary Opal said, "I'm fine, I just slipped and fell. Don't tell the others, it would just embarrass me." At about that time, Rachael heard Jesi and Nicole rounding the corner from the basement stairs. Rachael was bending down to help Aunt Mary Opal get up off the floor, but instead, she quickly dropped to the floor, with her body stretched out away from Aunt Mary Opal, only their heads touching. She had no idea why she had suddenly decided to lay down on the floor with Aunt Mary Opal, but there she was, faceup and head-to-head with Aunt Mary Opal as a way to keep the fall a secret.

Carrying the table and chairs, Jesi and Nicole entered the room. They stopped when they saw Aunt Mary Opal and Rachael lying on the floor with their heads touching. There was a long, awkward moment of silence that was broken by Jesi's laughter. "What in God's name are you two doing on the floor? Or do we want to know?"

"Meditating," Rachael quickly replied. Again, she had no idea where that thought came from, and she was even more confused when Aunt Mary Opal expanded on her answer.

"I read an article that said if you meditate while lying on the floor with your heads touching that whatever you're meditating about will happen sooner. We meditate every day." Aunt Mary Opal spoke with such conviction that it was easy for Jesi and Nicole to believe their story.

"I'm in!" said Nicole. She and Jesi promptly put down the card table and chairs and laid on the floor so that all of the women's heads were touching.

In her usual pushy fashion, Jesi said, "And if I find out other rituals you two are hiding from us, I'm going to have my feelings hurt. Now, let's meditate. What are we supposed to think about?"

Rachael couldn't believe it. One moment she was trying to help an elderly woman off the floor, and the next she was laying head-to-head in some sort of meditation. Aunt Mary Opal was so convincing that Rachael was actually wondering where she read the article. It was almost too much for Rachael. She began laughing so hard that she had to jump up and run to the bathroom, or she was certain she would wet her pants. As she ran out of the room, she yelled back, "I don't think I can meditate now!" When she returned to the living room, they were up off the floor and arranging the card table and chairs. Aunt Mary Opal gave Rachael a quick wink and a grin.

There was something so adorable about Aunt Mary Opal when she thought she was keeping a secret, and Rachael would never tell anyone the truth. The only problem would be when Jesi and Nicole wanted to come over for meditation sessions. She couldn't believe that Aunt Mary Opal told them they meditated on the floor every day.

"Let the ladies light luncheon begin," Nicole announced. She was the most reserved of the four ladies. To make an announcement of any kind was out of character, so it was a surprise and a delight to see her so enthusiastic.

"Nicole, you sure seem happy. Anything you want to tell us? Anything new?" Jesi flirtatiously inquired.

"Not really." Nicole pretended that nothing had conspired downstairs between she and Jesi. "I love to meditate, but I've never heard of people meditating together with their heads touching. I love that. What time to you usually meditate? I'd like to come over if that would be okay with you." She looked at Aunt Mary Opal with a look that would melt a heart.

Aunt Mary Opal looked at Rachael with that same look she always got when she was telling a story with artistic privilege. "It varies. Tomorrow, probably around 4:45, just a little bit before I pour. You're welcome to join us. In fact, why don't you decide what we'll meditate about? It'll be nice to get some fresh ideas in here."

Jesi's internal radar for secrecy was clearly piqued. "Where did you see that article? I'd like to read it. Maybe it would give us some ideas about what to meditate on." Rachael wondered if Jesi had picked up on something going on between Aunt Mary Opal and herself.

"Oh, just some magazine at the dentist's office. I'm sure you can find it on the Internet, if you look." Aunt Mary Opal was really good at going with the flow when it came to making up a good story.

Rachael felt nervous throughout the entire conversation. "What did we start?" she thought. "How can we keep this up?" She could hardly wait to tell Jake about this new turn of events.

TWELVE

THE LAST THING Aunt Mary Opal wanted to do was give Rachael something more to take care of. But after Jesi and Nicole went home, she and Rachael talked nonstop for forty-five minutes about how to handle the unfortunate incident that created a story about head-to-head meditation.

"What happened?" Rachael said. "Why did you fall?"

"I just tripped on that new table."

"Aunt Mary Opal, I know you love buying more antiques, but I think we need to clear some things out of here," Rachael said. "You can't be falling. What if we hadn't been here? What would you have done?"

Rachael seemed sincere in her concern, and Aunt Mary Opal knew she was right. "Maybe you can help me with that. I don't go to my antique store in Ellijay anymore. It's just too much trouble."

"I can help," Rachael said. "There's this guy I know who owns a prop shop for the film industry. We need to get him over here, and you need to make sure which things you're willing to let go of." Rachael seemed quick to create a plan for how to help Aunt Mary Opal with what she understood was the problem. Aunt Mary Opal felt relieved. It had not seemed to occur to Rachael that something bigger was going on.

As they moved the conversation back to how to keep the secret about the fall, they went from thinking it was hilarious to worrying about how Nicole would take it if they told her the truth. The other issue was that Jesi would not stop until she had researched the new type of meditation, and they worried about what would happen if she didn't find anything. Aunt Mary Opal said she was afraid that if Jesi found out that there was never an article on the subject, she would also realize that they made it all up. If that happened, then Aunt Mary Opal would probably have to tell the truth about having fallen in the middle of the room because of her pain. She wasn't ready to give up that secret.

As soon as Rachael left, Aunt Mary Opal drove directly to the library to get some help on finding anything that would give Jesi any kind of information about head-to-head meditation. She had never wanted a computer, but she realized that it would have made her life a lot easier if she had embraced the computer world. She arrived at the library, and a young, African American librarian, someone who had always been eager to help her, was thankfully working that day. It was Sunday, and she was hoping that there would be someone there to help her look up articles on the computer.

Aunt Mary Opal was no stranger to the library. After her last appointment with her therapist, she had reached a conclusion from her research there. The subject she had focused on was death with dignity. Aunt Mary Opal hadn't asked anyone at the library for help on the subject because she was afraid that someone might suspect what she had in mind.

But today was different. "Excuse me," she said to the librarian. "I'm Mary Opal Shook, and I'm sorry to bother you with this, but I am sure you could help me with my subject much faster than I can research on my own. Do you know how to search on the Google?"

The librarian smiled from ear-to-ear. Dee Joplin-Royce had worked at the library for more than ten years but had never heard reference to "the Google." "Yes, what can I help you with?"

Aunt Mary Opal quickly decided that Dee, with her large smile, seemed to find humor in her ignorance of the computer. But she ignored the librarian's attitude and stayed on the task of asking for assistance. "Well, I need to know if there are any articles written on meditation, the kind where people lie on their backs with their heads touching. Kind of a group thing." Aunt Mary Opal fumbled on the words a bit and motioned to the computer, as if the librarian needed to sit and work at her command.

But Aunt Mary Opal could see that Dee had no attitude. She seemed completely delighted to help her. Often, when Aunt Mary Opal felt out of control of a situation, she would put on an attitude of arrogance and project it onto the person trying to help her. That practice had become more prevalent as she had begun to notice changes in her body, including more pain and less flexibility. She didn't mean to speak with arrogance, and any time she realized she was treating others with disrespect, she always apologized, repeatedly.

But that day, she was in a hurry. Their first group

meditation was upon her, and she had no idea what to do, or if there was even such a thing as head-to-head group meditation.

"Okay now, let's see what we can find for you, ma'am." Seated at her computer, Dee patted the chair next to her, indicating a seat for Aunt Mary Opal.

"Do you think this will take long? I am so very sorry to rush you." Aunt Mary Opal began to back off of her attitude, probably due to the sweet tone Dee continued to offer, even when she had not been so kind in return.

"Well, let's see what Google has to offer us. I'll type in *head to head meditation*, and poof, what are the answers?" Dee laughed a little, clearly hoping that Aunt Mary Opal would join in, but she didn't. What Aunt Mary Opal didn't know was that Dee had noticed her in the library over the last few months and had restocked a few of the books that Aunt Mary Opal had been reading. Dee had taken note that the articles and books that focused on cancer and suicide. "Okay, here are the results. Actually, it looks like you have quite a few options."

"Are any of them articles in magazines? Tell me yes." Aunt Mary Opal felt grateful for her help.

"As a matter of fact, yes." Dee laughed again, but this time Aunt Mary Opal was not threatened by the laughter. In fact, she joined in.

"Whew!" Aunt Mary Opal let out her favorite celebratory chant and leaped up, circling in her usual dance around the chair.

Dee chimed in right behind her, matching the same tonality and laughter. "Whew!" They grabbed each other's hands as if they had found a pot of gold. Suddenly, they became conscious of the fact that they had gathered the attention of everyone in the library. It wasn't the norm for people to cheer out in the library, and it certainly wasn't what a librarian should be encouraging or joining in on. They both tucked their heads with a little embarrassment. Aunt Mary Opal saw the head librarian give Dee a stern look, clearly a man who had never found joy in anything.

Aunt Mary Opal let out a sigh of relief at their discovery. But getting in trouble at the library was something she had avoided her entire life, and she didn't intend to start then. She leaned in closer to Dee and whispered, "Most people call me Aunt Mary Opal. Could you print a few for me? I have a friend who will want to read them."

"Of course, Aunt Mary Opal, I'll make you copies," Dee said. "But you know they're twenty cents a page. If you want, I can just email them to you, and you can forward them to your friend. That way it won't cost you any money."

This librarian had clearly overestimated Aunt Mary Opal's computer skills, because this email thing was not going to happen. Not only did Aunt Mary Opal not have email, she really had no idea what Dee just said.

"No, I'm fine paying for the copies."

Once Aunt Mary Opal had the copies in hand, Dee walked with her to the door. "You know, if there are any other things you might want to research, it really is very easy for me to help you," said Dee in a serious voice, as her smile narrowed.

Aunt Mary Opal suspected that Dee might know about her secret research on death with dignity. If so, she would have to deal with that later, or never go back to that library again.

~

By the time Aunt Mary Opal arrived home, Rachael and Jesi were in Rachael's Mini that was parked in front of her house. Instead of pulling into the driveway, they were waiting on the street, anticipating that Aunt Mary Opal would want to drive her car close to the door, as she always had. Just as she pulled into the driveway, Nicole drove in behind her. The sound of the '68 Cadillac had a unique roar, and the smell of the exhaust was even more distinct.

As they all made their way into the house, Nicole couldn't help but express her excitement about the meditation. "I am just thrilled about this. I've meditated for years, but I haven't heard of meditating head-to-head."

Aunt Mary Opal looked across to Rachael, who seemed nervous about the whole thing. She could see from Jesi's body language that she was still skeptical.

She placed her purse on the counter and was about to pull out the articles when Jesi began talking about her Internet search. "I spent some time searching the Internet for that article you described, and I'm not sure if I found the one you read."

"Is the Internet the same as the Google, Jesi?" Aunt Mary Opal asked.

The ladies all glanced at each other with a smile and, once again, Rachael chimed in to save the day for Aunt Mary Opal. "Oh, it's okay. Don't worry about those articles, because we've done just fine with our head-to-head meditation so far. I'm sure tonight will be just fine, too." Aunt Mary Opal slid her articles back into her purse. There was no reason to rock the boat.

Jesi looked unconvinced, but agreed. "Okay, I think we all need to have a Jack before we get started."

"Whew!" Aunt Mary Opal was the first to agree. She walked into the sunroom to get the Jack Daniel's. Rachael picked out four glasses, Jesi opened a new box of jalapeño cheese straws, and Nicole put ice in all the glasses. When it came to cocktail hour, they all knew what to do. The question was, what would they do during the head-to-head meditation?

Usually, beginning the evening with a Jack on the rocks meant they never got to what they had planned because they ended up drinking more than one or two Jacks and had no interest in anything else, but Nicole was eager to get to the planned event. "Okay, y'all, I've decided what we need to meditate on." There was a pause filled with silence. "I think we need to meditate on getting Jesi to settle down."

Rachael spit her Jack Daniel's across the table and right into Nicole's face. She then threw her head back and laughed out loud.

"That's not funny." Jesi was not amused.

"I didn't mean it as funny, Jesi," Nicole said in her defense. "What's wrong with you, Rachael? What is so funny about helping Jesi settle down here in Atlanta? We've all talked about it."

Jesi held out her hands, as if to slow down the conversation. "Wait, you've all talked about it?" Jesi seemed even less amused as Nicole continued.

Rachael stopped laughing. "I'm sorry. You mean settle in Atlanta. I'm not laughing at the idea of Jesi settling down in Atlanta, if she wants to. I'm just not sure that it's a good subject to meditate on. Don't you think it needs to be about something bigger? More important?"

Jesi stood up from the table and poured another Jack. "Oh great, first y'all want to discuss, behind my back, how to get me to settle down. And now I'm not important enough for a silly meditation?"

It seemed that there was no way a head-to-head group meditation would take place that night. As the exchange continued to escalate, Aunt Mary Opal sat in silence, hoping no one would take note. But Nicole did. "You seem whiter than normal," she said. "Are you okay?" Nicole took Aunt Mary Opal's hand. "Oh, you're cold as ice."

They stopped the bickering and turned all of their attention on Aunt Mary Opal. "I'll be okay," she said. "I just have a little pain in my chest. It'll pass." They all moved into action around her. Rachael ran to the closet and pulled down a wool blanket from the top shelf. Jesi removed everything from the table and moved the table back from Aunt Mary Opal. Nicole grabbed the phone and was about to call 911 when Aunt Mary Opal held her hand in the air for them all to stop. "Please. I promise this will pass. Just give me a minute. Please." Confused and worried, they all took a seat back at the table, now repositioned about four feet away from where it had rested for decades.

"What's going on, Aunt Mary Opal?" Rachael slowly stroked her hand.

For a long few minutes, Aunt Mary Opal remained silent. And then, whatever it was that had caused her to appear so sick left her body. Blood flowed to her face, and she warmed up. They all sat in silence, waiting for her to say something, to explain what had just happened. "I'll have another Jack," she finally said. "I think we should meditate on world peace."

"No way. You cannot have another drink." Jesi sounded so sure of herself.

"Jesi, I know you like to be in charge, but you are not the boss of me," Aunt Mary Opal said. "I'm going to have one more drink before we start our first head-to-head group meditation on world peace. And that is the end of the subject." She moved her eyes to Rachael, not with a pleading tone but with one of certainty. "Please." They all knew that the subject was not over. They also knew that, for then, it was best to just follow her lead. Jesi intentionally poured a little less Jack Daniel's than normal, hoping that Aunt Mary Opal wouldn't notice, but she did. "Jesi, do you think we're running short on Jack Daniel's? I have another bottle if that one is empty." Aunt Mary Opal knew exactly what Jesi was up to, but she promised herself that as long as she was able to sit at the kitchen table, she would go on with life as she had always lived it. Jesi reluctantly filled their glasses to the normal level. They finished their cocktails, but not with the same enthusiasm as usual. They were all worried, including Aunt Mary Opal.

The easiest place to make room for all four of them to lie on the floor was in the family room. All the other rooms had way too much furniture to move. At least there they only had to move three pieces of furniture. Before they all lay on the floor, Aunt Mary Opal set the tone. "Now I want you all to listen to me. I am fine. I am old, but I'm fine. Sometimes old people just have pains. Don't dwell on it, or it will make me feel older than I am. Okay? Let's just enjoy our time together. Besides, world peace is depending on us to get this right." They each forced a smile and nodded their heads in agreement as they lay flat on the floor with the tops of their heads touching. "Jesi, those articles you read, what did they say we should do? I don't think Rachael and I were doing it correctly."

Jesi shook her head in disbelief, knowing that someone was lying, but she joined in. "One article said that once we have our heads touching, we're all supposed to picture what we are meditating on, world peace, and then we all make the sound of *ohm*. Another said the same thing, but that we need to also hold hands."

Jesi had made up the whole story, Aunt Mary Opal was sure. Jesi had never found any articles on head-to-head meditation. But right then, whatever the truth was seemed unimportant. They all agreed that holding hands was a good choice. Until then, none of them had considered that one day they might lose Aunt Mary Opal. Rachael started to make the *ohm* sound. It was lower than she usually spoke. The others joined in, but none of them focused on world peace. Each one focused on Aunt Mary Opal, visualizing her living life pain-free, dancing a jig, and laughing.

THIRTEEN

AFTER THE MEDITATION SESSION, the three younger women waved goodbye from the driveway and met up at Red's Lounge to talk about what had happened. The talk was brief but focused. From that point on, they would take turns every day to make sure that Aunt Mary Opal was okay.

Jesi continued her research for the articles that Aunt Mary Opal might have read, and once again, she came up dry. It wasn't in Jesi's nature to fall asleep crying, but that night, she did just that. Something must be really wrong with Aunt Mary Opal. While she always antici- pated losing her Noni while she was traveling to some other country, she was accustomed to that feeling. Now she had to hold the idea of losing Noni alongside the idea of losing Aunt Mary Opal. It was nearly unbearable.

The next morning, she awoke knowing exactly what to do: Settle in. Staying at Rachael and Jake's studio had been easy for Jesi because she had her own entrance and everyone respected each other's privacy. But that morning, Jesi sent Rachael a text, asking her if she wanted to meet around the pool for coffee.

They sat with their feet in the water. "I'm thinking about getting an apartment and maybe see what it feels like to settle down for a while," she announced. Jesi knew Rachael would be surprised. "Do you think you could help me decorate if I find a cool place?"

Rachael screamed out loud and leaped up from the side of the pool. Without a word, she ran into the house and returned with a stack of design magazines. "Are you kidding me? Yes, I can't wait to tell Aunt Mary Opal. She just asked me last week if I thought you might stay here for a while. And after last night with Nicole and her meditation suggestion, well, I was hoping that maybe it was possible for you to settle down." Rachael plopped down on the side of the pool next to Jesi and opened up a magazine to a page that she had tabbed. "Look at this. It is the coolest sofa. You are going to get a loft, right?"

Jesi had expected Rachael to be happy about her announcement, but she was surprised and delighted at just how excited Rachael seemed to be. "Yeah, I was thinking a loft would be really great."

OVER THE NEXT FEW WEEKS, Rachael, Aunt Mary Opal, Nicole, and Jesi looked at what seemed like every loft for rent in the city. Aunt Mary Opal told Jesi that she was thrilled at the decision but was a little concerned about her decision to live in an old building, until one day the quartet drove to a freestanding building located off Chattahoochee Avenue. Jesi's parents knew the owner of the building and, as it turned out, he was in financial trouble. If Jesi liked the building, her Noni was going to buy it so that Jesi could have her own place, rather than rent from someone else. For Jesi's parents and her Noni, this would be a dream come true.

When they walked into the old brick building, there was a smell of gasoline from an old car that appeared to have been parked in the garage for a long time. Aunt Mary Opal announced that she was worried for Jesi and was a little scared to walk any further. But Jesi appealed to Aunt Mary Opal's sense of never wanting to miss out, so the older woman followed the three younger women onto the freight elevator that took them to the second and third floors. The second floor was empty and clean, with wide floor planks and only two doors, which respectively led to the stairwell and an immaculate, expansive bathroom. By the time they got to the third floor, Aunt Mary Opal told Jesi that she was feeling more secure with the idea that Jesi might live in this building.

The third floor consisted of one large room with brick walls and a floor and ceiling made from wood with a rough-hewn texture—exactly what most people wanted in their lofts. On this floor, too, there were only two doors—one to the stairwell, and the other to a large bathroom. The simple kitchen overlooked a small, overgrown courtyard.

"What do you think, Jesi?" Aunt Mary Opal asked. "Is this place something that you could live in?" She almost didn't even have to inquire. Everyone in the room was excited. This would become Jesi's new home.

"Oh yeah. I love it," Jesi said. "But Aunt Mary Opal, I have to know that you'll come see me. When we get it fixed up, of course." Jesi motioned to Rachael, indicating that she would help with the renovation.

"I love it if you love it," Aunt Mary Opal said.

∽

OVER THE NEXT FEW MONTHS, Rachael worked every day on the designs, and as soon as the purchase was complete, she and Nicole joined in, working day and night with Jesi to make her loft a home. Jesi had pulled in contractors who worked for her dad. With Rachael in charge, they were able to complete the renovation in record time.

On the day they completed the work and the building was ready for Jesi to move in, the quartet celebrated by ordering dinner from a neighbor's Italian artisanal market. When a woman delivered the food, Jesi remarked, "Damn, I was hoping that hunk of a man who owns the store would deliver the food."

"Jesi, are you switching teams?" asked Aunt Mary Opal, who was surprised at Jesi's apparent attraction.

Jesi laughed and waved her hand as if she were just kidding. "No, I was thinking you might like him."

"Oh, no, no, no, no. I am done with that part of my life. The last thing I'm interested in is another man to tell me how to live my life."

Rachael joined in. "Is he cute? How old is he? Maybe I'd be interested."

While they all knew Rachael was loyal to her marriage, it didn't surprise any of them to hear her express interest in another man. Rachael loved Jake, but they all knew Rachael had become more introverted than normal, something they attributed to what Jesi referred to as Jake's energy-sucking ego trip.

Aware of the long silence in the room after her comment, Rachael flung open the French doors at the rear of the living room and took in a long deep breath of fresh air. "What a perfect night to celebrate a new beginning."

FOURTEEN

AUNT MARY OPAL realized that the kind and helpful librarian might be a good person to confide in. It seemed obvious that Dee had been keeping track of the books she had checked out of the library. Every book had to do with cancer and ending life while still having dignity. She hoped that Dee could help her by providing information from the Internet that would be more detailed and up-to-date than the books on the shelves. That's what she decided when she pulled into the parking lot.

The library was particularly cold that day, and Aunt Mary Opal was thankful to have brought her shawl. "Dee, do you think it would be okay if I sat with you at your computer for a moment?" Aunt Mary Opal had decided that she had to take a chance on confiding in someone. She hoped that she wasn't wrong about Dee and her ability to keep her secret.

"Aunt Mary Opal, of course. Sit right here next to me. Were the articles on meditation helpful?"

"Oh my, yes. I'm so sorry. I should have thanked you sooner. You were so kind to help me."

"No, you're just fine. What can I help you with today?" Dee said. "Oh, it's chilly in here, isn't it?"

Aunt Mary Opal felt especially sensitive to the cold and was selfishly grateful that Dee had noticed. Dee turned on the small heater that she kept under her desk, and she pointed it toward Aunt Mary Opal. "Thank you for warming me up," she said, after a long, deep breath. "I guess you know what I have been reading about."

"I'm glad you came back," Dee said. "You know, Aunt Mary Opal, part of my job is to make sure that books are placed in their correct location on the shelves. I hope you know I was in no way trying to find out what you were reading."

"No, no, no. You have been completely professional. But I do realize that you may be able to help me get better information than what I can find in the books. You know, on what they call death with dignity." Aunt Mary Opal moved her chair a little closer to Dee and to the heater. She was talking softly so they couldn't be over-heard. "Can we keep this our little secret?"

"Yes, we can. Your secret's safe with me." Dee winked at Aunt Mary Opal and gave her a little shoul-der-to-shoulder nudge. "I was hoping you'd come back in, so I took the liberty to print off some articles on the subject. I kept them in my briefcase to make sure that no one would see them."

Aunt Mary Opal was surprised. "Was I that obvious?"

"No. It's just that when I saw you reading the book *At Liberty to Die*, I knew you were dealing with something very serious." Dee shifted her body a little closer. "I have an idea. How about we meet at a coffeehouse in the morning, and we can visit? Take these articles, and we can talk about all this tomorrow. Would that work for you?"

"Are you sure it's okay? It won't interfere with your workday?" Aunt Mary Opal quickly glanced up to where the library supervisor usually stood, overlooking the main floor, but he was nowhere to be seen.

"I'm off work tomorrow, and I would love to get to know you." Dee slipped the articles into Aunt Mary Opal's purse. She wiped the perspiration that had formed on her forehead, even though Aunt Mary Opal still seemed to be chilled.

"Well then, you must come to my house, and we can have some privacy." Aunt Mary Opal knew that getting out of the house too early was becoming more difficult for her and that meeting there would be best. Even her aerobics class had become challenging. They exchanged phone numbers, and Aunt Mary Opal wrote down her address for Dee.

"Okay, then. I'll see you at your house at 8:30," Dee said. Instead of shaking her hand on the agreement, Dee gently wrapped her arms around Aunt Mary Opal and held her in a long embrace.

Aunt Mary Opal suddenly felt a little less alone. When she got to her car, she bowed her head and prayed for a few minutes. "Thank you for my new friend. Thank you for sending me someone I trust enough to share the most important secret of my life, perhaps my last secret."

Over the next few months, Aunt Mary Opal and Dee met for coffee at least once a week. Sometimes they talked about her plans to take her own life, but mostly, Aunt Mary Opal shared about her adventures with Rachael, Jesi, and Nicole. When the subject turned to Aunt Mary Opal's health, Dee always made her feel as if there was nothing wrong with her plans to take her own life. Aunt Mary Opal worked up the nerve to ask Dee if she might be willing to help her if she ever needed help. "I know this is a lot to ask of you. And if you're not comfortable with helping me, then it is just fine. You have to be honest. I have all the things needed, including the helium tank. I just need someone to do a couple of things."

"Aunt Mary Opal, I would be honored to help you if that's something you're certain about," Dee replied. "But you do know that me helping you can never be discussed with anyone, even your friends."

"Oh no, I would never tell anyone. And my friends don't even know anything about you. This is our little secret, remember?" She motioned back and forth between them with her right forefinger, indicating that she was talking about their friendship.

FIFTEEN

THAT EVENING, Dee got home from working at the library just in time to get in a five-mile run before cooking dinner. In addition to her golden retriever, Babe, and her sweetheart, Dr. Paula Gregory, exercising was one of the top three most important things in her life.

Dee usually took Babe on her runs but, as the years passed, Babe had difficulty keeping up. She missed having her dog with her, but she would rather go back out for a short walk than to eliminate the exercise that kept her feeling healthy or to push Babe beyond her limits. Dee was a petite woman, but her body was strong and well-defined. She kept her hair short, which accentuated her high cheekbones and deep brown eyes.

Dee and Paula had been married for eight years. They lived a charmed life in an exclusive area of Atlanta. While Dee earned a librarian's income, Paula was an oncologist and loved being the main breadwinner of the family. They met at a New Year's Eve party. The night Dee walked into the party, Paula told her that she couldn't take her eyes off her. "You were like a magnet,"

Paula had said. From the time they went on their first date, neither of them had any interest in dating anyone else. They joked about the lesbians who showed up on their second date with a U-Haul trailer. Dee often told people, "That's us, we both drove up with trailers!"

After Dee's run, she walked Babe around the block and headed home to shower and fix dinner. Their home was contemporary, with windows that stretched from floor to ceiling and expansive covered balconies. Because it had three floors, it was difficult for Babe to maneuver the stairs as she aged, so they had installed an elevator. If Babe wanted to get to another floor, she sat at the elevator entrance and barked until someone acted as her elevator operator. Babe knew which floor she wanted. If they stopped on the second floor but Babe wanted on the third floor, Babe backed up into the corner of the elevator and cried until they closed it and continued to the floor Babe wanted to exit on. "I think we've created an elevator monster," Paula told their friends. "I can just see us spending all our time trying to get to the right floor for Babe." But they didn't care. They loved her as if she were their child.

Just as Dee undressed and climbed into the shower, she heard Paula call out, "Dee, I'm home, and I'm starving!"

"I'm getting in the shower, and I'll fix dinner when I'm done." Dee knew she was running a little late and was hoping Paula would take her out to dinner. She pictured her wife of eight years, the long blonde hair that she kept curled tight against her head while working. Paula didn't think it was professional of her for patients to see hair stretching down her back. But Paula's habit was that as soon as she walked into the front door of their home, she pulled the pins away and shook her head so the tension in her scalp was relieved and her hair could flow freely. She always told Dee that she felt as if this was a ritual to let go of the pressures of the day and the stress of helping her cancer patients.

Just as Dee covered her hair in shampoo, the shower door opened and Paula slipped in. Paula wrapped her arms around Dee and pulled her body close to hers. She loved being able to slip up on Dee from behind, especially in the shower. "I know I said I'm hungry, but let's spend the whole evening making love. We can order a pizza if we need food." The hot water poured over their bodies as they made love.

As they stepped out of the shower, Paula leaned into Dee and said, "I want more of that." Paula often came home from work with an insatiable sexual appetite, and Dee was thrilled to be her wife.

"Me too, but I'm starving," Dee said. "I can fix dinner, we can go out, or order in. Which is it, Dr. Love?" Dee often called her Dr. Love, but only in private. If their friends found out, they would never let them live it down.

"I feel like celebrating tonight," Paula said. "Let's go to La Tavola. I'll call and let them know we're on our way."

Dee and Paula were regulars at La Tavola and never had to call in advance for reservations. Everyone at the restaurant loved them both because they were always so pleasant and because they tipped better than anyone else. Paula knew how to get a server's attention and keep it — that way, she was always certain to have a positive experience.

"What are we celebrating?" Dee had to decide what to wear.

"You and me, babe, our life." Paula often liked to have random celebrations. As an oncologist, she saw a lot of suffering, and she was clear that if life was intended to be joyful, then it better be celebrated.

"I'll be ready in ten." Dee took off running into her closet and chose a brightly colored sundress, one loose enough that she didn't have to wear anything underneath.

During appetizers, Dee shared her experience of meeting Aunt Mary Opal, "She's an adorable woman, probably about seventy years old. I kept trying to get her to let me help her, but she was always so private, and sometimes she's a little snippy."

"She's snippy and you like her?" Paula frowned.

Dee laughed. "Yes, you'd just have to meet her to understand. Anyway, I've been meeting her for coffee, and I love our new friendship."

"How long have you known her?"

Dee hesitated, because she knew that keeping secrets was not something they did in their marriage. "A few months."

"A few months? And this is the first time you're telling me about her?"

At this, Dee had a sinking feeling. Did Paula think there was more to the story than just Dee having coffee with a snippy old woman? But she let the thought pass. Paula had always respected Dee and her choices, and she sat across the table, waiting for Dee to share more.

∾

FOR THE NEXT TWENTY MINUTES, Dee shared stories of how Aunt Mary Opal danced around her chair when she learned new things. Paula smiled at the endearing stories of Aunt Mary Opal's life, including stories about Rachael, Jesi, and Nicole. "I feel like I know them, even though I've never met them," Dee said. "I'm hoping to someday. And, Aunt Mary Opal and Rachael think Jesi and Nicole are in love with each other." Dee smiled at Paula and rubbed her foot up the side of Paula's leg. "The first time Aunt Mary Opal let me help her was when she made up a story about what she calls head-to-head group meditation," Dee continued. "She was so nervous to get my help that she was grouchy and kind of mean. But when I pulled up some articles for her, it was like all her stress left. That's when she jumped up from the chair and danced around in a circle." Dee leaped up from the table, mimicked Aunt Mary Opal, and concluded with a "Whew!"

Paula smiled. "That is why I love you so much. You have a way of connecting to people and a way of expression that is so pure, so loving."

When Dee sat back down, she slid in next to Paula, seductively telling her that she had nothing on underneath her dress. She then jumped up from the table and sat back across from Paula.

"You are such a tease," Paula said.

They stared in each other's eyes for a long moment before Dee continued and the server arrived to fill their wine glasses and let them know their food would be right out. "This next part is what's hard. Aunt Mary Opal asked me to help her research death with dignity."

Paula put her glass of wine on the table and leaned in. "Is she sick?"

"Yes." Dee held her breath for a moment and waited for Paula's response. Dee knew that Paula couldn't resist helping people in need. She knew Paula was an oncologist because she loved to help people. The money was a bonus, but helping people who were suffering was her passion. "One time she was reading about that group here in Georgia that helps terminally ill people die by using helium as the means for suicide."

"That group went to jail, Dee," Paula said. "Does she know that there are places she can move to where it's legal, like Oregon? Does she have a doctor?"

Dee was completely aware of the issues. She also had never been one to walk away from someone in need. Paula knew that about her. But Dee wasn't about to tell Paula that Aunt Mary Opal had asked her to help with her plans. They didn't talk much more about Aunt Mary Opal. When the topic shifted, they were clear that the subject of assisted suicide was not something that Paula could talk about. Paula was Dr. Paula, the oncologist. Her ethical and legal boundaries were clear.

A COUPLE OF DAYS LATER, just as Dee had hoped, Paula returned home early and said, "Dee, I've been thinking about the woman you know from the library. Do you think you could get her to talk to me? Does she seem like she's in pain?"

"I do think she's in pain," Dee said. "How about I see if I can get her to go to lunch one day, say, Friday?" Friday was Paula's day off.

"Perfect, I'll put it on my schedule. Let's meet at

Mick's, the one close to the hospital. If there's anything I can do, we'll be close to the office."

The next morning, Dee called Aunt Mary Opal and asked her to have lunch at Mick's that Friday. "Do you want me to pick you up?"

"Oh no, no, no," Aunt Mary Opal said. "I'll meet you there. I have some errands to do, so a lunch break will be perfect. Maybe we can start with some chocolate pie."

Dee was thrilled. "Perfect. I'll see you there." There, her job was done. She had complete confidence in Paula to take it from there. It was not the first time Dee had found herself with someone who needed Paula's help.

That evening, the couple hosted dinner guests, Paula's brother and his wife. Dee skipped her run in order to marinate the steaks and get dinner pulled together. It was another boring evening with them and, thankfully, short. As Dee served cheesecake topped with strawberries, she mentioned to Paula, "Oh, by the way, I confirmed lunch at eleven on Friday."

"Great, I'll just meet you there. I may run a little late." Dee already knew the drill. Paula would show up about fifteen minutes late and act like she hadn't expected to see them. Then she'd do her magic.

THAT FRIDAY, Dee waited on the bench outside Mick's as Aunt Mary Opal walked up the hill. "I just can't breathe quite as good as I used to when walking uphill," she said as she arrived. "Please forgive me if I'm breathing heavy." She reached out and hugged Dee.

Dee could feel the older woman shaking a little, so she kept holding on for a moment as Aunt Mary Opal steadied herself. "Thank you so much for meeting me for lunch. I love this place. Do you ever come here?"

"Oh yes, many times. I love that chocolate pie." Aunt Mary Opal seemed to be feeling better, so they made their way into the restaurant. The hostess seated them in a booth with a view of Peachtree Street.

They ordered, and Dee started by talking about meditation. "Here are copies of some more articles on meditation. I love meditating. How is your group meditation going?"

"Well, sometimes, I just go to sleep," Aunt Mary Opal said. "They don't even know it, and I'm not going to tell them either. My friends are much younger. I don't know why they keep me around, but I don't question it. You're so kind to think of me and to make the copies."

Just as Aunt Mary Opal was about to offer to pay for the copies, Paula walked up to the table. "Dee, so good to see you."

"Paula, great to see you," Dee said. "This is my friend, Mary Opal Shook." Dee motioned to Aunt Mary Opal as she slid over in the booth for Paula to sit down.

"People call me Aunt Mary Opal." She smiled and extended her handshake. "Are you going to join us for lunch? We just ordered."

"I'll have a cup of coffee if that's okay. I have a meeting at the hospital in a few minutes."

"Oh, are you a nurse?" Aunt Mary Opal asked.

"Actually, I'm an oncologist at Piedmont," Paula said. "I love being a doctor, especially in my field. I feel so needed by my patients, and that feels good."

Dee smiled. Paula had started her magic.

"Oh, how stupid of me. Of course you're a doctor," Aunt Mary Opal said. "Please forgive me. I'm old."

"That's quite alright. I love nurses, and sometimes I think they could run the hospital without us." Paula grinned at Aunt Mary Opal, checking to see if she was feeling comfortable.

"How long have you been at Piedmont?" Aunt Mary Opal asked. Dee felt certain that the older woman understood that Dee had set her up to meet Paula.

"Sixteen years," Paula said. "My office is closed today, but I have a patient who wants to visit with me. Sometimes I meet her in Piedmont Park. We sit on a bench and talk about what's going on in her life. That's part of why I love being a doctor. I can help people sometimes by just giving some good advice."

Dee saw that Aunt Mary Opal was curious. She and Paula waited for her to continue the conversation. They knew that Aunt Mary Opal needed to engage in the conversation if a window of opportunity was to open. Dee excused herself to go to the bathroom, and she let the server know that Paula would like a cup of coffee. Afterward, she would learn of what happened.

Assured of privacy, Aunt Mary Opal began to speak. "So the woman you meet in the park is a patient of yours?"

"Not really," Paula said. "She's decided not to go through treatment. The problem is that she doesn't want to live with the inevitable pain. So I just meet with her as her friend and keep a check on her. If it gets to where she needs something more, I'll have to talk to her about some pain treatment. Then she'll need to be my patient."

Aunt Mary Opal reached across and patted Paula's arm. "You're very kind, Dr. Paula. She's lucky to have you as a friend."

Paula pulled out a business card, wrote down her cell

number, and slid the card across the table. "Aunt Mary Opal, here's my personal cell number. If you ever need a friend, call me. Okay?"

Dee returned to the table just as Paula stood up and took a quick sip of her coffee. "I'm so sorry I have to rush off," Paula said. "It was so very nice to visit with you, Aunt Mary Opal. Dee, I'll catch you later." She squeezed Aunt Mary Opal's right shoulder as she walked away.

ONLY A WEEK LATER, just as Paula had anticipated, Aunt Mary Opal called her. "Dr. Paula, I could use a friend. Do you think you could meet me for a stroll through the park?"

Paula met Aunt Mary Opal every Friday for two months, hoping that their conversations would go from death with dignity to treatment options. Neither of them shared their visits with anyone else, even Dee. Aunt Mary Opal knew that Paula wanted nothing more than to try to help her with treatment. Aunt Mary Opal simply wanted permission to end her life. As much as Paula wanted things to be different, she gave Aunt Mary Opal exactly what she wanted—permission.

SIXTEEN

AUNT MARY OPAL's furniture was pushed back to make room for the women to lie on the floor, faces up, heads touching. It was Rachael's day to make decisions. "Today, we're going to meditate on how to make it so Nicole and I have as much free time as y'all."

Nicole exhaled loudly. "Thank you, Rachael. I just squeezed a week of work into the last three days just so I could take off today and tomorrow to play with y'all. I am exhausted."

"Me too," Rachael agreed. "And I need some things to change—a lot of things."

"Like what?" Nicole asked.

"For one, I am sick of living alone. I know Jake lives with me, but he's never there. He comes in long enough to make a mess and then he's gone. I want to do something exciting with my life instead of just cleaning up after him all the time." Rachael sensed that her words had landed. Her friends all knew things weren't perfect at home for her, but she knew that they heard in her voice more than just the usual frustration.

"Let's come up with some ideas, and we can all medi-tate on them," Nicole said. "You could plan a vacation, or you could volunteer at a senior center."

"What about taking flying lessons?" Aunt Mary Opal interjected. "Your dad was in the Air Force. Maybe that would help."

It was Jesi's turn to come up with something. "You could get a divorce."

At that, Aunt Mary Opal and Nicole gasped. Rachael burst into laughter.

"Believe me, I've thought about it," Rachael said.

Jesi picked up on this. "I mean, if you live alone, why not really live alone? I'm not sure if it would give you more time away from work, but it sure would free up your off time."

Nicole rolled her eyes. "That's a little drastic, don't you think?"

"Why?" Jesi said. "What's the point of having a rela-tionship if you're always alone?"

"Jesi, the answer to problems is not always to walk out on them," Nicole said. "Sometimes it takes staying power."

Jesi, in her usual style, said, "How well did that work for you? I mean you stayed and just got screwed."

At that comment, Nicole sat up. "Let's not turn this conversation about Rachael's marriage into a way to remind me of how stupid I am." She turned and looked down at Rachael. "Rachael, I'm just saying that maybe there are some ways to be happy even if Jake's not around."

Jesi sat up and reached out to touch Nicole's hand. "I'm sorry. I didn't mean to be so mean."

"Yes you did, and I don't care," Nicole said. "It's true.

I suck at choosing someone to be with. But Rachael, you and Jake seem to have so many things that work for you, don't you?" Her voice was pleading. As the tension escalated, Aunt Mary Opal made her way up from the floor and sat in her rocker. Jesi, Rachael, and Nicole sat cross-legged in a circle around the chair.

"Yeah, we do," Rachael sighed. "It's just that I'm pretty certain that Jake's seeing someone. I mean someone he really likes." Other than the grandfather clock announcing that it was 3:00 p.m., the room was quiet. "I've always known he would have flings, but this seems different," Rachael said. "You know, with him being on tour all the time. I knew what I was getting when we got married. I didn't care. But now I think I do care." She sat in silence as the room filled with emotional outbursts.

First, Jesi: "That asshole."

Then Nicole: "That makes me sick to my stomach."

Then Aunt Mary Opal, her voice raised: "Men have always treated women like they're just supposed to shut up while they go do anything they want. I know. I lived through it."

Jesi jumped up from the floor. "I'll get the bourbon. We need a drink."

Rachael waved her hand back and forth. "I can't, Jesi."

"What do you mean you can't? You just drop that bombshell on us and think you don't need a drink? You better think again." Jesi poured four double jacks on the rocks.

～

THE NEXT MORNING, Rachael awoke with a pounding hangover. For a moment, she was confused about where she was. The ceiling was lower than at her own house, and the room was packed with antiques. There was a slight musty smell. She then realized that she was in Aunt Mary Opal's basement. The ladies light luncheon had turned into a Thursday throw-down, and the Friday morning sunlight pierced right to the back of her eyeballs. The musty smell came from the green shag carpet and pine-paneled walls. She slowly made her way upstairs and into the family room. Aunt Mary Opal stood in the kitchen, unaware that Rachael had entered.

Rachael found the whole scene to be odd, as if Aunt Mary Opal were in a trance. As Rachael approached the kitchen, she noticed a hand towel on the floor. Aunt Mary Opal was frozen in space, holding onto the kitchen counter, staring at the towel with an expression of fear. After a moment of confusion, it finally hit Rachael. Aunt Mary Opal was not able to bend down to pick up the towel. She walked into the kitchen, bent over, and picked up the towel. She slapped it into Aunt Mary Opal's hand and gave a look of fake exasperation. "Did you throw that on the floor just to watch me pick it up? Me? With this hangover?"

Aunt Mary Opal snapped out of her trance-like state and began to laugh, joining in with Rachael. "I sure did. I wanted to see if your head could bend down that far this early with that much alcohol." They both poured their coffee and sat at the kitchen table, and they never mentioned the towel again. At about the same time they started on their second cups of coffee, in walked Jesi and Nicole. They had dark rings under their eyes, and their faces were both as white as a sheet. "Oh my!" exclaimed Aunt Mary Opal. "Let me get you some coffee."

"What happened?" Nicole asked.

Rachael noticed that her eyes were bloodshot.

"The last thing I remember was playing dominoes and Rachael was winning," Nicole said. "Then I woke up with all my clothes on and I feel like I have a sweater on my teeth."

"Don't talk to me," Jesi said. "I haven't had my coffee yet."

Jesi was always a little dramatic in the mornings, Rachael thought. Usually, they all tiptoed around her, but it was not to be that day. With her voice intentionally louder than necessary, Rachael hoped to annoy Jesi as much as Jesi had annoyed them all the night before with her insistence on just one more drink. "Good morning, sunshine!" she sang out. "Rise and shine, it's gonna be a beautiful day!"

"Oh, God. Please lower your voice," Jesi whispered, as she held her left hand up as though it could stop the conversation.

"Please!" Nicole pleaded. "I want to know why we thought we had to do what she wanted. Not next time. Next time I'm going to remember this. I'm never going to listen to you again, Jesi. You are evil."

Jesi still wasn't able to speak above a whisper. "Okay, okay, but no one twisted your arm."

Nicole looked up from her coffee at Aunt Mary Opal. She stared at her for a few moments and studied her perfectly back-combed hair, her peachy skin, and her sharply pressed blouse. "How can you look so rested, with your hair in perfect shape, when we all look like this?"

"I am a professional," Aunt Mary Opal proudly proclaimed. "I paced myself. Unlike you, I don't have to do everything Jesi tells me to do."

"That's it? That's all you have to say?" Nicole asked. "You don't have some kind of secret pill or spell you take that you've kept from us? One of your little secrets?" Nicole was pointedly sarcastic, no doubt thinking of all the secrets Aunt Mary Opal seemed to keep. The conversation digressed. Jesi and Rachael sat straight up in their chairs but stayed quiet. They moved their eyes back and forth between Nicole and Aunt Mary Opal, waiting to see what would transpire from Nicole's challenging tone.

"Well, I do take a supplement before I go to bed," Aunt Mary Opal said. "That may help."

"I knew it. You're holding out on us. It's another secret. What is it?" Nicole said.

"It's nothing, really. I read an article that said if you take Airborne after you've been drinking and before you go to sleep, you'll feel better in the morning. I'm not sure if that's why I look like this, but it may be." Aunt Mary Opal wrinkled her nose up and smiled at Jesi and Rachael, evidently sure that Nicole was not ready to let go of her sarcasm.

Nicole stepped it up. "Well, do you think you might share some with us?"

Aunt Mary Opal got up from the table and set the Airborne on the table, along with three glasses of water. She wrapped her arms around Nicole and squeezed her, whispering so that it wouldn't hurt her head, "Take this, honey. You'll feel better in a bit." Nicole rested her head on Aunt Mary Opal's shoulder for a long moment. Looking at the two of them, Rachael felt like she was watching a mother and daughter. She remembered all the times her own mother held her close.

SEVENTEEN

NICOLE AGREED to host the next ladies light luncheon. Rachael and Aunt Mary Opal had been packing up items that the prop shop had purchased, and Aunt Mary Opal's house was in no condition to host. Nicole moved all the furniture to the walls of her living room just in case a meditation session was in order.

After lunch, Nicole finally got up the nerve to ask the question she had always wanted to ask. "Rachael, why do you have so many tattoos? I get people putting one tattoo somewhere to remind them of some special person. But you're covered. What's that about?" Rachael giggled, while Aunt Mary Opal and Jesi remained quiet. They seemed like they could hardly believe that Nicole was asking that question.

"Well, Nicole, I am so happy you asked me," Rachael said. "Have you been wanting to ask that for a while?"

"Ever since that day we met in the grocery store," Nicole said. She finally felt secure enough in their friendship to open up.

"Wow," Jesi said. "You've wanted to ask that since

the beginning but you're just now getting the nerve? I am so proud of you, Nicole! Let me pour you drink."

"No, Jesi. I don't want another drink," Nicole said. "I just want to learn more about Rachael. So don't pour me a drink, and I mean it. You know what happened last time, and I have no intention of repeating that. I was hung over for two days." She turned her attention back to Rachael. "Are you okay talking about it? Because if you're not, it's okay." Suddenly, Nicole thought maybe she shouldn't have asked.

"No, no, I mean yes, it's okay to ask," said Rachael, raising her left pant leg. "Do you see that black design right there?" She pointed just above her left ankle at a black winding design. "That's the eternal knot of love, my first tattoo. I got that when I was eighteen. My best friend and I got the same one right after she was voted most likely to become a nun in our senior year prophesies. We thought the tattoo would keep us connected if she did become a nun. She's actually a cop. We aren't close anymore, but I love the memory." They gathered in a circle around Rachael as she continued. "Then, the one just above it, see how the knot of love kind of weaves into that dragon?" They leaned in closer to see the purple-and-red dragon whose tail was an extension of the eternal knot of love and extended up the side of her entire left calf. "I designed that one myself. It was when I was twenty-one and feeling like men kept getting the design jobs I wanted. Sophie, that's the dragon's name. She reminds me that my strength and talent begin with love and then rise up."

Rachael held their attention for over an hour. They were mostly quiet while listening to the tremendous emotional history Rachael was sharing. Occasionally,

Rachael's eyes filled with tears at the stories of her tattoos, especially her most recent one. It read *Mildred*, which Nicole knew was Rachael's mother's name.

When Rachael finished, Nicole leaned in, took Rachael's hands in hers, and said, "Rachael, now I know. Now I know how you are so sweet all of the time. You put everything right here." She touched Rachael's torso. "And that way you don't have to live the past. You've written it all down."

Tears welled in Rachael's eyes, and then her sweet smile came. "Yeah, I guess that's what I do."

"I have an idea," Jesi broke in. "Let's all get tattoos."

Nicole gasped. "What?"

"Well, why not? I think we could all come up with something that would be like our own design. What do you say, Aunt Mary Opal?" When Jesi began her maneuvering, neither Rachael nor Aunt Mary Opal knew what to say or do, so they turned their gaze to Nicole.

"I am not getting a tattoo, and neither is Aunt Mary Opal," Nicole said. "So stop it, Jesi."

Rachael's eyes were no longer filled with tears. They were as wide open as they could be. Angry dissent was not easy for her to be around. To Nicole, it seemed like she and Jesi had been pushing each other out of their comfort zones lately.

Nicole knew that Aunt Mary Opal never liked people telling her what to do, even Jesi. "I will get a tattoo if I want to," Aunt Mary Opal said.

Nicole gasped. "Aunt Mary Opal, don't let Jesi manipulate you."

"She is doing no such thing," Aunt Mary Opal said.

"As a matter of fact, you are the one telling me what I will and will not do."

Nicole could hardly believe what she was hearing. "Fine, if Aunt Mary Opal gets one, then so will I. But Aunt Mary Opal has to get her tattoo first, before I will. I don't want to get one and then both of you back out." She spoke to Rachael, but she was looking at Aunt Mary Opal and Jesi when she said it.

Aunt Mary Opal took Nicole's hand. "I have an idea, Nicole. Let's get tattoos at the same time. All four of us, together."

Rachael and Jesi, both glancing back and forth at Nicole and Aunt Mary Opal, began laughing at the thought of seeing them get tattoos. "Oh, now, what have we gotten started?" Rachael said, hardly believing she was actually hearing Aunt Mary Opal agreeing to get a tattoo. "Aunt Mary Opal, are you sure you want to do that?"

"Well, if I am, we all are, so what are we going to get tattooed?" Aunt Mary Opal seemed confident.

For two weeks, they shared ideas of designs, and finally, they all came to the same conclusion: They would let Rachael create a design showing all four of them in their weekly meditation, head to head to head to head. That would be unique and would symbolize their connection to each other.

Nicole suspected that the tattoo day would never become a reality, but she knew one thing for certain: She would not go first. In the past, some of Nicole's friends had tried to persuade her to get a tattoo, and she always responded that she would "rather change her jewelry."

The plan was put into action. They would all meet at Aunt Mary Opal's house for coffee, and Rachael would drive them all to the tattoo parlor in Aunt Mary Opal's car. After they finished getting tattoos, they would have lunch at Mick's on Peachtree Street, with a slice of chocolate pie as a reward.

Three days before the agreed-upon date, Nicole felt guilty about how she had spoken to Jesi and Aunt Mary Opal. She had never wanted to hurt their feelings or be harsh to them. Actually, she wasn't really worried that she might have hurt Jesi's feelings, because Jesi was pushy all the time. But Aunt Mary Opal was sweet and old. Nicole created a plan to heal any hurt feelings.

EIGHTEEN

It was Sunday morning, and Aunt Mary Opal was just returning from church when Rachael and Jesi arrived a few minutes early. They announced that Nicole had sent them a text: "Running late, meet you there."

"She better not back out," Jesi said. "If she does, I'll have a hard time forgiving her." Jesi's face turned red at the thought of Nicole backing out.

"Let's just give her the benefit of the doubt, okay?" Rachael said.

Aunt Mary Opal said nothing when she learned that Nicole was not going to follow the plan. The truth was that she was scared too. On the drive to their destination, she stayed completely quiet, and so did Rachael and Jesi. It seemed that each person was contemplating what they had agreed to do and wondering what Nicole would do.

Samson's Tattoo Parlor was a small corner business and located next to a florist. The neon lights were already on, and the window was filled with photographs of people's tattoos. Aunt Mary Opal had frequented the florist but had never paid much attention to Samson's.

A man with tattoos trailing down his arms greeted them at the door. Samson had piercing blue eyes and dark, wavy, shoulder-length hair that was perfectly parted down the center of his head. After admiring how handsome Samson was, Aunt Mary Opal noticed the tattoo that trailed down his right forearm: *Fuck'n A*. She did her best to hide her disapproval of the tattoo, but she was certain that everyone in the room noticed the frown on her face, including Samson.

Samson smiled and offered them the option of Coke or water. When he motioned for them to move into the back room, the front door opened. They all turned around, hoping that it would be Nicole, only to be disappointed to see that it was simply a delivery man with doughnuts. The note on top of the box read: *To Rachael, Jesi, Aunt Mary Opal, & Nicole. Have a great time. Love, Jake.*

"Oh, that Jake." Aunt Mary Opal adored Jake, even though she knew the doughnut delivery was just a sign of his ego and that his ego was probably going to bring about the end of his marriage.

Jesi was focused on Nicole. "Where is she?" she asked. "Do you think she's backing out?" Just then, Nicole entered. They all gasped and bursted into hysterical laughter. Samson and the other tattoo artists looked around quizzically. There stood Nicole, her hair cut, bleached, and back-combed to look just like Aunt Mary Opal. Nicole laughed with them. Tears ran down all of their faces. Their nerves had been on edge for two weeks, and relief showed up in the form of laughing and crying at the same time. Samson looked around, not sure what to do. He left the room, and Aunt Mary Opal wondered if he was hoping that they were not all intoxicated.

"Now, I'm going to look like two of my three favorite people, back-combed and tattooed!" Nicole could barely get the words out between laughing and crying.

Soon, they settled into their chairs. Rachael had lined up four tattoo artists so they would all get the same tattoo at the same time, just as Nicole had insisted. The room was cramped with the four women and four tattoo artists. Before them, on the wall, completely covered from floor to ceiling, were Mardi Gras beads in designs for suggested tattoos. Rachael had explained that Samson had been in the Ninth Ward of New Orleans and had turned the wall into a Mardi Gras shrine as a great way to remind him of home. Every color and design that could possibly represent New Orleans was on that wall.

Reaching an agreement on the tattoo design was difficult, but determining the location of the design was easy. Aunt Mary Opal had let them know that there was no way that she would go through with getting a tattoo unless the design was in a discrete place, not to be seen by anyone unless it was in an intimate situation. She was certain that meant never for herself. What she didn't share with them, as she demanded that the tattoo be placed just above her left breast, was that her cancer has been identified as originating there. She adored her young friends, but a secret was a secret, and she would never divulge anyone's secrets, even her own. Luckily, Rachael had not already been tattooed above her left breast, so the decision was easy for her. Nicole and Jesi agreed, albeit with a bit of dissatisfaction, but they went along with Aunt Mary Opal—after all, she was their elder. That was their unspoken rule. They treated her a little gentler than they might treat each other.

Samson offered to work with Aunt Mary Opal, to which she raised her right forefinger in the air and waved it back and forth in protest. "No, no, no, no, that won't do." She thanked Samson for offering, but that was not going to work for her.

"But Aunt Mary Opal, Samson is the most experienced, and he owns the . . ." Jesi said.

Aunt Mary Opal quickly held up her hand to stop Jesi from talking. "You may all choose your life the way you want, but I will not have a man drawing on my chest, ever." She smiled sweetly and commandingly at the eldest of the three women tattoo artists.

In a short amount of time, it was decided. Jesi sat with the youngest of the female artists, Nicole with the remaining female, and Rachael with Samson. Once they were all seated, Aunt Mary Opal said, "There, you see, everything always works out exactly as it should!"

During the negotiations, Samson had not said a word. But at Aunt Mary Opal's proclamation, he let out a laugh that filled the room. "Well then, there you have it!"

What had seemed so scary to Aunt Mary Opal and Nicole was over in a short time. As the four women sat at the mercy of tattoo artists with needles, one of Samson's employees snapped photographs. She seemed especially interested in Nicole and Aunt Mary Opal, who sat next to each other, both sporting the same hairstyle. Aunt Mary Opal was still surprised that Nicole had actually bleached her hair to match hers. It was one thing to get your hair back-combed. That was easily removed. But to cut and bleach her red hair was a commitment. Aunt Mary Opal looked forward to the chocolate pie at Mick's so they would have time to find out exactly what Nicole was thinking to be so bold.

When they were finished and once the bandages were in place, the entire staff at the store stood up and applauded. Again, they seem to pay special attention to Nicole and Aunt Mary Opal. As each woman reached to retrieve money to pay, Samson held up his hands. "Nope, it's all taken care of."

Rachael seemed surprised. "What? Who paid you? Are you sure?"

"This is on one of the lovely tattooed ladies with white back-combed hair," Samson said, laughing and motioning toward Nicole and Aunt Mary Opal.

Aunt Mary Opal danced a little jig, as she did so often when she was happy with herself. "Okay, I did. But truthfully, I wasn't sure I would go through with it, and you know I don't like to miss appointments. These people are trying to make a living here." Rachael, Jesi, and Nicole began telling her that there was no way she would pay for all of them, at which point they were interrupted. "A simple 'thank you' is the most polite thing to say," Aunt Mary Opal said. She held her head up, walked past the ladies, slapped Samson's shoulder with the back of her left hand, and threw him a wink. Samson graciously and demonstratively bowed at the waist as she passed him. She walked out of the store and to the passenger side of her car, where she waited for Jesi to open the door.

Rachael looked back at Samson as if he were in trouble with them, to which he smiled and shrugged his shoulders. "What can I say? I have a weakness for older women."

On the drive to Mick's, Rachael reminded them not

to get the tattoo wet for forty-eight hours. She knew that would be difficult for Aunt Mary Opal, who showered every morning at 6:30 a.m. "Aunt Mary Opal, I know you don't want to follow those instructions, but you have to. If you want, I can tell you a lot of really gross stories about what happens when you don't follow the instructions after getting a tattoo, but you really don't want to hear them. They're disgusting. So promise me you'll follow the rules this time. I won't ever ask you to follow rules again. Deal?" Jesi and Nicole laughed and waited for Aunt Mary Opal to agree. When she said nothing, Rachael began to pull the car over. Only then did Aunt Mary Opal agree to keep the tattoo dry for forty-eight hours.

The chocolate pie was at least four inches high, half of it meringue, with a chocolate and graham cracker crust and dark chocolate shavings on top. They each ate their own piece with a cup of dark-roast coffee. Rachael pulled out a flask of Jack Daniel's and poured into each of their cups, careful not to be caught by the waitstaff. They were in Georgia and it was Sunday, and the blue laws prohibited drinking alcohol on Sundays before 12:30 p.m. Aunt Mary Opal always said it was because the Christians didn't want people to get ahead of them. So everyone had to wait until church let out before anyone could drink.

They raised their cups for a toast, and they all said "Whew!" in high-pitched voices. As they toasted, Rachael, Nicole, and Jesi jumped out of their chairs and mimicked Aunt Mary Opal's jig. By then, every head in the restaurant, including the manager's, had turned in their direction.

The manager stopped by the table to tell them how

happy he was that they had chosen Mick's to celebrate, and he asked if Aunt Mary Opal was their mother. "Actually, we're twins," Nicole said, wrapping her arm around Aunt Mary Opal and pulling her close, careful not to disturb either of their tattoos. The manager seemed not quite sure what to do, so he gave a slight smile and wished them a good day. That was quite fine with them because, as usual, they were selfish with their time together, so selfish that their usual ladies light luncheons were typically in the privacy of Aunt Mary Opal's house. But that day was special, and it had warranted a change of pace.

Aunt Mary Opal asked Nicole why she decided to get her hair bleached and back-combed.

Nicole started to explain, but she stopped talking about how she had felt guilty. "I just thought it would be a fun thing to do," she said. "You know, pretend to be someone I admire." She winked at Aunt Mary Opal with the same grin she usually reserved for Jesi.

Aunt Mary Opal blushed a little and shrugged it off with laughter. It was obvious that Nicole would not tell any of them what was really going on with her to have her hair bleached and back-combed. Aunt Mary Opal knew the truth. She knew that Nicole was reaching out to let her know, in her own way, that she didn't feel like an outsider anymore. Aunt Mary Opal had the feeling that Jesi must have known the impact when she pushed them all into agreeing to get tattoos together. It created a sense of belonging to each other.

To Aunt Mary Opal, Nicole was different after that day. She was more emotional with them and stopped apologizing all the time. It was as if she finally felt a part of something bigger than herself.

NINETEEN

THE CITY HADN'T SEEN the Sun in more than a month, and the mist kept everything wet and chilly. The seal around the windshield of Nicole's '68 Cadillac Diva had far outlived its usefulness, and the water had seeped inside, moistening the dash. Nicole cut her workday short in order to drop in to visit with Aunt Mary Opal. She stood at the back door with the heavy mist highlighting where her red curls were finally beginning to take over the bleach from the day they all got tattoos. "I hope it's okay that I just dropped in on you. I was driving up Briarcliff Road and realized how close I was." Nicole stretched out her arms. "So here I am."

"Of course, dear, you're always welcome," Aunt Mary Opal said. "You know, most people don't like drop-in guests, but I love them." Aunt Mary Opal pulled a hand towel from the kitchen drawer and handed it to Nicole so she could wipe the misty rain from her face. "I am so sorry. I had the awning taken down to get it repaired, and they haven't brought it back yet."

Nicole wanted alone time with Aunt Mary Opal. "I

know it's not five o'clock yet, but would you happen to have a bottle of red wine we could open? I brought some cheese and crackers."

"Run downstairs to the spare room and pick out what wine you want," Aunt Mary Opal said. "I'll get the cheese and crackers ready." She pulled two crystal wine glasses from the cupboard.

Nicole placed the bag of groceries on the counter as Aunt Mary Opal pulled out her favorite cutting board and carefully placed the cheese in perfect symmetry. She then ran down the stairs to retrieve a bottle of red wine. As she started back upstairs, she noticed that the store-room door stood wide open, with the lights on. "That's strange," Nicole thought. "That storeroom is always locked." As Nicole poked her head into the storeroom, a chill came over her. Her breathing stopped for a long moment as she scanned the equipment. She'd seen this before. Neatly lined up was the exact setup for assisted suicide that Nicole herself had gathered before she had fallen into Aunt Mary Opal in the store. Helium. Plastic tent. Arm restraints. "Am I really seeing this? Is Aunt Mary Opal sick? What should I do? Talk to Aunt Mary Opal? Rachael and Jesi?"

In a split instant, incidents from the past with Aunt Mary Opal began to add up. The pain she saw in her eyes, the night she had a pain in her chest, the cough that seemed to worsen each month, and more. Nicole held her hands over her mouth and quietly cried. She was certain that Aunt Mary Opal was dying. Why? Why hadn't she told Rachael, Jesi, and herself? "Oh my God, she can't do this. What am I going to do?" Nicole stood in silence until she heard Aunt Mary Opal, who must not have been aware that she had left the storeroom open.

"Nicole, did you see where the wine is?"

Nicole quickly wiped her eyes with the sleeve of her jacket and yelled back. "Yes, just had to use the bathroom. I'm picking out the wine now. Be right up." She pulled it together and made the decision not to say anything at that point. She needed to think about how to handle the devastating discovery. Then she turned the lights off and closed the door.

That night, Nicole did something she hadn't done since she was a child. She knelt down next to her bed and prayed. "God, I know it's been a really long time since I prayed, but I really need your help. I believed it when you said you were always there for me, and right now I need you to be really clear with me. What do I do about Aunt Mary Opal? I know you know what I'm talking about. She's going to commit suicide, and I don't know if I am supposed to try to stop her, help her, or just butt out. Please give me a sign, anything that will tell me how to handle this. I'm afraid that if I talk to her about it, she'll push me away. But if I don't, what if she does it and she's all alone?" Nicole cried aloud and, in an instant, got the answer she was needing.

THE NEXT MORNING, Nicole called Aunt Mary Opal and thanked her for being okay that she had dropped in. "I made some egg salad sandwiches for lunch. How about I stop by in an hour or so and we can have lunch together?" She knew Aunt Mary Opal loved egg salad sandwiches.

"That would be delicious," Aunt Mary Opal said. "I have some Cheetos hidden in the cupboard. I'll pull them out, too." Nicole also knew that Aunt Mary Opal loved Cheetos, the originals that she kept hidden and only pulled out occasionally. Jesi would sometimes move them from Aunt Mary Opal's hiding place just to watch her search for them. It was an ongoing joke between the two. But then Aunt Mary Opal asked, "Nicole, are you okay?"

Did Aunt Mary Opal know something was up? "Oh, yes, I'm okay," she said. "I just made this salad, and it seemed like something you'd like." Time for a lie. Nicole wasn't a very good liar. She never had been, and from the sound of Aunt Mary Opal's question, Nicole figured she was caught.

Nicole was prepared when she arrived at the house. Her plan was to eat lunch and engage in small talk. She would then pull out her books and articles on assisted suicide. She was a nervous wreck. As soon as she walked into the door, she tripped on the step and nearly dropped the glass bowl that held the egg salad. Nicole knew she had tripped on the voices in her head, and the fact that she almost tripped was just an outward display of what was going on inside.

Egg salad sandwiches and Cheetos filled the platter as they sat in their usual chairs. Nicole nervously moved the Cheetos back and forth across her plate and felt eyes staring at her. "Aunt Mary Opal, do you remember the day we met?"

"Well, of course I do," she said, with a giggle. "You fell right into my arms and pushed me into Rachael. We all fell flat out on that dirty grocery store floor."

Nicole reached out and placed Aunt Mary Opal's hands in hers. She held them gently and continued. "Well, the truth is that you saved my life that day. I haven't ever told anyone this, and it's not an easy thing to tell someone."

Aunt Mary Opal pushed the dishes aside and leaned into Nicole, her eyes never looking away from Nicole's face. "Go on, honey."

Nicole's eyes filled with tears as she described the plans she had for that night. "I wasn't buying my solo dinner as a celebration like I said. It was going to be my last dinner. Everything in my life seemed to be so hard. The woman I had been with, the asshole, was abusive, and I couldn't seem to forgive myself for allowing that abuse for so long. I just wanted it all to stop, so I was planning to take my own life that night. But then I tripped on that damn case of wine and you caught me. It was as if you and Rachael were my angels. And there was Jesi staring down at me with those beautiful eyes and that laughter. It was like you all gave me a whole new chance on happiness. I got home that night and cried for hours. I hadn't cried like that in so long. Living with a woman who sucked all my energy away was kind of like real identity theft. After I finally left her, a friend of hers, who is a psychologist, told me that I had been living with a sociopath. I didn't even know what that meant, but when I looked it up all those years of confusion slowly got really clear. Another one of her friends told me the asshole had lied to me from the very beginning. She never owned the business she said she owned — she was a bartender, not a bar owner. She never went to culinary school, and all those stories she told about people wanting her to be their business partner were all just lies. That's when I lost all faith in myself. I lost trust in my ability to make decisions. I just wanted out. Out of everything. Out of living. The night we met was the beginning of forgiving myself, the night I started to love myself again, and love you."

The answer to Nicole's prayers was clear. In order to expect Aunt Mary Opal to trust her, she had to trust Aunt Mary Opal with her own secret. They sat together all afternoon talking about Nicole and her years of living with someone who had no conscience and what it had done to her. Aunt Mary Opal mostly just listened, but sometimes she asked questions just to keep Nicole talking.

"I realized that everything she did was about manipulating circumstances for complete control," Nicole continued. "A few years before I finally left, I decided to write a response and practice it so when she tried to get me to do things that I didn't want to do, I could say the same thing every time." Nicole pretended to talk to her abusive ex. "There is nothing you can do or say that will convince me or manipulate me into doing what you want." She repeated it a couple of times while Aunt Mary Opal watched and listened.

Nicole felt that Aunt Mary Opal must know what she was trying to do, to get her to open up. But the conversation was one-sided—Aunt Mary Opal did not share, but she just asked questions for Nicole to answer. "Nicole, have you gotten some help with all that? I mean, learning to put your needs ahead of others? You have to do that if you haven't already."

"Yes, I'll probably always have to get therapy for that. When I told my therapist that my partner had said I was self-centered and only considered my own needs, she laughed out loud and told me that in all the years she had been a therapist, I was the one client she worried most about putting everyone else before me. It's not easy for me to make plans without thinking about helping someone else. Even in my job, all I do, all day long, is find out what other people want and help them get it. I blame it all on my mom." Nicole broke the tension with laughter. "I always say she made me into a really good lesbian. Hold the door open for her, make sure I tell her that her hair is pretty, run errands, driving Miss Mom."

After about three hours, the room was silent. Nicole was done sharing stories that she had never shared with anyone except her therapist. She sat quietly, hoping that Aunt Mary Opal would open up to her. After a long stretch of silence, it was clear that it was not going to happen that day.

≈

A FEW DAYS LATER, Nicole received a call from Aunt Mary Opal, who invited her to stop by for a cup of coffee. Nicole had a busy day, so it was about 3:30 before she was able to break away. All day long, she was filled with anxiety and wondered where their conversation would go. As they sat at the kitchen table drinking Mello Joy coffee and eating bagels with cream cheese and plum jam, Aunt Mary Opal leaned back in her chair and casually said, "You know, don't you?"

Nicole held her breath and stared back. "Yes. I wasn't snooping," Nicole said. "The door was open and the light was on." She held her breath again, hoping that she wouldn't be in trouble with Aunt Mary Opal.

"I know," Aunt Mary Opal said. "I realized a couple of days ago when I went down there and the door was unlocked. When you rang the doorbell that day, I had been in the storeroom. I forgot to lock it in my rush to get to the door. Thank you for turning the light off and shutting the door." Nicole watched the tension in Aunt Mary Opal as she sat in her chair with her arms curled tightly around her waist.

Nicole simply nodded her head in acknowledgment of what was happening. "Would you like some more coffee?"

"Yes, but I think I really need some bourbon." Aunt Mary Opal's head tipped forward, still with her arms around her waist.

Nicole stood up from the kitchen table and retrieved the Jack from where it always rested in the sunroom. It was still cloudy and rainy. The rain had seeped inside one of the windows in the sunroom and was dripping onto the terrazzo floor. The conversation was surreal, as was the entire day. She began to think about how the rain had come inside the house. "Things just get in, even when the house is built really well," she thought to herself. "The older the house is, the easier it is for the rain to creep inside." She stared at the creeping water for a moment, put the Jack Daniel's back on the stand, and walked into the kitchen. She moved her chair close to Aunt Mary Opal and sat down. They held hands in silence. Aunt Mary Opal began to cry. Nicole had never seen her friend show this emotion. Nicole sat in silence and waited for Aunt Mary Opal to speak.

"Is that how you were going to take your life that day?"

"Yes." Nicole knew that the ice was broken and that this was her chance to help Aunt Mary Opal change her plans. Aunt Mary Opal looked up and uncrossed her arms. "Did you have someone to help you?"

Nicole looked across the table into her sad and

pleading eyes. "No. That was the scariest part. Is someone helping you?" Nicole was afraid of how Aunt Mary Opal would answer.

"No. I wouldn't want anyone to have to do that for me. I know there's a chance it won't work, but I'll take that chance." She didn't tell Nicole about her new friend Dee.

"But why, Aunt Mary Opal? What's happening? Please talk to me. Maybe I can help you. Maybe I can be your angel like you were for me." Nicole's heart raced with panic. She wanted to respect Aunt Mary Opal's wishes, but she also wanted to do everything within her power to stop it.

"It's cancer. It's back, but this time it's really bad. I don't want to go through the chemotherapy and radiation. It won't do anything but make me sick for the time I have left, and I am not going to live the rest of my life being sick from the very thing that's supposed to make me get better. I know my body, and I know my limits. The problem is the pain. It's getting worse, and I want to die with dignity, not screaming in pain or knocked out with painkillers. I've made up my mind." Aunt Mary Opal sat back in her chair, crossed her legs, and took a long, deep breath.

"Can we just talk about it some more? Look at some other options? I know there are some alternative therapies, and I could go with you. There is a place in Mexico I read about," Nicole pleaded.

Aunt Mary Opal placed her hand on Nicole's mouth. "I am loving my life exactly as it is, Nicole. I am at peace with my decision. My situation is not like yours. Your pain is emotional, and you can change your thoughts to lessen your pain. My cancer is physical. And besides,

I've already studied all those alternative therapies, and not one of them says you can drink Jack Daniel's at five o'clock every day, and none of them recommend head-to-head group meditation. If I start treatment, all I would do is live in fear, fear of not healing, and I'm seventy-six years old. My life has been full, and never more full than when you, Rachael, and Jesi are with me." They sat staring at each other until Aunt Mary Opal broke the silence. "Let's keep all this between us, okay? Our little secret."

Nicole nodded without saying a word. She didn't know what to say.

"So, Miss Nicole, I think it's five o'clock somewhere in the world, and if I am not mistaken, that bottle of Jack you went in there to get is still sitting in the same place." Aunt Mary Opal smiled and winked at Nicole.

Nicole reluctantly walked back into the sunroom to pick up the Jack Daniel's from the table. The water from the window had pooled on the floor. "Strange," she thought. "I guess that's how Aunt Mary Opal feels right now. She can't stop it from coming in. She's old, just like her house."

It wasn't even five minutes later when the doorbell rang. Jesi and Rachael had been at the grocery store getting ready for the ladies light luncheon scheduled for the next day, and they decided to drive by Aunt Mary Opal's house to drop off the perishables, assuming her car was in the driveway. When they saw Nicole's '68 Diva in the driveway, it was like Christmas morning. "Great minds think alike!" Jesi yelled out.

When Nicole opened the side door, Rachael and Jesi were standing in the rain and singing "Oh what a beautiful morning, oh what a beautiful day." Nicole looked at both of them in disbelief, slammed the door in their faces, and walked back to the kitchen.

"What was that?" asked Aunt Mary Opal.

"Wrong house." The doorbell rang again, and at the same time, Aunt Mary Opal's phone rang.

Aunt Mary Opal walked to the door and let them in. "Nicole has just been talking about some work issues and isn't in a very good mood," she said.

Nicole was not surprised to hear such a story told in such a casual and convincing manner. She had heard Aunt Mary Opal make up so many stories. "What more does she cover up?" she wondered.

Nicole flinched as Jesi wrapped her arms around her shoulders. "You need to let that work stuff go sometimes, Nicole. You can't let it drag you down all the time." Jesi wasn't usually affectionate, and Nicole welcomed her effort to comfort, even though the whole thing was based on one of Aunt Mary Opal's artistic privilege stories. Nicole returned the affection by resting her head on Jesi's arm. Jesi stroked Nicole's hair a couple of times — both were unaware that Aunt Mary Opal and Rachael were watching the sweet moment with high attention.

Nicole decided to go along with Aunt Mary Opal's story. "Oh well, maybe I'll just quit my job some day and travel around with you, Jesi."

"Come on! Let's go to Paris," Jesi joyfully responded.

"Let's have a drink instead," Nicole said, brightened by the thought. She gathered two more glasses from the cupboard. But before she poured their drinks, she gathered paper towels and walked to the sunroom. The puddle of water had crept across the floor, almost to the rug. As she cleaned up the water from the floor, she felt the sun peering through the clouds and warming the side of her face. It had stopped raining, and the blue sky seemed to be more vibrant than she could remember. As she soaked up the last of the water, she watched her tears drop to the floor. She quickly wiped the tears from her face and made her way to the bathroom to clear her eyes and her thoughts. "Like Aunt Mary Opal said, I can change my thoughts to lessen my pain."

Over the next few weeks, Nicole regularly stopped by Aunt Mary Opal's house. She delivered articles and books that contained stories of people who had healed themselves from cancer. Each time, Aunt Mary Opal thanked her, but she simply set the gifts aside.

TWENTY

JESI'S MOTHER spoke with a strain in her voice. "Jesi, you need to come home. Noni's not doing well."

It was a bitterly cold Sunday morning in Atlanta. The mist was so thick that the headlights reflected back, making it difficult for Jesi to see the turns in the road. She gripped the steering wheel so tightly that her fingers were white as she played her mother's voice over and over in her mind, hoping that she would make it to be with her Noni before she lost her. Jesi's car moved slowly up Interstate 75 until she exited at Collier Road. By then, the mist had turned into a mixture of ice and rain, and her windshield began to cover with a thin sheet of ice. She turned on the defogger, which cleared the windshield enough to safely drive the next two miles to her parents' home.

Their home was an expansive two-story white stone house built in the 1890s. It was perched at the top of a hill at the end of a winding, wooded private drive. As Jesi turned into the drive, she noticed that every light in the house was on. The window just outside the room where her Noni was resting was propped open. Noni believed that it was helpful to open a window for the soul to leave and that souls coming to help her in her passing could easily come and go. Jesi remembered that her mother had always said Noni went a bit too far with her belief in spiritual assistance at death. Jesi had a fleeting thought that perhaps there might always be a struggle between a mother and daughter.

As she made her way through the well-lit house, it felt as if the residence was full of visitors, even though she knew that only her parents and her Noni were there. There was also a familiar smell, a sweet kind of smoky scent. That incense seemed to be in places where Jesi was feeling a lot of emotion. She remembered the scent from the day her brother, Antony, had died. "It must be some sort of incense that mother lights during a death," Jesi thought. She tried to find the scent at stores when she traveled but was never able to find that specific aroma.

Noni had been clear about her desires when the time came for her transition—no doctors, lights on, a window open, only three people with her—her daughter, her son-in-law, and her granddaughter, Jesi. The truth was that Noni really only wanted her daughter and grand-daughter present. Jesi felt that they all knew the truth, so as she made her way up the staircase, she was not surprised to see her father at the kitchen table instead of at Noni's side. She also knew her mother would never leave Noni.

As she walked down the long hallway, she was keenly aware of the family photographs that lined the dark wooden walls. Jesi's mother and Noni had argued for days about the arrangement of the photographs. In the end, Noni, as usual, had won the argument.

Jesi removed a photo of her grandfather, Noni's husband, and clutched it as she entered her Noni's room. As she moved toward the bed where Noni lay dying, she opened the window next to the bed. Jesi's mother looked up as if to say something, but she simply lowered her head and continued her prayers. Jesi placed the photograph on the bedside table between the bed and the window. She sat on the bed next to her Noni. Noni never opened her eyes, and nothing was spoken. Just silence.

Noni was emaciated. Her skin had more wrinkles and was whiter than at any time in her life. Jesi was not prepared for seeing Noni in that state. While Jesi had always known that Noni would someday leave this earth, the reality of losing her became more than she could bear. She launched into stories about her trip to Nepal. "Noni, let me tell you about my trip." She tried to talk, but instead she became quiet and curled up on the bed with her back next to Noni, her head resting on Noni's pillow.

When Jesi was very young, she and her brother would each rest with their backs to Noni while she told them stories of their ancestors. Jesi never understood how they could be so deep in sleep that Noni was able to get up from the bed without waking either of them. As Jesi lay there in a state between consciousness and sleep, she heard Noni's voice, which seemed different and deeper, but familiar. Jesi didn't move, but she was aware that her mother had lit incense again. The scent was very strong. She seemed to slip in and out of awareness of hearing a voice.

"Remember when you fell off your bike? I helped

bandage you. But you don't remember my tears for your pain. You didn't know that when your rabbit died in your arms, I grieved until I thought my life would also end. I know what you are doing."

Jesi nestled even closer to her Noni and began to weep. Not since her brother's death had she allowed another person to see her tears.

"I've watched you since the day you pushed everything from you that would make you feel the depths that life can give you," Noni's voice said. "You have to stop now, Jesi. You must let in everything that life offers you, not just the top of the mountain. Without the valley, the mountain becomes nothing. When you're left alone, grieve. Grieve so hard that you think your heart will break. Jesi, life is about freedom. But freedom is nothing without the deepest love."

Jesi wept so hard that the mattress shook with her trembling. Then there was no sound of crying, no sound at all. It was just as Noni had always told her: "A woman will always be with you—when you are born, when you live, and when you leave." Jesi always thought her words were about self. But in that moment, she felt that it was about her Noni, her mother, and herself.

Jesi and her parents spoke very few words. They quietly walked through the motions of calling the doctor, who was aware of Noni's wishes and was prepared to take over. Within a couple of hours, the ambulance was gone and the bedroom was cleaned. Jesi watched as the housekeeper, who had arrived to help, reached to close the window next to Noni's bed. Her mother stopped her. "Not yet. She's still here." Jesi was surprised to hear her mother say those words. Her mother had always said that the spirit needing an open window to come and go was an old wives' tale.

"Mother, what is that incense you're burning?" Jesi wanted to know so that if she ever needed it, she would be ready.

"I didn't light incense," her mother said. "You know I don't like smoke in my house." Her voice sounded strangely distant.

"But that smell. It's the same as when Antony passed." Jesi felt confused.

"What smell?" her mother asked. "I don't know what you are talking about, Jesi. There isn't a smell." Her mother gave Jesi a frustrated look and continued cleaning the house so that there would be no evidence of death. That was exactly what her mother did the day Noni yelled at her after Antony died. From then on, her mother had always kept the house spotless.

Even though she was sure there was incense, Jesi felt it best to drop the subject.

Her dad had made a pot of coffee and had placed the ham from the refrigerator on the counter, along with a loaf of bread, mustard, and mayonnaise. Jesi looked around for chips, hoping that there would be Fritos; she liked the crunch when eating a sandwich. They all sat around the table eating, and for about ten minutes, the only sound was the sound of Jesi crunching the corn chips that she had found.

"I wish she could have said something at the end," said Jesi's mother, softly. "I just wanted to hear her voice one more time."

Jesi spoke without even swallowing her food. "She did, Mother. You were right there."

"No, Jesi. I was there, but she had not spoken in at

least ten hours. She wasn't even conscious." They straightened up and squared off at each other.

Jesi noticed that her dad sat back. He had seen conflict between them for so long that nothing could surprise him.

"Yes, she did," Jesi said. "You had to have heard her. She reminded me about when she helped bandage my leg when I fell off my bike, how she grieved for my pain when my rabbit died. You had to have heard that, Mother." She stood up, and her body vibrated with frustration.

"No, Jesi," her mother said. "She did not speak." Her mother's voice was now raised to match Jesi's. "And even if she had, you were sleeping when she passed."

Jesi burst into tears and starting pacing. "Mother, yes she did. You heard her. She told me how I watched her yelling at you after Antony died, that you had to stop it, and that you had to be there for father and me. You heard her. You know you did. Why are you doing this?"

"No," her mother said. "You are wrong, Jesi. Your Noni wasn't even there when you fell off your bike or when your rabbit died. Antony was there. It was Antony who helped me and it was Antony who cried so hard that I thought he was going to get sick. Now stop it."

Mother and daughter stood face to face, Jesi in complete confusion.

The room fell to total silence. Only the sound of the refrigerator could be heard. Jesi turned and walked out of the kitchen, and she made her way back upstairs to her Noni's room. She closed the window, climbed into bed, covered herself with the white woven bedspread, buried her face in the down pillow, and cried until she fell into a deep sleep. When she woke, she was aware that the sweet, smoky scent was gone. The rain was also gone, and the Sun streamed through the window. As she made her way down the hallway, Jesi saw her mother in her bedroom, kneeling in prayer next to the bed. She found her father in the living room, half asleep in his red leather chair that was comfortably close to the roaring fire in the fireplace. The stone fireplace was cut into a wall that expanded up to the fourteen-foot-high ceiling. The room was filled with a mixture of Sicilian art, along with modern American art. While it was a large room, her mother had arranged the furniture so that it felt more like three separate, cozy dens. Jesi curled up in a black leather chair next to her father.

"Has she gotten any sleep?" Jesi expected that her mother had been praying all night.

"No," her father said. "She hasn't stopped praying. I've never seen her so strong. I expected her to be over-whelmed with grief. But now, it's like she's at peace. She'll get through this. Don't worry about her, Jesi." Her father always tried to protect Jesi from sadness, and that day was no different.

TWENTY-ONE

THE FUNERAL WAS HELD in Agrigento, Sicily. The entire extended family was there to pay their respects to their elder. The Agrigento Cathedral was a small, ornate cathedral in the historic core of Agrigento, the same cathedral where everyone in the family had been christened, married, and buried.

As Jesi entered the cathedral with her parents, her mother reached out to her. "Jesi, your friends," she whispered. Jesi swiveled her head as her mother motioned toward the other entrance. There stood Rachael, Nicole, and Aunt Mary Opal. Jesi let go of her mother's arm and fell into the loving arms of her friends. Her legs felt weak. Aunt Mary Opal, Rachael, and Nicole reached out and held her close. None of them spoke. They all simply wept. It was not what any of them expected. Jesi's happy-go-lucky façade had dropped, and she felt that their love for her had deepened.

Jesi had never even considered that her friends would be at her Noni's funeral. The entire day felt surreal, her worlds colliding together. She looked forward to hearing how Rachael and Nicole had persuaded Aunt Mary Opal to fly to Sicily. They had all heard so many stories about how Aunt Mary Opal had no desire to visit anywhere in Sicily after her experience of losing her luggage in Palermo all those years ago.

Jesi's family was used to her staying at a distance, so after the funeral, it was not questioned when she was seen leaving with her friends. "Come on, ladies," she said. "We won't have a 'light luncheon,' but it will be delicious." Jesi escorted them to a cozy corner restaurant and ordered red wine for everyone. She told them it was tradition, following a funeral, because she was certain they would say no to celebrating instead of grieving. Call it tradition, or call it Jesi needing a drink to calm her nerves. She was a little embarrassed that her usual tough demeanor was gone and that they had seen her cry, even though she knew that if anyone would see her cry and not hold it against her, it would be Nicole, Rachael, and Aunt Mary Opal.

An awkward silence fell over the table until Nicole spoke. "Wow, Jesi, I don't think I've ever seen you in a dress." Nicole flashed her usual flirtatious grin.

Jesi's face turned red, but she didn't back down. "Well, Nicole, I've never invited you to a funeral now, have I?"

Aunt Mary Opal chimed in. "Jesi, I think you look beautiful in a dress. I think you should wear dresses more often. It might just get you more dates." Aunt Mary Opal reached over and poked Nicole in her side as she laughed and flirted with them both.

Jesi was aware of Rachael's silence and tried not to look in her direction, knowing that Rachael would likely say something that would make her cry again. Rachael had a way of getting to the heart of any situation. Finally, Rachael spoke as she reached up and put her arm on Jesi's shoulder. "I am so sorry, Jesi. We know this can't be easy for you." Rachael stroked Jesi's hair as she lowered her head to rest on Rachael's shoulder. She tried to hide her tears, but the emotion was just too much for her, so she let the tears flow.

After a couple of minutes, Jesi quieted, her tears stopped, and she looked up. "I will always remember seeing you all standing there at the church," she said. "You have no idea how deeply that touches me." For the next forty-five minutes, Jesi slowly and emotionally shared with them the events of her Noni's passing, the voice she heard, the argument with her mother, and then her mother's words, which shook Jesi's reality. "It was Antony the whole time," she whispered. "He never left me." The stillness at the table stretched into more than a fleeting moment as each of them quietly considered the idea that Jesi had actually heard the voice of her deceased brother.

Jesi took a deep breath in and out, which snapped them out of their contemplation. "I just have one question," she said. "How did y'all get Aunt Mary Opal to Sicily? What the fuck, y'all?" Jesi laughed out loud as she wiped the tears from her cheeks.

After a brief shock and hesitation, Rachael said, "It was easy. We just told her that if she'd go with us, we'd carry her luggage."

The wine and pasta flowed. While the luncheon wasn't light food, it was light in terms of energy, and that was the best thing for Jesi.

TWENTY-TWO

FOR THE NEXT FIVE DAYS, the women enjoyed Sicily, with Jesi as their guide and narrator. This made it easier for Rachael to take notes and photographs of everything. They stayed at a charming hotel in the Valley of the Temples, originally built as the home of a princess. The back side of the hotel was welcoming, with an expansive stone terrace that stretched the length of the structure. Surrounding the hotel were olive trees with trunks that would take all four of them to wrap their arms around.

The entire experience was as if they were dropped into some type of fairy tale. Every day was an adventure. The most heartwarming memory was the experience of seeing Jesi flourish in her birthplace. She was the first to be ready each morning with a schedule of activities. To Rachael, Nicole, and Aunt Mary Opal, it was as if they were seeing Jesi for the first time. Her love of Sicily seemed to bring out the best in her. The hard edges Jesi normally used as a way to protect herself seemed to evaporate. What replaced her hardness was a desire to share her passionate love of history and art.

Rachael, knowing that she would have opportunity to photograph beautiful landscapes and Greek temples, had brought along almost all of her camera equipment. She snapped one photograph after another as Jesi led them through an olive grove toward one of the best preserved Greek temples in the world. "Where we are walking, these olive trees are older than Christ," Jesi proudly shared. "The temple on the hill is one of the most magnificent architectural accomplishments in the world. Look how beautiful it is. When I was small, we could run in and out of the columns. Today, there are guards to keep people from destroying things."

Rachael was thrilled and intrigued with the images. "I have an idea," she said. "Let's come out here at night and let me photograph the temples. Last night, I noticed that when they light up the temples, it's like they're golden. What do you say, Jesi?"

"Oh no, we can't," Jesi said. "They keep guards out here."

Rachael couldn't believe that, of all people, Jesi was averse to an adventure. Nicole and Aunt Mary Opal watched them banter back and forth about whether to sneak into the olive grove at night, an argument that Rachael was sure she was destined to win. Her desire to photograph the temples for her design business had overtaken her sensibilities, and she was playing to Jesi's adventurous side.

"Shit, Rachael," Jesi said. "Okay, but if we do, you have to listen to me if I think we're going to get caught. Promise?"

"Yes, I promise," Rachael sarcastically responded. "If we get in trouble in the danger zone, we can leave."

FOR THE REST of the day, they lounged on the terrace and drank red wine, snacked on prosciutto and cheese, and listened to Aunt Mary Opal's stories of living in Europe.

"Tell us more, Aunt Mary Opal," Nicole pleaded.

"Oh, no, no, no," she said. "That's enough. I need to take a nap if we're going on an adventure tonight." She picked up her bag and headed for the elevator. They followed her, with no questions asked. But Rachael suspected that Aunt Mary Opal had other plans. She had seen that look on her face before, and it usually meant that she was conjuring up a story of some kind. "I don't need you to escort me," Aunt Mary Opal said at the elevator. "Go find something fun to do. I'll see you after I rest."

As soon as they left the hotel lobby, Rachael held back for a moment and looked back just in time to see Aunt Mary Opal calling for a taxi. "What is she up to?" she wondered.

JUST BEFORE SUNSET, the four of them gathered in Rachael's room, where Rachael had laid out her camera equipment on the bed. Rachael was keenly aware of Jesi's attention to all of the equipment. It was when Jesi put her hands on her hips that Rachael knew she was going to have fun with the conversation that was going to happen.

"You're not taking all that into the danger zone," Jesi said.

"Yes, I am," Rachael said. "And you're going to help me." She pointed at Nicole and Jesi. "I'm not getting in there just to realize that I need some other accessory." She smiled as she watched Jesi look to Nicole and Aunt Mary Opal for help. Instead, they stepped back, making it clear that they were not helping Jesi.

"No way, this is between the two of you," Nicole responded. "I'll go and I'll help, but I won't get in this conversation." Aunt Mary Opal didn't say a word. She simply wrapped her arm around Nicole's arm, and they stood next to each other, with determined looks on their faces. At that, Jesi turned back to Rachael, who assessed Jesi to figure out how far she was willing to continue objecting. As Rachael stretched her head upward to exaggerate her towering presence above them, she made it clear to Jesi, just through a look of certainty, that she and Nicole were going to carry equipment into the danger zone.

Once that was settled and they were leaving Rachael's room, Aunt Mary Opal turned the other direction, toward her own room, rather than follow the others. Jesi, who was in the lead, looked past Rachael and Nicole. "Where are you going?" she said. "We need to go out the back door."

Each looked a little confused at Aunt Mary Opal's response. "No, I'm too old for this," she said. "You go ahead." Just as Rachael had suspected, Aunt Mary Opal was up to something. She just didn't know what.

"What? You can't stay here. It's one for all, and all that." Nicole reached out to wrap her arm in Aunt Mary Opal's.

"Yes, I can, Nicole," Aunt Mary Opal announced. "And I am going to stay here while you all go on an adventure." The tides turned, Rachael and Jesi stepped out of the way of this exchange.

Nicole and Aunt Mary Opal stood facing each other. "Well, then I'm staying with you," Nicole said.

"Nicole, you go," Aunt Mary Opal said. "I'll be right here waiting for you when you get back. I promise."

"What the hell? Will the secrets ever stop?" Rachael stood further down the hallway, shaking her head. "Okay, Nicole, either go with us, or give me my equipment." Nicole didn't move. "Nicole!" Rachael said. "Come on, time's a ticking."

Nicole seemed to snap out of her silence as she turned to join them. "Fine, I'm coming," she said. "And Aunt Mary Opal, we'll see you in just a bit. Okay?" Aunt Mary Opal waved her hand high in a circle and danced a brief shuffle.

As they exited the grounds of the hotel, they looked around to make certain no one was looking, and they slipped into the darkness behind an olive tree that was just taller than Rachael.

"Okay, I checked it out earlier," Rachael said, leaning down so they were not overheard. "If we go a little to the left, we can sneak from tree to tree until we get to that little building." Rachael pointed to a small guard shack halfway up the hill toward the temple. "Can you see it?" There were no lights to illuminate the olive grove, so they needed to be very careful and make sure they stayed close to each other, especially with the uneven terrain. "That's where there's a break in the fence and a little bridge," Rachael said. "From there, we can go straight up the hill to the temple. Ready?"

Nicole and Jesi followed Rachael from one olive tree to the next, always keeping a lookout for either a guard or the Sicilian police. As they passed through the break in the fence and over the small bridge, Rachael used her body to shield the computer monitor and camera in the little building. "If Nicole sees this, it's all over," she thought to herself, as she motioned them past her just to make certain they didn't see inside the building.

Once they made it up to the perfect location, Rachael lowered her tripod to the ground and began taking photographs. Within a couple of minutes, Jesi spotted a car on the other side of the wall, next to the temple, slowly driving toward them. "Rachael," Jesi whispered. "A car."

Nicole stretched up to look over the wall just in time to see the oncoming car. "Oh my God, it's the police," she said.

In an instant, the entire adventure into the danger zone turned into something much more serious. "Run!" Rachael whispered, in a panic. She threw her tripod, camera still attached, over her shoulder. She ducked as low as she could so that she was below the top of the wall, and she ran behind Jesi and Nicole to the largest olive tree they could find. They held on to each other while Jesi peeked out to see if the car was still coming toward them. The policeman slowed the car and cast his spotlight across the olive grove, searching for the trespassers.

Jesi quickly tucked her head back behind the tree. "Don't move. He's trying to find us with a spotlight." The light moved through the grove and across the tree that hid them. Once the light was past them, the car began to move further down the road, the spotlight still scanning the grove. "Rachael, I think we're safe," Jesi said, as she motioned for Nicole, who, in terror, was clutching the back of Jesi's jean jacket, to let go.

Rachael relaxed once she saw the police car moving further down the hill and away from them. The air was dry, almost as dry as Rachael's throat felt when she considered that they could have all gone to jail. She giggled quietly and motioned for Nicole and Jesi to follow her. She had considered staying longer to take more photographs but figured that Nicole had probably reached her limit with excitement. She thought the stress was gone until she heard Jesi's tense voice burst out. "Here he comes again! Run!"

In unison, they all three took off in a sprint toward the small opening to cross the footbridge as the spotlight moved across the olive trees toward them. As soon as they reached the bridge, their bodies collided, nearly knocking Jesi to the ground. "Move it!" Rachael commanded as she glanced back over her shoulder in time to see the policeman get out of his car and jump over the knee-high stone wall. Other than their panicked whispers to each other, the night was quiet—at least it was quiet until a deafening siren blast shocked them and, as Rachael saw, shocked the policeman as well. They ran back up the hill toward the hotel and Rachael, looking back over her shoulder, watched the policeman jump back over the wall, get in his car, and rush toward the direction of the sound. They had made it without getting arrested.

Rachael, Jesi, and Nicole stood on the expansive stone porch of the hotel, laughing and gasping for air. "Shit, we almost got caught. Did y'all see that camera in the little building? They knew we were out there."

Nicole burst out laughing. "Thank God that alarm went off."

Rachael was just glad Jesi and Nicole were still speaking to her. "Come on, let's go find Aunt Mary Opal and tell her what happened." Rachael had never heard a car alarm that sounded like that, and she had a suspicion that maybe Aunt Mary Opal had something to do with them not getting caught. They made their way into the hotel lobby just in time to see Aunt Mary Opal rushing toward the elevator. "What the hell?" Rachael exclaimed. The three of them burst toward Aunt Mary Opal, and they all collapsed on the chairs in the lobby, laughing hysterically.

Aunt Mary Opal listened and laughed with them as they recounted the adventure in the danger zone and being saved by a random horn that distracted the policeman. Nicole reached up and removed her hair clasp to let her red hair flow freely. "Aunt Mary Opal, one of the funniest things is when we realized we were safe. I heard Jesi say, 'Stupid Americans, go to Sicily and get thrown in jail.'"

As they continued to laugh about the escapade, Rachael noticed Aunt Mary Opal watching a policeman walk into the hotel's front door. He started toward them. Aunt Mary Opal motioned to Rachael to hide her camera equipment. They carefully pushed the bags and the tripod under the loveseat where Nicole and Jesi were sitting. Aunt Mary Opal stood up and spoke to the policeman. "Well, hello again. Did you catch your suspect?" She wrapped her arm through his and walked him in the opposite direction. The distraction worked.

Rachael saw her camera poking out from under the loveseat, so she slid Aunt Mary Opal's purse in front of the camera. It seemed especially heavy. As she pulled on the purse, she inadvertently opened the top just enough so the label on the sound horn was exposed. Rachael gasped, quickly ripped off her hat, and placed it on top of the purse. Aunt Mary Opal continued to talk to the policeman about how Sicily had changed since she had lived there, even though she had never lived there. It was clear to Rachael that the officer only understood a few of Aunt Mary Opal's words. Rachael watched as Aunt Mary Opal escorted him out of the hotel lobby. With her other arm, she motioned to Rachael, Jesi, and Nicole to head to the elevator.

FOR AN HOUR, Aunt Mary Opal's room was filled with laughter, stories of the great escape, and lots of red wine.

"Aunt Mary Opal, how did you know to buy that sound horn?" Rachael sat cross-legged with her back against the headboard.

"It's something I picked up in the CIA. If I tell you my secrets, I might have to kill you," Aunt Mary Opal said, with a mischievous grin and a wink.

TWENTY-THREE

RACHAEL PREPARED an Italian feast for Jake, Aunt Mary Opal, Jesi, and Nicole. Early in the day, Aunt Mary Opal called to let her know that she had not been feeling well and thought it best to stay home. About forty-five minutes before Jesi and Nicole were supposed to arrive, Rachael received a text from Jake that his recording session was taking longer than expected. "Don't wait up."

Rachael didn't doubt Jake's love for her, but something snapped as she read that text. Rachael was sick of being left alone. With Jake, it was always his music before his relationship. Rachael walked into the kitchen and threw all of the food she had prepared into the trash can. She made her way out the back door, dropped all her clothes, and dove into the pool. She swam lap after lap. Her emotions ran from anger to hurt to a quiet resolve. She wanted more from a relationship.

The only close connections she felt were her friendships with Aunt Mary Opal, Jesi, and Nicole. Over the past year, she had tried many things to get the feeling of inclusion and love she desired from Jake. She had considered having a baby to help her feel the unconditional love that she knew was missing in her relationship. Fortunately, she realized that having a baby would probably just make Jake move even further away. She came to the conclusion that Jake loved her as much as he was capable of loving, and that this just wasn't enough for her. She would have to leave Jake because Jake would never leave her. Everything was just fine as far as he was concerned.

When Jesi and Nicole arrived, Rachael, her hair still wet from swimming and a lit joint hanging in her mouth, greeted them at the door with martinis and two joints resting in the middle of a sterling platter. The two visitors danced around with their hands above their heads. The evening turned into a slow and laid-back time of sharing. Rachael ordered pizza, and they lounged around the pool as she filled them in on her decision to leave Jake.

"Wow, Rachael, that's a big step," Nicole said. "I know you've been struggling with things, even though you haven't talked about it much. Are you sure that's what you want?"

Jesi didn't say a word.

"I love Jake. I always will. It's not his fault," Rachael said. "He's just doing what he needs to do for his life. And that's one of the things I love about him. It's just that I want to do things for me, too. I want someone to adore me the way he adores his music and the way I adore him. There has to be a man out there like that!"

"Have you told him how you feel?" Nicole asked. "Maybe if you go to therapy, you can both work it out."

"I've tried," Rachael said, with an ironic chuckle. "He won't even talk about it. When I try to get him to deal with it, he just writes another damn song for me. I can't even tell you how sick I am of hearing him sing me another love song." The pot and the martinis were helping. She felt lighter already.

Jesi finally opened up. "Rachael, didn't you make a promise? 'Til death do you part?"

"Jesi, shut up," Nicole blurted out. "Didn't you hear anything she said? She's tried everything."

"Yeah, I heard her, but she still made a promise," Jesi challenged back.

"Well, that is so selfish of you, Jesi," Nicole continued. "You live in your fairytale world while everyone else deals with reality." She stood and paced back and forth.

Rachael saw that the conversation had turned into something that had nothing to do with her. She also knew that Jesi lived in a fairytale sometimes. As the conflict escalated, Rachael slowly backed away from them. Nicole headed to the door, and Jesi followed.

Jesi turned back to Rachael. "I'm sorry, Rachael," she said. "I love you. I certainly didn't mean to be as selfish as Nicole thinks I am. Let me know what I can do to support you." With that, Jesi walked out to Nicole's car, where a shouting match ensued in the middle of the road. Rachael opened the window in order to hear every word.

"No, you are not going to bully me, Jesi!" Nicole screamed. "I know exactly what you do. You think that because you come from a family that hung the moon you can just push everyone with your childish judgments. Well, let me tell you, Miss Jesi, I am not ever going to be pushed around by you." Nicole raised her voice even further as she waved her right arm in the air for emphasis. She yelled some more. "You'll never be in charge of my life!"

The more Nicole screamed, the more Jesi focused on her. Nicole's red hair seemed to intensify in the moonlight. It was the first time Rachael had ever seen Jesi so quiet. Jesi put her arms around Nicole's waist and pulled her close. Nicole pushed Jesi back. "Stop it! You think you can just make everything okay by acting like you want to be close? Stop it." Rachael continued to watch as Jesi pulled Nicole even closer. The more Nicole resisted, the tighter Jesi held her. Rachael was stunned, as the passionate sparring that had engulfed Jesi and Nicole turned on its axis in a split second. Then, all of a sudden, tires screeched, headlights glared, and Nicole screamed in terror as a car rounded the corner at a high speed. The car's bumper smacked into Jesi and knocked her to the pavement. Rachael then heard a siren wailing as a police car turned the corner. The lights from the police car seemed like a strobe light in a nightmare, and as Rachael watched in horror, she saw Nicole jump in front of the police cruiser, between the headlights and Jesi. The police car jerked away from Nicole, but not fast enough. It struck Nicole and knocked her to the pavement, next to Jesi.

It all happened so fast. One moment she was watching what looked like a lovers' quarrel, and then a horrific tragedy took place. Rachael grabbed her phone to dial 911 as she ran out the front door to help them. The policeman who had been driving was yelling into his phone. Rachael was confused as she overheard the officer saying that it was the other car that struck both of them. "Please, please, you have to help me," Rachael said to the 911 operator. "My sisters are hurt!"

∾

AT THE HOSPITAL, Rachael paced in the waiting room as Aunt Mary Opal watched. "It was my fault," Rachael said. "I was going on about maybe leaving Jake, and you know how Jesi is. She got so pissed off and started to take sides when Nicole told her to shut up."

Hours passed in the waiting room, with Rachael and Aunt Mary Opal the only people keeping vigil for Jesi and Nicole. Jesi's parents were out of the country and were working on a plan to get home as soon as possible. Nicole had no family in Georgia. When Rachael was able to reach Nicole's brother, Pete, he greeted her with questions about a last will and testament. She felt as if Nicole's only worth to her brother was if she could provide some sort of financial benefit. Her only thought was that Nicole was not going to die. Rachael decided to never call Pete again.

The next three weeks were long and difficult. Rachael had never prayed the way she did during those weeks. Both Nicole and Jesi had experienced a close brush with death that night, and Rachael watched the whole scene, unable to stop any of it. She played it over and over again in her head, each time cringing with regret and fear.

Jesi's parents stayed at the hospital twenty-four hours a day and took turns with nonstop prayer. Fortunately, for both Nicole and Jesi, Aunt Mary Opal was close friends with the hospital's chief of staff, who permitted them to spend as much time as they wished with Jesi and Nicole, even though they were not blood relatives. They were also able to arrange for Jesi and

Nicole to share the same hospital room after leaving the critical care unit.

"Rachael, why did you tell the 911 operator that they were your sisters?" Aunt Mary Opal asked her one day.

Rachael heard the confusion in Aunt Mary Opal's tone. "Because I knew that if I said I was family, the hospital would move things faster," Rachael said. "A friend almost died one time because the hospital waited for her sister to get there to sign documents. I will never forget her sister's words. She said, 'All I know is that when I ran into the emergency room, my sister lay there dying. Her face started turning dark from the bleeding. I just started signing, and as soon as I signed the last document, they rushed her into the back.'" Rachael turned to look Aunt Mary Opal in the eye. "Aunt Mary Opal, when I got here, I signed all the documents for both of them. I told them I was their sister. I even signed that I guaranteed payment. I'm glad I did." She bent forward, rested her head on Aunt Mary Opal's lap, and cried as Aunt Mary Opal quietly stroked her hair.

TWENTY-FOUR

JESI'S PARENTS had hired a nurse to be at their house for Jesi's care, around the clock. What they didn't expect was for Jesi to insist on staying at Nicole's. Jesi knew her mother had seen their closeness as they rested in the hospital room, but she didn't feel the need to discuss it with anyone, especially her mother. Jesi's mother rebooked the trip to Sicily as soon as Jesi confirmed that she would be staying with Nicole.

"Narcissism is alive and well," Jesi spoke sarcastically of her mother. "She wanted me to be at the house so she could tell everyone how hard it was on her to have an injured daughter. So now that I'm not allowing that, a vacation is the best thing to have." There was no anger or bitterness from Jesi, just a cool observation. She adored her mother and was clear that her way to cope was to escape, a trait that they apparently shared.

"We'll be okay, Jesi," Nicole said. "We need some time alone together. Besides, after all this, I don't think Aunt Mary Opal and Rachael are about to leave us alone too much, and my house isn't big enough for them and your parents. If that happened, you and I would probably have to take a vacation." They tried not to laugh. The pain was still alive and well for them both.

Jesi was scheduled for physical therapy for the next few months, with an expectation of a full recovery from the knee surgery. Nicole's shoulder and left arm would probably always have some issues, but considering what they had been through, they felt lucky to be alive.

The police officer initially tried to put the blame for the accident on Nicole and Jesi. But with Rachael as a witness, an investigation was quickly completed, and it found that the high-speed chase through such a populated residential area was "inappropriate and reckless conduct" on the part of the officer driving the car. The city offered them money to settle the entire incident. At first, Jesi and Nicole had decided not to accept the settlement offer, but the city's attorney explained that there was a bigger issue at stake. There were internal problems at police headquarters, and she explained that they would hear about the results in upcoming news reports. They later learned that signing the nondisclosure agreements and accepting the money was just one more step by the city attorney, who had prepared a case against the chief of police for mismanagement. Their incident, plus the cost to keep them quiet, was like icing on the cake for the city attorney. They had been used like pawns in a game of chess. Their own attorney assured them that accepting the money from the city was not only legal but was just punishment for the actions of the officer.

Even though Jesi and Nicole had signed nondisclosure agreements with the city, they felt safe disclosing the details to Rachael and Aunt Mary Opal, since everything said during the head-to-head group meditation was held in strict confidence, never to leave the room.

"Wait, they offered you what?" Rachael burst into infectious laughter.

Nicole, holding her arms close to lessen the pain, laughed with Rachael. "They did. They gave us each $200,000 just to keep us quiet."

"Well, you deserve it after what you went through," Aunt Mary Opal said, still angry about the entire incident. "That policeman should never have been chasing that other car so fast. What if you had died? Or worse, crippled for life? I won't be laughing at any of this. The more you laugh, the madder I get." She sank down in her chair and looked up at their faces. "Really, I'm just afraid of losing my friends. I've come to love you more than anyone in my life. It's not that I don't love my daughters; it's just that you don't treat me like an old person. I feel like we're all the same, like sisters."

"Aunt Mary Opal, it's okay," Jesi said. "We made it through, and as the song says, what doesn't kill you makes you stronger." Careful not to move too quickly, she sang out the verse. Then Rachael and Nicole joined in.

"In your case, what doesn't kill you makes you richer," Aunt Mary Opal said, seeming to let go of her stress and joining in with the laughter and singing. Jesi knew that Aunt Mary Opal had prayed for hours every day for them to have a full recovery, just like her parents had.

Soon after, Jesi wondered if maybe she and Nicole had made a mistake by not letting Jesi's parents and the nurse take care of them. Just getting out of bed was painful for both of them, and they wished for someone to do things for them, such as getting a glass of water. By the fourth day, Jesi heard Nicole call out from the kitchen, offering to cook breakfast for them both. "Jesi, would you eat a waffle if I make it? I could make scrambled eggs if you don't want the carbs."

Clearly, Nicole was feeling better than she was. "How can you do it, Nicole? I can hardly move right now." Jesi moaned a little, looking for sympathy. When Nicole didn't respond, she said, "I'm starving, Nicole. Thanks for fixing breakfast. Anything is fine. But before you do, will you come back in here? I have something to say." Jesi patted the mattress, and Nicole sat close. "Nicole, I know we have a lot of differences, and I get it that we're not the same age. But Nicole, I really, really care for you. Do you think we could maybe talk about if there could be a chance for us?" She was so nervous that her usual cool demeanor was gone and her body trembled slightly as she spoke.

"We can talk about it, Jesi," Nicole said. "But the thing is that I can't have a relationship with someone who plays around. And all your stories about three-ways and men and women, all of it makes me nervous. Jesi, I love our friendship too much to screw it up with something that could doom it from the start."

Jesi felt a jolt. Nicole had obviously put some thought into the possibility of them being a couple. She immediately wished that she hadn't opened up about her escapades to Nicole. "I get that, Nicole. I know. But I've never felt about anyone the way I feel about you. I've never wanted to be with anyone else since the night I met you. There you were lying on top of Aunt Mary Opal and Rachael in the grocery store with that shocked look on your face and your phone playing 'Sexual Healing' so loud that I think the whole store could hear it. Nicole, I love you so much. All I think about is you. We can take our time and make sure we're moving at a pace that's healthy. But Nicole, I know what I want. You know how I am—when I know, I know. And there's nothing in my life that I am more certain about, and that's you and me."

Nicole remained quiet.

To lighten the conversation, Jesi said, "Now, as far as that argument we had in front of Rachael and Jake's house, no more of that, okay? I don't think we can survive another run-in with the law!" They tried to laugh, but neither was able to handle too much movement without pain.

Jesi watched Nicole's face and noticed how her deep red hair framed her face in a way that made her hazel eyes seem to widen. It was as if she was looking for answers, for the truth, as if she were doubting the decisions she'd made about love. How could Jesi assure her that she would not act like her last lover? They came from such different pasts, different cultures, and different families.

Nicole finally spoke. "Jesi."

"Yes."

"Jesi." Nicole was trying to say something, but words didn't seem to form.

"What is it, Nicole? Talk to me." Wincing from pain, she leaned toward Nicole.

Nicole shifted closer so that her breasts and shoulders melted into Jesi. As their bodies fused together, Jesi moved her lips across Nicole's forehead and slid them onto Nicole's mouth, where they held still for a long moment, both women breathing each other's breath. Nicole pushed Jesi's dark hair back away from her face and gently placed her hands on Jesi's cheeks. They began kissing each other with no inhibition, no fear, only trust and passion. Nicole again stared intently into Jesi's eyes. "I love you, Jesi. I've loved you from the beginning."

The next hour was slow and passionate. It was the only time in Jesi's life that she had allowed herself to be completely present with another woman. Having so much pain in their bodies helped to slow things down and gave both of them time to be aware of every touch, every kiss, every move, every feeling.

TWENTY-FIVE

AFTER FALLING asleep and waking up holding each other, Nicole and Jesi made love again. They were unaware that Rachael and Aunt Mary Opal had come by with chicken soup and movies for entertainment. Rachael had a key to the house, so they let themselves in, fully expecting to see them both sleeping. Having an open floor plan meant that whatever was going on in one room was visible from anywhere in the apartment. Rachael entered the house in front of Aunt Mary Opal and looked up just in time to see Jesi and Nicole wrapped up in each other in a position that was obviously not for sleeping or physical therapy. Rachael was so shocked that she screamed and dropped the stack of movies. Aunt Mary Opal didn't see what Rachael saw, but she screamed and froze in place so she wouldn't drop the chicken soup. Rachael tried to run back out of the room to block Aunt Mary Opal, but it was too late.

"What are you doing, Rachael?" Aunt Mary Opal yelled. "Good grief! I almost dropped this whole dish of chicken soup all over the floor." She sounded really irritated.

"What the fuck, y'all?" Jesi let out a moan.

Even though Rachael had tried to block Aunt Mary Opal from seeing what she had seen, it was too late. They both began to laugh uncontrollably, and Rachael, as she often did, fell on the floor, laughing so hard that she could hardly breathe. Aunt Mary Opal had to put the chicken soup down on the floor because it was too hot for the table. When she bent over, she passed gas so loud that Jesi and Nicole heard it in the next room. Rachael crawled out of the living room and onto the porch so she could stop laughing, and Aunt Mary Opal, doubled over, sat down on one of the dining room chairs. After a few moments of laughter and moans from Jesi and Nicole, Aunt Mary Opal said, "Well, that settles that. From now on, we need to knock." They all laughed for a few moments longer before it became too painful for Jesi and Nicole, who had covered themselves with a comforter.

"Stop it," Jesi said. "Please, we can't take it anymore. If you keep this up, you have to leave." Jesi yelled so that Rachael could also hear her from the porch.

"Well, I promise. We aren't staying," Rachael said, stepping back in and placing the chicken soup and movies on the kitchen counter. "We love you both. You're supposed to be resting. And I mean it. Call us, or we won't come back."

As Rachael drove Aunt Mary Opal home, they continued processing what had taken place. "Lord, I didn't know what you were screaming about until I turned the corner and it looked like those carvings in

Khajuraho, India," Aunt Mary Opal said. "I couldn't tell whose leg was where."

"I don't know why I thought I had to make you back up!" Rachael said. "Maybe I was just trying to knock you down so I could get out!"

Rachael and Aunt Mary Opal joked about the whole scene, but they agreed that they were happy to see Jesi and Nicole expressing their love for each other instead of getting themselves run over. "Well, now maybe they can start being a little nicer to each other," Aunt Mary Opal said. "Before the accident, I thought we were going to have to conduct an intervention."

TWENTY-SIX

OVER THE NEXT FEW WEEKS, their recovery was faster than the doctors had anticipated but slower than what Jesi wanted. She and Nicole were finally open to exploring their love for each other, and they were eager to be able to touch each other without pain. They often laughed about not knowing if the other was moaning because it felt good or because it hurt. It took a lot more communication than either had been used to while making love. In a weird kind of a way, it made them completely present with each other, totally attending to themselves and each other physically, spiritually, and emotionally. Their connection was deeper than either of them had ever experienced, and they were thankful to have this downtime to be together.

"Jesi, I feel like we're both letting go of the pain from our past, together," Nicole said.

"Me too," said Jesi, who could feel her relief. "It's so weird to feel so free. It's like I needed to have my life threatened just to let go of feeling like I was alone."

Both of their lives had been threatened. Nicole, first

by living with an abusive woman and then by the strike of that car as it took her down when she was just trying to protect Jesi from getting hit again.

"We have to get out of this house," Jesi said. "I want you to spend time with me at my parents' house in Agrigento. I know they have issues, but they really love me and I really love them. I want you to feel that love with me. I know they'll pull you into our family." Nicole hesitated, and Jesi teased her. "Please, please, please. I promise not to throw you in front of the bus, or car, or anything else except my love."

"I don't know about that," Nicole said. "I'm not saying no. I'm just saying don't push me. Okay?"

Jesi knew Nicole needed to take things slowly when it came to family. She understood that Nicole had finally opened up her heart to Aunt Mary Opal, Rachael, and Jesi, but extending that trust was another level that Nicole wasn't sure she wanted to handle.

"Nicole, I won't bring it up again," Jesi said. "You tell me if that's going to be an option. I promise I won't push you, except to get out of this house for a while. I think we need to go for a walk in the park and maybe out to dinner tonight. Let's call Rachael and see if they can go with us." Jesi was getting bored, and that's the last thing that she wanted to happen in her life.

Nicole flashed Jesi her flirtatious smile, picked up the phone, and called Rachael. "Hey Rachael, call us back. We're thinking that the four of us should go out to dinner tonight to celebrate our freedom from bondage over here." She threw her head back and laughed into the phone. "Call me."

It wasn't more than a few seconds before the phone rang and spelled out on the caller ID that it was Rachael.

Before Nicole could even say hello, Rachael said, "So, you *came* up for air."

"Yep, over and over." After a brief shared laugh, Nicole continued. "What are you and Aunt Mary Opal up to tonight? Can you join us for dinner?"

"I'll call her now, but I know she's really missed both of you," Rachael said. "We went to lunch yesterday. I think something's going on with her. I'm not sure what it is, but she just seems kind of low on energy or something. I can't seem to get a grip on what it is. Let me know if you sense something, okay? Maybe she is just missing you guys. I'll call you right back."

After Nicole hung up the phone, she turned in time to see Jesi packing a bag. Jesi had decided that she needed to spend some time in her own home for a few days. She knew the look on Nicole's face was concern. "Don't worry, you're not getting rid of me that easy. I just need to spend some time in my house with my pillow and my clothes. You can go with me if you want. But I think time apart is healthy too. Don't you?" Jesi had been loving her time with Nicole, but she missed her own routine and didn't want to make a big deal of spending time alone or time together at her house. The new relationship thing was going to be something she was going to have to negotiate. She knew not to get into a pattern where she felt trapped—that's when she would leave town.

Nicole was processing what she was seeing and hearing from Jesi when her phone rang. It was Rachael again. "Hey, what's up? Are you meeting us?"

Jesi yelled from the other room. "Be there or be square."

They met at La Fonda, a wonderful Latin restaurant in West Midtown. When they arrived at the restaurant, they were all so happy to see each other that they lingered at the table and shared story after story until after nine o'clock.

"Aunt Mary Opal, tell us about when you got your number to be in the CIA," Jesi began. "But don't tell us too much, because I know you'd have to shoot us. Did you really have a number?"

Aunt Mary Opal laughed. "Yes, I really did. Times were different then. Everyone jumped in to help anywhere they could. I remember one time my husband coming home from a trip to London with a small package hidden inside the lining of his coat. He asked me to take the envelope and go to a coffeehouse close to the airport and just wait for someone to show up and call me by my alias. And no, Jesi, I can't tell you my alias because I really would have to shoot you." They all giggled and refocused as Aunt Mary Opal picked up the story. "Sure enough, I was sitting there having coffee, and this really tall man with white hair came over and sat down in the booth across from me. My hair was dark back then. He could barely even fit into the booth, and I remember thinking how stupid I was to sit in a booth instead of at a table. Anyway, he called me by my alias and left some money for the coffee. I got up and left the coffeehouse, but I left the envelope inside the newspaper on the table. I assumed that he got the newspaper and left with it. I don't know. I didn't look back to see what he did when I left the coffeehouse."

"Did you just hand it to him? Or did you have to kind of sneak it to him?" Jesi asked, leaning forward, eyes wide open. Her dark hair draped her face and fell in front of her shoulders.

"No, I had it sitting on the table as soon as I got

there," Aunt Mary Opal said. "I put the envelope in the newspaper before I even got to the coffeehouse. I wasn't about to let someone see me with it."

"What was in it?" Jesi asked.

"Who knows?" Aunt Mary Opal said. "That kind of thing happened all the time, and no one ever asked any questions. I just did what I was told."

To Jesi, Aunt Mary Opal seemed to be getting a little nervous, and it wasn't just about the stories. She stood up and announced, "Wow, can you believe it's after nine? Let's get out of here. It's almost past my bedtime."

Rachael stood with Jesi. "I sure have missed you both. How about our ladies light luncheon? Our regular day is in two days, and we haven't had one since you know what, the big bang." She burst into laughter and covered her mouth.

Jesi pushed Rachael aside and laughed because she knew Rachael's comment didn't come out the way it was intended. "Oh my God, Rachael, I can't believe you just said that!" Jesi was laughing, but she was a little embarrassed to hear those words come out of Rachael's mouth, especially in front of Aunt Mary Opal. Even though they all knew Aunt Mary Opal was just one of them, they were all three very careful to respect her as their elder and as a woman who attended church every Sunday.

"That's not what I meant," Rachael said. "Good grief. I meant when you both decided to have a screaming fit in the middle of the road and get hit by not one car, but two. That's what I meant. What should I call that? It wasn't a hit and run; it was more like some cosmic wakeup call." Rachael was joking, but shivers went through her as she recounted the horrific event.

They all agreed to meet at Aunt Mary Opal's in two

days. Before Rachael and Aunt Mary Opal walked toward the car, Rachael turned to Nicole and Jesi and said, "Listen, y'all. I'm going to Charlotte for a couple of nights to see my friend Lea. I should be on time for the luncheon, but just in case I'm running late, I'll call. Keep your phones on."

They held each other tight before they left the restaurant. As they parted, Aunt Mary Opal, who has holding Rachael's hand, turned back to Nicole and Jesi. "I love you both. Please be careful. We can't take much more of that."

They each hesitated, and Aunt Mary Opal said, "Bring something special to the luncheon on Thursday. Bring each other, okay?"

TWENTY-SEVEN

RACHAEL'S DRIVE to Charlotte gave her four hours to contemplate her recent decision to leave Jake. She was looking forward to sharing her plans and getting support from her best friend, Lea. She anticipated that Lea would ask her to think about "What does Rachael want?" She also anticipated that the answer would be that she had no idea. She just knew that living every moment trying to anticipate what everyone else in her life wanted was about to drive her crazy. One of the last pieces of advice from her mother before her death was, "Don't make the same mistake I made. Figure out what you want from life and go get it. Please don't accept something just because someone else has a dream to fulfill. Find your own dream."

Rachael knew that her friendships with Aunt Mary Opal, Jesi, and Nicole were mutual and reciprocal. While she nurtured them, they did the same thing for her as well. But in most of her life, it was a one-way street— she nurtured, others got nurtured. She wasn't used to balance, and it felt really good. At that point in her life, they were the only people who knew about her decision to seek a divorce.

Rachael could not have been more surprised at Lea's reaction. She struck out at her: "You think it's only about you? I don't even know who you are or why you're here. You are so selfish. It's like you think your breakup is only about you, like it doesn't affect me. You just need to get over it and forgive him for whatever it is. Stop being so selfish." Lea had always had an edge to her way of communicating, but those words struck deep inside of Rachael. Lea's words—*selfish, don't even know who you are, just need to get over it*—echoed in her mind.

"Only about me? What are you talking about? It's my relationship." Rachael was stunned, but not for long. When she left, she not only drove away from Charlotte, but away from her long-term friendship.

Her mother's words repeated in her mind over and over. "The last thing in the world you need to worry about is if you are a kind and loving person. It's just in your nature." Her mother was right, and the person she had referred to as her best friend for all those years was wrong. She shortened her drive to Atlanta by not making her usual bathroom break until just before she got to Lake Hartwell. She made her way directly to Aunt Mary Opal's house so she wouldn't miss a minute of time with her real friends.

As they all four lay faceup in the middle of the family room, heads touching, Rachael shared with them Lea's reaction to her leaving Jake. "She told me that I was just being selfish and that I need to forgive Jake."

Jesi reacted first. "Fucking bitch. I don't like her."

"Jesi, please," Aunt Mary Opal said.

"I don't either," Nicole joined in.

"I'm sorry. I didn't mean to call her a bitch," Jesi said. "Actually, she's too low to be a bitch. I think we should get a picture of her and burn it in the fireplace." Jesi, in true fashion, was always the defender.

Nicole started the laughter. "I'm with Jesi. Let's burn her picture in the fireplace, but first, let's all have a Jack on the rocks and make up some sort of voodoo spell."

"Stop that!" Aunt Mary Opal said. "Rachael's feelings are hurt, and you two are being silly."

"Okay, maybe we won't make up a spell, but let's burn her picture," Nicole said, doubling over with laughter.

Rachael enjoyed this lightheartedness, but most importantly, she loved that her friends were standing by her and defending her. That was far from what she got from Lea.

Without saying anything else, they all picked themselves up from the floor, Rachael helping Aunt Mary Opal, and stepped into their roles of getting their cocktails poured. As Aunt Mary Opal walked into the sunroom to get the Jack Daniel's, she said, "Rachael, you need to put that friendship in the past. Do you have a picture we can burn?"

They didn't burn Lea's photograph that day. They spent the rest of the day and evening listening to Rachael talk about her relationship with Jake and her decision to leave him. As Rachael expected, they all rallied around her decision and gave her complete support.

~

A MONTH LATER, Aunt Mary Opal was right: An apology never came from Lea. Later, Rachael saw photographs on Facebook of Lea and Jake together at a small music festival, and Jake was not performing. She printed the photograph, and on the next evening of head-to-head group meditation, they lit a fire in the fireplace, wrote a voodoo spell, and burned the picture.

Voodoo, who do. Into the fire we send you.
Never again will you have the power,
Never again to make Rachael cower.
Get out, get back, we hear nothing you say.
From here to eternity, you are sent away!

They had to repeat the spell three times because the fire kept going out. Jesi kept relighting the fire to make sure the entire photograph was burned to ashes. Once Rachael was clear that the entire photograph had been turned into black and white ashes, she brushed her hands together. "Done." That was the last time any of them spoke of the "best friend."

TWENTY-EIGHT

RACHAEL ARRIVED EARLY at Caribou Coffee to make sure she was able to get a table in the corner. She was meeting Nicole and wanted to have a conversation without interruption. She had told Nicole that they were meeting for coffee before going shopping at Lenox Square. But the truth was that Rachael was concerned about Aunt Mary Opal and had a feeling that Nicole knew something that she wasn't sharing with her. She had been noticing looks between Aunt Mary Opal and Nicole, the quiet way they talked to each other, and the way they became quiet when anyone else walked into the room. She had driven by Aunt Mary Opal's house a few times during the previous couple of weeks, and Nicole's car was there almost every time. She was trying not to be jealous of their friendship, but she realized that she was feeling left out. Because Aunt Mary Opal was the queen of secrets, she was hoping to get to the truth through Nicole.

Nicole arrived late and rushed in. "Rachael, I'm so

sorry. I had to stop and get gas, and there was a line. Can you believe it? There are a dozen gas stations in the area and I pick the one with a line!"

"It's okay, Nicole. Grab some coffee and come on over."

"I think I'm going to hold off," Nicole said. "I had coffee with Aunt Mary Opal this morning, and you know her coffee. It's so strong. I think if I drink anymore, I'll stay up for days."

Hearing that Nicole had just had coffee with Aunt Mary Opal threw fuel on the fire for Rachael. "Nicole, I need to ask you some questions, and I really need you to be up-front with me." Rachael's voice was unusually stern. She seemed to forget the fact that she had not shared her own secrets about Aunt Mary Opal falling, head-to-head meditation, and other things with Nicole.

"What? What's going on? Are you okay?" Rachael noticed that Nicole looked confused.

"You've been spending time with Aunt Mary Opal, and it feels like you've been keeping it a secret from me. Am I just making it up? Or is something going on?" Rachael had obviously startled Nicole into speechlessness. She sat back in her chair as she waited on an answer.

Nicole sat straight up in her chair and pushed her red curls back away from her face. "Rachael, are you jealous of my friendship with Aunt Mary Opal? If you are, you need to get a grip. Aunt Mary Opal loves you. What's up? What's this really about?"

"I want to know why you always seem to be at her house," Rachael said. "You don't tell me about it. Is something going on?" Rachael shifted forward in her chair and her voice turned from defensive to concerned.

"I don't know, Nicole. I just have this feeling that something is going on, and I can't figure out what it is. Haven't you ever had something like that happen? It's like there's something wrong, but everyone acts like everything is fine. It makes me feel like I'm crazy. If you tell me I'm wrong, I'll let it go and just chalk it up to my hormones or some messed-up thing like that. I don't know, maybe it could even be about Jesi." Rachael tucked her head down. She had wondered whether Nicole was having issues in her relationship. That was why she wanted to meet with Nicole alone, even though she and Jesi had agreed to talk to Nicole together to find out what all the secrets were. Rachael's frustration made tears well up in her eyes.

"Fine, here's the deal, but you can't tell Aunt Mary Opal I told you. Okay?" Nicole said. Rachael watched Nicole's demeanor shift from concern to what looked like a little anger, and that confused her.

Rachael leaned in close and nodded her head. "Okay. What's up? Is she okay? So it's not about Jesi? Is she mad at me?"

"Do you want to know or not?" Nicole snapped.

"Yes, I do." Rachael was startled at Nicole's tone.

"Then shut up and let me talk." They stared at each other. Rachael waited as she watched Nicole wrestle with her answer. "So this is the deal," Nicole said. "Aunt Mary Opal called me one day and asked me to come over. She told me that I couldn't say a word to anyone, so I didn't." Nicole hesitated before continuing. "She told me that she was having a bad reaction to drinking alcohol, especially Jack Daniel's. After she drinks, she gets a rash, and then she has pain in her joints and stomach."

Rachael gasped. "That must be what happened to her

that day at the house when she looked like she was in pain. So we quit! What's the big deal?" Relief filled Rachael after hearing that it was only about alcohol.

"Shut up, Rachael," Nicole said, which shocked Rachael. She wasn't used to hearing such anger come from Nicole. They were both so emotionally charged that the couple sitting at the table next to them moved across the room to another table. Rachael's eyes widened, and she leaned in closer to Nicole, uncomfortable with how the conversation had escalated. "Aunt Mary Opal is afraid that if she quits drinking, she'll lose you and Jesi," Nicole said. "When we get together, we drink tea that makes our bodies more alkaline. We've even been talking about switching our diets to vegan. She has this crazy notion that there are some things that divide people and some things that bring them together, and alcohol is a big one. You know, Rachael, it's like this. How many friends do you have who don't smoke pot except Aunt Mary Opal? She doesn't even know that everyone smokes."

"None."

"Exactly. That's what Aunt Mary Opal is afraid of. And if you tell her I told you, I will never talk to you again. And I mean it, Rachael. You have to promise not to tell her I told her secret."

Rachael breathed out a long breath and sat back in her chair. "I promise. But what the hell?"

"So there, are you satisfied now? Now just because you're so insecure, you made me give up a secret of Aunt Mary Opal's. If she ever finds out, she'll probably never trust me again with anything. I hope you're happy. Do you still feel crazy? 'Cause I feel like a lying creep. I have to go, Rachael." Nicole stood up from the table and dramatically walked away, leaving Rachael still in shock at how exaggerated Nicole's anger was at her.

Rachael's eyes followed Nicole as she left the coffee-house and walked to her car. "That was weird," she thought. "Something doesn't seem right."

TWENTY-NINE

NICOLE HAD LIED TO RACHAEL. She was so wound up about having to lie to cover up Aunt Mary Opal's secret that she had to leave the coffeehouse. She left Caribou Coffee and drove straight to Aunt Mary Opal's house. If she was going to create a web of lies, she had to make certain that she had all her bases covered.

On the drive to Aunt Mary Opal's, she concocted a story. When the door opened, she started into an emotional outpouring. "I can't believe it. Rachael called me to go shopping but instead trapped me at the coffeehouse and told me something that I am supposed to keep as a secret. But I have to tell someone, and I know you know how to keep a secret."

Aunt Mary Opal guessed. "Don't tell me she's sick!"

"No, not really," Nicole said. "But it is about her health."

Aunt Mary Opal gasped and covered her mouth with her hand. She motioned for Nicole to walk into the kitchen, as they usually sat at the table for conversations.

Nicole waved her hands in the air. "No, I can't stay. I

have an appointment," she lied again. She expanded on her emotions just to make sure she had Aunt Mary Opal hook, line, and sinker. "God, what is it with everyone around me and health issues? She said that every time she drinks alcohol, especially Jack Daniel's, she gets a really bad stomachache. But the thing is, she's convinced that if she quits drinking, none of us will want to be around her. She has this stupid belief that drinkers hang out with drinkers and that they don't hang out with nondrinkers."

"Well, that's ridiculous," Aunt Mary Opal said. "We don't spend time with Rachael because she drinks."

Nicole was pleased with herself. Aunt Mary Opal was believing the story. "I know that, but you know how she is," Nicole said. "She always wants to please people, and she thinks you'll feel weird drinking in front of her. Aunt Mary Opal, you have to swear not to tell her I told you, promise."

"I promise, Nicole. I know how to keep a secret." She winked as she poked Nicole in her side.

"Okay, we have to figure out how to fix this without her knowing." Nicole looked at Aunt Mary Opal, hoping she was able to pull off her deception.

Not wanting to stay long for fear that she might mess up her web of lies, Nicole left the house, and as she drove off, she could see the concern in Aunt Mary Opal's face. She was standing in the driveway and waving goodbye to Nicole, but without the usual smile. The seeds were planted on both sides. She just hoped it didn't cause World War III between all of them. Mostly she just wanted her friend to live, with no pain. And she wanted Jesi and Rachael to stop looking at her as if she was betraying them.

THIRTY

Knowing that Jesi would be home, Rachael drove straight there after leaving the coffeehouse. Spring had arrived in Atlanta, and Bradford pear trees lined the streets with white blooms, looking like dense, fluffy clouds had fallen from the sky. Rachael's hair blew wild as she raced through the back roads with the top down on her car. Having been convinced that Aunt Mary Opal was having a hard time drinking alcohol, she needed Jesi's help in creating a solution to the problem. She called Jesi to let her know to meet at her house. "We need to talk. I'll be there in ten."

When Rachael arrived, Jesi stood in the kitchen and was pulling chips and dip from the cabinets. Rachael did not hold back as she spilled everything about her effort to discover from Nicole what all the secrets were. After a few minutes, Jesi put down the chips and, without swallowing, squeaked out, "Rachael, what are you talking about? You asked Nicole about the secret she's been keeping?"

Rachael sighed. She and Jesi had been going round

and round for weeks about how to handle Nicole's penchant for secrecy. They had agreed not to bring it up until they could be together with Nicole. But she had felt impatient with this solution. Her fear was that Nicole's secret might be about her relationship with Jesi. She was afraid that Jesi was going to get hurt. She'd wanted to protect her, not betray her. "Jesi, I'm sorry. It just happened." She didn't think it was necessary to tell Jesi she had planned to confront Nicole without her there. "We were going to the mall, and instead, we went to Caribou for a coffee. It just came out," she said. "It's okay to be mad at me, but please don't be mad for too long. We have some planning to do."

Rachael had a way of flirting with Jesi to get her to lighten up. It worked every time. Rachael ducked her head down and flashed a grin, and she ran her right forefinger down Jesi's left arm.

Jesi pulled her arm away. "Stop it. That's not fair. We agreed that we would talk to Nicole together."

Rachael kept teasing Jesi until she started laughing. "Okay, okay, you know I can't be mad at you." Just as Rachael had hoped. Jesi always gave in when Rachael was so flirtatious. "So tell me, was it about me?" Jesi said. "Is Nicole going to dump me? I know you were thinking she's leaving me, Rachael. I had the same thought. Is that it? Talk!"

Rachael moved the chips and dip to the dining room table, where the sun was streaming through the dogwood trees that had not yet bloomed. The sun felt good on her back as she sat facing Jesi. "Not even close!" Rachael was relieved to tell Jesi that it had nothing to do with her. "Now here's the deal, not a word. If Aunt Mary Opal finds out that Nicole told me, it could ruin everything. Girl Scout's honor?" Rachael held up her right hand with the three middle fingers straight up and her thumb crossing her pinky finger, as Girl Scouts do.

Jesi gave the same sign. "Girl Scout's honor!"

"This is really serious. Aunt Mary Opal has been getting sick after she drinks, but she thinks that if she quits drinking, we won't want to be around her."

"Well?" Jesi shrugged her shoulders and gave a look to Rachael as if it seemed to be a reasonable conclusion for Aunt Mary Opal.

"What the hell, Jesi? You'd block her out just because she doesn't drink?" Rachael was surprised.

"No, I'm just saying that I can see how she gets to that conclusion. Thanks a lot, Rachael. I'm not that shallow."

"Oh, sorry, I just thought . . ."

"You are such a bitch sometimes, Rachael," Jesi said, laughing out loud. She pushed Rachael back in her chair, which almost flipped backwards.

Rachael shifted into a more serious tone and leaned in for emphasis. "Okay, focus. What are we going to do? We can't let Aunt Mary Opal know, but we need to make up some story about why none of us should drink. And, you can't tell Nicole that you know. Man, she'd get really mad at me if she knew we were talking about this."

"Let's tell them you're pregnant," Jesi said, as she jumped up from the table.

Rachael groaned. Jesi had to know Rachael would have a strong reaction to that idea. She decided to play it light. "Oh, great idea, stupid." Rachael grabbed the bag of chips and threw it at Jesi. Potato chips scattered across the dining room floor.

As they cleaned up the mess, they covered the list of

possible solutions. Finally, they decided on one: They would tell Aunt Mary Opal and Nicole that Jesi was going to train for a marathon and that her coach had prohibited her from drinking. It was partially true. Jesi was going to run a ten-kilometer race, but it was an almost-naked run and only for fun. There would be cocktails served at every mile marker. "If they ask me, I'll tell them you can't come over because it would be too hard, and that you don't expect us to change anything just because of her," Rachael said. "I'll lay it on hard." Rachael started acting out a melodramatic scene. "It's awful, Aunt Mary Opal. Jesi's having to deal with a lifetime of feeling alone and desolate. She thinks no one loves her enough to compromise for her."

Jesi picked up the onion dip and pushed it into Rachael's face as they both laughed until Jesi snorted. After Rachael cleaned the dip from her face, she opened a bottle of champagne, and they toasted what they thought was the perfect plan.

Rachael knew she had been pushing Jesi's buttons when she teased her about feeling alone. She also knew that Jesi had stayed in one city for longer than she had in years and, more importantly, Jesi had fallen in love with Nicole.

THIRTY-ONE

TWO DAYS LATER, Aunt Mary Opal had gotten home from getting her hair back-combed, and she prepared all the beds for guests, knowing that the luncheon could turn into a slumber party. Sometimes she wished that they would all stay for a few days. She couldn't get enough time with them.

Nicole and Jesi arrived a few minutes before Rachael, which gave Jesi enough time to fill in Aunt Mary Opal and Nicole on her trip to San Diego.

"I'm sorry to say that I can't have alcohol," Jesi said.

Aunt Mary Opal was confused. It was Jesi who couldn't have alcohol? Nicole had told her it was Rachael. "Something's up," she thought. She noticed a look of shock on Nicole's face as she stared, wide-eyed, at Jesi. She eyed Nicole with suspicion. "Are you sick?" she asked Jesi.

"No, my trainer told me I can't drink," she said. "I'm going to run a marathon, and he said that if I don't agree to follow his rules, he will stop being my trainer."

Aunt Mary Opal decided to play along with Jesi's

story. "Well, then I won't drink either. Jesi, why don't you put that Jack Daniel's back in the bar?" She motioned Jesi toward the sunroom. "One for all, and all that stuff." As soon as Jesi turned her back, Aunt Mary Opal leaned in very close to Nicole. "She's trying to cover for Rachael. Just go with it. We can talk about it later."

"I'm in!" Nicole whispered back, while giving Aunt Mary Opal a wink.

When Rachael arrived, they were all drinking iced tea. "What's this?" she asked. "Where are our cocktails?"

Aunt Mary Opal felt a thrill. The plan to help Rachael was working. "Jesi's running a marathon and can't drink, so we decided not to drink either," she said. She stood next to the table with a wooden spoon in her hand, holding it in the air as if she had just made a proclamation.

"A marathon? That's great, Jesi. Then I'm all in."

Aunt Mary Opal winked at Jesi and Nicole just before she danced her jig. "Whew!"

THIRTY-TWO

Drops of moisture melted from Jesi's face and dripped onto her chest. It was all she could do to pry her thoughts from nightmare to reality. It was late afternoon, and she sat on the sofa, trying to focus on the room where she waited. Not her apartment. Nicole's house. She must have fallen asleep. Nicole should be home from work soon. Yet the tears kept flowing, and her breathing was labored. Like a panic attack, she thought. Like the nightmare was real. She grabbed her cell phone and dialed Nicole. Straight to voice mail.

"What's happening? Is this real? Is Nicole sleeping with someone else? Is it Rachael?" Jesi's mind reeled. So many secrets, but she couldn't keep her head clear long enough to figure them out. And that nightmare. Could Nicole be having an affair with Rachael?

Jesi had gone along with the secret plot of not drinking, but that wasn't all. She was sure there was still some sort of secret that Nicole was keeping. She just felt it. Her heart raced. She stood up from the sofa and gathered her things, and she placed a note for Nicole on the kitchen counter.

Nicole, I tried to call you, and I stayed here until it seemed weird to be here waiting on you. I don't think I can do this anymore. I'm going to New Orleans for a few days just to get away and get my head clear. When I get back, we need to talk about what's going on.

Jesi returned to her building and packed a bag. Even though it was late, she rolled down the top of her BMW and turned her car south on Interstate 85 toward Montgomery, Alabama. She planned to get a hotel somewhere on the road and drive into New Orleans the next day. She felt confused. She had always known that when she got those feelings, something was going on—someone was being deceptive. While she couldn't always figure out the details of who or why, it often turned out that someone was lying about something big.

When Rachael had told her that the big secret was Aunt Mary Opal needing to stop drinking, Jesi was hopeful that this cleared up everything. But the feeling hadn't gone away. Nicole was lying about something, and her instinct to run away was in full force. She also fully expected that Nicole would call her, but Nicole didn't call. "Nicole had to have read my note," Jesi thought. "She has decided not to call me." This seemed to confirm every fear she had.

So she kept driving and hoping, driving and hoping. Instead of stopping for the night, she arrived in New Orleans at 3:15 a.m., exhausted and numb. She felt like a fool. "How could I let my guard down? I can't ever trust Nicole again."

She checked into the Bourbon Orleans, in the 700 block of Orleans, across from her second-favorite restaurant in the French Quarter, the Orleans Grapevine. Irene's, a Sicilian restaurant with a southern Louisiana flair, was her favorite. When she ate at Irene's, it was like turning to her ancestral home of Agrigento. By the time she finally got to the room, she could barely hold her eyes open. She turned her phone off, pulled the curtains tightly closed, and climbed into bed. The emotional drive all night long had wiped out all her energy. Jesi put in earplugs and proceeded to sleep for nine straight hours.

It was after 1:00 p.m. before Jesi got out of bed and showered, which made it 2:00 p.m. in Atlanta. She walked around the corner to the Gumbo Shop for a cup of gumbo. As she sat there, still feeling numb from what she believed to be happening in her world, she realized that she had forgotten her phone in the room. "Oh well, things happen for a reason." Jesi was resigned to the idea, factual or not, that Nicole was seeing Rachael.

While waiting on her food, Jesi skimmed through the *Gambit*, a local newspaper, when she saw that one of her favorite bands was playing at the House of Blues. She really loved the sound of Donna The Buffalo and was surprised to see that they were playing in New Orleans. She had a fleeting thought that she needed to get two tickets, one for herself and one for Nicole, but quickly pushed the idea aside. After paying for her gumbo, Jesi stood to leave, thinking that a walk on the riverfront would be a good idea. But then she heard a familiar voice.

"Jesi?" A petite, dark-haired woman with olive skin peeked out from behind the wall next to her table. Jesi turned to look at the person who had called her name, and a soft, confident voice said, "Wow, it is you! You are so beautiful, and you look like you just woke up. Still pulling all-nighters?" Jesi recognized that flirtatious tone.

Awinita Arkeketa, Wini for short. The woman was still smiling, which made Jesi blush.

Jesi had traveled with Wini and her husband, Elon, for six months in their RV. Wini and Elon met growing up in an orphanage for Cherokee children in Ponca City, Oklahoma. They had been together since she was ten and he was fourteen. Jesi had met them years earlier at a powwow in Anadarko when Jesi was on a road trip from Atlanta to San Diego. When she first saw them, Wini and Elon were dancing to the beating of drums that pounded out a song for protection. Wini had worn a long headdress made of hawk and eagle feathers. Her tanned leather dress had been covered in beadwork that was carefully hand-stitched. Elon had towered over her while he danced with his arms stretched out above her head, as if the meaning of the dance was to protect what belonged to him. He had worn dark stripes on his face and bright blue feathers draped down his back. They had both moved with exaggerated gestures filled with passionate emotion. Jesi had not been able to look away from them. As they danced, they had noticed the attention they were getting from Jesi, and when the dance was done, they had walked up to Jesi. "Why are you here?" Elon had asked.

"To see you, of course." Jesi flirted with both of them and was certain of the energy that came back to her. For six months, they traveled, laughed, cried, made love, fought, and then parted ways. It was an intense time in each of their lives, and when they parted, it was a painful but necessary split. Jesi had begun to lose herself in them. Wini and Elon had, for the first time in their lives together, felt a distance between each other. Jesi had known the right thing to do, and above all, that was to protect Wini and Elon's love. Afterwards, Jesi's travels never left her in one place for more than a month, until she arrived in Atlanta.

Standing in the Gumbo Shop, Jesi asked Wini, "Why are you here?"

Wini smiled. "To see you, of course." They both blushed slightly at the memories they shared, and they embraced for a long, warm moment.

Jesi looked over Wini's shoulder, expecting to see Elon.

"Elon's in a meeting. We're here for a Cherokee conference." Wini looked into Jesi's eyes as Jesi wondered if she could sense her sadness. "He's going to be so happy to see you, Jesi. Do you live here?"

Jesi backed away. "No, Atlanta."

"Do you have some time? Can you join me for coffee?"

Jesi wondered if Wini had seen her pain, which she was trying so hard to hide.

Wini always wore a shiny stone hanging from a thin leather strand around her neck. If she needed to call on her ancestors for help, she held the stone and rubbed the back with her right thumb. It was a habit, and Jesi knew that when Wini reached up and put the stone in her right hand, it meant she was calling for help. Jesi also knew that Wini's focus was intensely on her and that she felt emotionally exposed, the last thing she wanted to feel at this time.

"I was going to see about getting a ticket to see Donna The Buffalo tonight," Jesi said. "You can walk over to the House of Blues with me if you'd like." Jesi was aware of how awkward she must seem to Wini.

"Okay. I can do that," Wini said. "I can skip some of the seminar. I'll send a text to Elon."

Jesi and Wini made their way up Royal Street and over to Decatur Street to the ticket office, where Jesi purchased one ticket. She didn't ask Wini if they would like to join her, because she wasn't sure if she really even wanted to spend time with them. On the way, Jesi kept the conversation on the surface, something that had never been the norm for her. She shared stories with Wini about traveling to Spain and about meeting a woman, but she didn't give any details about her friendship with Rachael or Aunt Mary Opal. She certainly didn't mention any details about her relationship with Nicole. Jesi felt like she was stuck in an emotional turmoil between numbness and panic, so she avoided anything that would touch her emotions. Jesi was afraid that if she opened up, she would break down into tears. She also knew that it was no coincidence that she had driven all night to New Orleans only to walk right into Wini. She kept checking her pocket for her phone. Each time, she remembered that she had left it at the hotel.

Wini noticed, and she asked if Jesi had lost her phone.

"Yeah, I feel so stupid. I left it in my room. That's okay. Listen . . ." Jesi's energy shifted. "Let's go get a cocktail and walk on the riverfront. We can hang out and watch the ships until Elon gets out of the class. How does that sound?"

"That sounds like a plan."

"It is New Orleans, and they serve drinks to go, right?" Jesi said, thinking about Aunt Mary Opal. That certainly lifted her spirits out from the dull ache of the past two days.

~

THEY ORDERED spicy Bloody Marys to go, and they strolled up toward the Mississippi River, next to the Aquarium. They didn't talk much. Jesi avoided conversation by pretending to read the names on the bricks of the walkway. As they walked up the hill, three young men who appeared as if they hadn't showered in a year hustled them for money. When the men didn't get what they were hoping for, they began making crude sexual comments toward both of them. Jesi's internal fire boiled up. Wini reached over and took Jesi's arm in hers. "Let it go, my friend. Pick your battles, remember?"

Jesi had always followed Wini when she tried to calm her spirit. They walked arm-in-arm along the linear park toward the Natchez steamboat. The sound of a calliope got louder as they walked closer. The same jovial and expressive woman that Jesi remembered from her previous trips to New Orleans was playing music and entertaining the onlookers.

Wini sent a text to Elon to join her on the Moon Walk. Within a few minutes, Jesi spotted Elon. He was just as handsome as he was the last time they had seen each other. She knew Elon had seen them because he let out a scream and his hands waved in the air. As Elon lifted Jesi and twirled her around, all three of them laughed. The rest of the tension Jesi had been holding vanished.

"Jesi, I forgot how little you are," Elon said. He had

a laugh that fit his stature—big and boisterous. "Was this planned?" He turned to Wini for confirmation.

"No," Wini said. "We both happened to be at the Gumbo Shop at the same time. 'Why are you here?' she asked me. And I said . . ." They all three chimed in at the same time: ". . . to see you, of course!" The laughter continued as they turned back to walk to the French Quarter.

"Go with me to my room so I can get my phone," Jesi said. "Do y'all have plans tonight?" That's when she realized how disconnected she had been from Wini. She turned to Wini with a red face, tears pouring from her eyes. They embraced. "I'm sorry," Jesi said. "Please forgive me." Jesi didn't have to say why she apologized. She knew Wini had been waiting on her to show her spirit.

Wini enveloped Jesi in her arms. "No, Jesi, don't do that to yourself. You're safe with me, just the way you are. When you want to share, then share. But only when you're clear that you are loved and safe." When she stared back into Jesi's eyes, it was as if she offered Jesi a place to feel innocent and vulnerable. They held each other silently. Only after Jesi took a deep breath and the energy lightened did Wini continue to speak. "Besides, we already have tickets to Donna The Buffalo."

They strolled through the French Quarter and down Bourbon Street until they got to Orleans Avenue. A couple of stores caught their attention, and at one point, they all bought the same T-shirt that read *Be Nice Or Leave.* Elon put his on over the shirt he already had on. The shirts were designed and printed by Dr. Bob, a local artist. The store attendant told them they needed to go to

Dr. Bob's studio in Bywater, a historic neighborhood located downriver from the French Quarter.

"Yeah, dawlin', just keep the river to your right," the attendant said. "Not long after you cross the tracks, you'll get to Dr. Bob's place. It's a good neighborhood, real artsy. Where y'all stay by?" The young woman seemed to be flirting with Elon in her New Orleans dialect, and Jesi couldn't help but think that it was a perfect match for Elon's big personality.

"We stay by Ardmore, Oklahoma," Elon said.

Out on the street, Wini and Jesi laughed about the flirtation. "Some things never change, do they?" whispered Jesi, as she grabbed Wini's arm and they made their way down Bourbon Street.

On the way to Jesi's room, they picked up a bottle of Maker's Mark, Wini's favorite libation, and a bottle of red wine for Elon. As soon as they got to the room, Jesi turned her phone back on. A cacophony of ringtones notified her of all the calls and text messages that had come in.

Wini raised her eyebrows. "Someone's trying to reach you. Do you need time alone to make some calls?"

Jesi shrugged as she listened to the first message. The first one was from Nicole. "Jesi, where are you? What's this note about? Call me. This is not a good way to start a Friday." She put her phone down and chose not to listen to any of the other messages.

Jesi poured them all drinks and filled them in on her relationship with Nicole and the web of secrets that had pushed her into a state of mistrust. "I don't know what happened," she said. "I just got this overwhelming feeling that there was something not right, like she's not telling me the truth about something, so I left. I just couldn't get my head clear."

Elon remained quiet as she talked about Nicole, Rachael, and Aunt Mary Opal. He listened and leaned toward Jesi, his long, straight, black hair spread across his shoulders. "Jesi, remember that time when you kept saying there was something not right about that teacher of yours? Richard, right?"

"Yes, I just had this feeling. He gave me the creeps. My friends loved him, but I still didn't trust him."

"Well, guess what? You were right," Elon said. "Remember how he used to talk badly about his gay son who rode in the rodeo?"

"Yeah, that always pissed me off," Jesi said.

"Well, here's what we found out. The whole time that he was married and putting down his gay son, he had a male lover on the side," Elon said. "My view is, I don't care if people are gay or straight; I care if they are honorable."

Jesi leaped out of her chair. "Oh my God! That's it! That's what I was sensing. What a fucker. He was so mean about his son. He even told me one time when he saw me with a lesbian not to ruin my life. The nerve of that asshole!" By then, Jesi was pacing, and her voice was raised enough so that if someone were outside her door in the hallway, they'd hear her. "What a jerk! What a hypocrite!"

"Jesi, what I'm saying is this," Elon continued through his grin at her emotional response. "You always know when something's going on, but sometimes it's not as bad you think. If you love Nicole, you need to talk to her. You can't just walk out. Maybe it's something simple."

Jesi flashed Elon a sarcastic look. "Something simple, like maybe she's got someone on the side? Yeah, that's pretty simple, alright." Her voice was still loud and angry.

Suddenly, there was a knock on the door. Jesi, still wound up from the conversation, opened the door to see Nicole standing in the hallway with a confused and hurt look on her face. Nicole leaned in to see Elon and Wini resting against the headboard of the bed, each with a cocktail. There was an awkward silence before they both jumped off the bed and stuttered as they introduced themselves, clearly not knowing who they were saying hello to.

Jesi knew it didn't look right, and it felt even worse. When Nicole stared into Jesi's eyes, seeking an answer, Jesi glared back and motioned toward Nicole and then back toward her friends. "This is Nicole. Nicole, this is Wini and Elon."

Wini set her bourbon on the bedside table and reached out to shake Nicole's hand. "Nicole, Jesi was just sharing with us how special you are. We're going to step across the street and get a glass of wine at Grapevine. If you would like, please join us there once you get settled in."

Elon followed Wini out of the room as he shook Nicole's hand and waved goodbye to Jesi, who was nearly shaking with tension. "We'll probably have dinner there, please join us," he said. "We have so much to catch up on, and we would love to get to know you, Nicole."

Wini gently smiled at Nicole as Elon set his wine glass on the dresser on the way out the door.

The door closed, and Jesi watched as Nicole dropped her burnt-orange bag to the carpeted floor. Jesi walked over to the dresser, poured a short bourbon for Nicole, and watched her as she ran her hand through her red hair and sat down in the chair below the window overlooking Orleans Avenue. Jesi waited on Nicole to say something.

Nicole didn't sip the bourbon. She drank it in one shot. "I can't compete with Tonto and Pocahontas, so don't waste my time, Jesi. What's going on?" she said. "I don't think you've ever lied to me. I trust you, so just say it."

"It's not what you think, Nicole," Jesi said, wringing her hands as she paced back and forth.

"You don't know what I think, Jesi," Nicole said. "You never asked me. You just put this message in the kitchen and left." She whipped out Jesi's note and set it on the end table next to her empty glass. "Is this it? Is this how you leave people? Out of my bed and into theirs?"

"That's not it, Nicole." Jesi watched Nicole sit back in the chair and cross her legs, relaxed but her face cold and angry.

"Then what is it? I just canceled my day and flew five hundred miles to find you, only to get here and find not one but two beautiful people in your bed drinking cocktails. What do I do with that? Am I still just a fool? I certainly was in my last relationship, lied to from the start. Is that happening again? Because really, Jesi, I don't think I can take it, so don't fucking lie to me."

Jesi felt overwhelmed with emotion. The numbness was gone, and she was crying so hard that she could hardly catch her breath. "Where were you last night? I waited for you for hours. You didn't come home and you didn't answer your phone. You tell me, Nicole. What is going on? Something's wrong. You're hiding something. I feel it in my bones. And don't tell me I'm wrong, because I know when someone is keeping something from me. I've been trying to figure it out for months, but I can't. Is it Rachael? Are you fucking Rachael?"

Nicole's mouth dropped open in shock. She nearly shot out of her chair but instead sat on the edge. "What? You think I'm having an affair with Rachael? That's why you make plans to come down here and have a fling with Tonto and Pocahontas? Man, are you wrong. I am doing nothing of the kind. But you sure are." Nicole flung out her arm and pointed her finger at the bed where they had been sitting when she arrived.

Jesi's voice quivered as her pacing intensified. "No, Nicole, you are wrong. I mean, yes, I had a thing with them years ago, but I didn't know they were here. I ran into Wini at lunch. I haven't had contact with them in years. When you knocked on the door, I was just telling them about you and how there's something wrong. So what is it, Nicole? I told you, now it's your turn. What are you keeping from me? I'll know if it's the truth; just say it!" Jesi stood crying and waited for Nicole to tell her something, anything.

Nicole walked to the dresser, poured another bourbon, and walked back to the chair. "Sit down, Jesi. There is something."

Jesi didn't sit down; she exploded. "I knew it! Who?" She stopped crying and wiped the tears from her face with her sleeve.

"Not who, Jesi. Please sit down so we can talk."

Jesi reluctantly sat down on the edge of the bed and waited for Nicole to begin. Her whole body vibrated. She bounced her right leg up and down with tension.

"I promised not to tell anyone, and it's been really hard keeping this a secret," Nicole said. "I knew you could sense it, but I promised. I never meant it to hurt you. It's . . . Aunt Mary Opal." Astonished, Jesi watched as Nicole clasped her face in her hands and cried. "She's dying. Aunt Mary Opal is dying. And she's planning on taking her life. She made me promise not to tell. I wanted to, but I promised. Please forgive me. I didn't know what to do."

Jesi had been crying. Now her tears stopped, and she was filled with calm. "When did she tell you?"

"About four months ago. I knew something was up, but one day I went to the basement to get a bottle of wine and the door to the storeroom was wide open. It had some things in there that told me something was wrong. I wasn't sure how to get her to talk about it. You know how she is about her privacy. There's no telling how many secrets she'll die with without ever telling anyone. I think she took that CIA thing a little too far." Nicole looked up at Jesi. "But anyway, I got her to open up. She has cancer."

Jesi felt a strange calmness. She couldn't be angry at Nicole because she had her own secret about Aunt Mary Opal. Two months earlier, in an effort to figure out what secrets had been kept, she followed Aunt Mary Opal. The first day, she watched from the end of a parking lot when Aunt Mary Opal entered a medical building and into the office of an oncologist. That was when she knew the secret: Aunt Mary Opal had cancer. The next day, she followed again and ended up at a therapist's office off Clairmont Road. She had made it a routine on many of her days to follow Aunt Mary Opal until one day she realized she felt like a stalker. But Jesi wasn't ready to tell Nicole about what she knew.

"Are you hearing me, Jesi?" Nicole said. "I told you Aunt Mary Opal is dying."

Jesi slid down to the floor and rested her head in Nicole's lap with her arms around her legs. "I'm sorry. I let my emotions get away with me. I've always had a problem with that, and this time, it almost damaged us forever. I'm sorry."

"Jesi, I love you," Nicole said. "I want us to be strong together, but you can't run away from me every time you sense something's a little off. You have to trust me."

Jesi reached up and covered Nicole's mouth to quiet her, and she moved Nicole's body from the chair until they were both on their knees, holding each other. At that time, Jesi needed to feel Nicole's touch, her spirit. They undressed each other, their voices were silent. All they heard was breathing, and they allowed their energy to reconnect, their bodies to move together.

As they rested in each other's arms, covered only by the white sheet, Nicole spoke. "Jesi, your friends, I'm sorry I called them Tonto and Pocahontas. Please don't tell them I said that. It seems so racist."

Jesi burst into laughter. Actually, she could hardly wait to tell Wini and Elon. "It's okay. I used to call them that to their faces."

"Were you going to have sex with them if I hadn't shown up? Tell the truth."

For the first time, Jesi became aware of a change in herself. While she had run away from Atlanta, she realized that she had not run away from her commitment to Nicole. "I hadn't thought about it. I started talking about you, and they told me that I might be jumping the gun with my conclusions about feeling some kind of deception, that maybe it wasn't an affair."

"I like them already." Nicole threw a pillow as Jesi walked into the bathroom to shower.

Jesi dodged the pillow. "Hey Nicole, I got a ticket to see Donna The Buffalo at nine. Let's get dressed and go. I don't think it's sold out."

~

WHEN JESI EMERGED from the shower, she saw Nicole still resting in bed. She leaned her head out to say, "I don't want to talk about Aunt Mary Opal right now. I want us to talk about her after we leave New Orleans. Is that okay with you?"

"Jesi, when you start to doubt us, stop for a second, talk to me. I'm strong for you."

"I'm sorry. I'll remember," said Jesi, thinking she was still not ready to tell Nicole of her secret about Aunt Mary Opal.

They held hands on their walk to the House of Blues to purchase another ticket. "Did you call your friends to see if they want to join us?" Nicole asked. The thick air had moved in across the Mississippi River into the French Quarter. While it wasn't raining, a mist had filled the sky, and it reflected the lights across the wet streets as the air was filled with glistening drops of moisture.

"No, I don't have their numbers. They said they're going to the concert, so we'll probably see them there. I need to make sure I get their numbers before we leave."

"Okay. But Jesi, I don't want to talk about your history with them until we leave New Orleans, okay?"

They both wanted to protect their time together in New Orleans and to make sure that nothing interfered.

They arrived at the House of Blues early, just as Jesi realized how hungry she was. She hadn't eaten anything since breakfast. "Let's grab a sandwich before the concert."

"Sounds good. I've eaten here at the restaurant before. It's pretty good, and the servers know people need to eat and get to the concert, so they don't hold you up." Nicole opened the restaurant door for Jesi and reached out to hug her as she passed. Jesi felt as if some sort of veil had been lifted from between them.

The server was a cute young blonde woman who was sporting a Donna The Buffalo T-shirt with what looked like signatures of all the band members on the front. "Love your shirt!" Jesi said, motioning toward her.

"Thanks. I collect them from all the people who perform here." The server shifted her weight back and forth as she held her pad of paper with pen in hand, ready to take their order.

"That's cool," Jesi nodded. "Do you have a Jake LeBlanc shirt? I think he was here a few months ago."

"Yeah. I love him," the server said. "Actually, my best friend Teri is dating him."

This unexpected answer got Jesi and Nicole's attention. They stopped looking at the menu and glanced at each other in shock. "Really?" Nicole finally said. "How long have they been dating?"

"A couple of years or so," the server said. "They met when he was playing here. She's a great singer and they just hit it off. She's actually traveling with him on tour right now."

"Where is she from?" Jesi asked.

"Australia. But she moved to Atlanta to be closer to Jake." Jesi thought the server seemed to enjoy being a part of the story. "Yeah, Jake was getting a divorce when they met. I think it's probably already done, but you know how the press is. They only publish things if it's controversial. We may never hear about it." The server held her breath as she stared back at the shocked looks on Jesi and Nicole's faces. "Um, do y'all know Jake?"

"Well, actually, he and his wife are two of our very best friends," Jesi said, forcefully. "And no, they were not separated and getting a divorce two years ago."

Nicole reached over and placed her hand on Jesi's to calm her down a bit.

That was the last they saw of their server, and a different server brought their check. Neither of them brought up what had just been shared. That subject would be added to the list of things to talk about on their seven-hour drive back to Atlanta.

As Jesi hoped, they spotted Wini and Elon immediately. The concert was just starting, so having a conversation was difficult, which she figured would be okay with Nicole. There was something magical about dancing to the music that night. As the concert neared its close, Nicole looked over just in time to see Wini and Elon embrace each other. Jesi watched Nicole stare at her friends. Nicole's tension had vanished, and a soft smile formed on her face when Jesi reached over and took her hand in hers.

After the concert, the sky had cleared in the French Quarter. All four of them strolled downriver through Jackson Square. Artists, musicians, and tarot card readers were out, making it clear that they were in a city with a rich history. They settled in at Café Du Monde on

Decatur Street for café au lait and beignets. Their conversations were filled with laughter, and Jesi was delighted as she watched the interactions between Nicole, Wini, and Elon.

Jesi felt exhausted from the emotional roller coaster, but there was an intense energy with Nicole, a kind of Tantric passion. They made love again when they returned to the room from the concert, and they fell asleep holding each other until the sun peeked through the curtains.

THE NEW MORNING brought Jesi calmness, and not a minute too soon. By nine, they were making their way east onto Interstate 10, the radio tuned to WWOZ, the sound of New Orleans. An hour in, Nicole reached over and turned the radio off. "Do you feel like talking about some things?"

Jesi smiled as she kept her eyes on the road. "I can't imagine what we would have to talk about."

"Right," Nicole chuckled.

"I don't need to know anything about what you talked to Aunt Mary Opal about," Jesi started. "I know she likes her secrets, and I want to respect that."

"I don't mind sharing with you," Nicole said.

Jesi stopped her. "No, don't. It's your little secret." She thought that if Nicole told her more, she would have to tell her what she knew. She changed the subject. "Do you have any questions about Tonto and Pocahontas?"

"No. I can see how you were so attracted to them. They're really beautiful people, and they love you."

"Of course they do. I mean, look at me!"

They made light conversation about possibly meeting up with them in the future.

And then all conversation stopped and the car was filled with silence. Jesi felt overwhelmed with anger at what they had learned about Jake. When she tried to talk, the only word she could say before her tears took over was "Rachael." Nicole reached for Jesi's hand. She could see out of the corner of her eye that tears streaked down Nicole's face. Finally, Jesi broke the silence. "What do we do with this? Do we tell Rachael? This is a really shitty thing to know."

"Let's think about it. Rachael has already decided to leave Jake, and it seems like it's going to be amicable," Nicole said. "Do you think she knows it's Teri?"

"No. I think if she did, she would have told us." Jesi felt her face grow hot with emotion. But then an idea occurred to her. "Let's ask Aunt Mary Opal what to do. She'll know."

"You mean like 'What would Aunt Mary Opal do?'" Nicole ran her finger across her arm as if to indicate a tattoo with the letters on her forearm.

"I guess the real question is: Would I want her to tell me if you were doing the same thing?" She stared at the road ahead, and they both grew quiet. Nicole turned the radio back on.

They arrived back in Atlanta and to the 14th Street exit, but instead of exiting to go to Nicole's house, Jesi continued north on Interstate 85. Jesi didn't ask Nicole if that would work for her — she just kept driving.

When they arrived at Aunt Mary Opal's, they saw another car in the driveway, one they didn't recognize. Jesi stopped the car instead of pulling into the driveway. The front door opened, and a chubby, gray-haired man stepped out. Aunt Mary Opal wore her robe, something that was out of the norm for her this late in the day. Nicole gasped. "Do you think Aunt Mary Opal is having an affair?" Jesi quickly drove forward so Aunt Mary Opal wouldn't see them lingering in front of the house. They both began laughing.

"I hope she is," Jesi said. She was thrilled at the thought of Aunt Mary Opal having a fling. "We can't go in there and get her upset now. Let's just talk to her later."

"No problem. Now we know 'WWAMOD.'" Nicole burst into laughter, and they drove back to Nicole's for a slow dinner and an early night.

THIRTY-THREE

AUNT MARY OPAL'S birthday was just a few days away, and Rachael wanted to make plans. "What do you think if we do a photo shoot with her, just the four of us?" she said to Jesi and Nicole. She knew that buying Aunt Mary Opal one more object for her house was a terrible idea.

"I love that thought," agreed Jesi, who looked to Nicole for a response.

Wearing a big grin, Nicole nodded. "What if we all get our hair done like hers?"

Rachael laughed out loud. "That's a great idea! Do you think we can get her to show her tattoo? We could all drop our sleeves off our shoulders and expose our tattoos."

"If we get her drunk, she will," Jesi said. "Let's take her to Pancho's. You know she loves margaritas, and she drinks more when she doesn't measure the pour herself. But don't tell her. Let it be a surprise." Jesi burst into laughter at the thought.

That was the plan—cut, bleach, and back-comb all of

their hair. Serve Aunt Mary Opal a few drinks and then take the photographs, tattoos exposed. Rachael was more excited about this upcoming photo shoot than she had been about any other.

When the day came, getting their hair done should have been a nonevent. But as the day proceeded, the word *eventful* was an understatement.

A photographer walked into the salon and interrupted them as he snapped pictures of Rachael. He was obviously not welcome, but Rachael was stuck in the chair as her stylist was putting the final back-comb in her white hair. She couldn't get out of the chair, so she held her hand up for him to stop. "What are you doing?"

The man smiled. "Sorry, Rachael, just trying to get a story on you for Jake's fans. Why did you leave Jake? Are you a lesbian?" He continued by taking photographs, not just of Rachael, but also of Jesi and Nicole.

Jesi laughed, and Nicole held her hand up to cover her face. Rachael was so surprised that she didn't know how to respond. She would never want to do or say something that might harm Jake. "No, I'm still so in love with Jake. He's the love of my life," she said, with a touch of sarcasm.

Rachael was a little worried when Jesi got out of her salon chair and started toward the photographer to try to block him from taking pictures of her. "Come on, man, leave her alone," said Jesi.

"Why are you getting your hair bleached, Rachael?" he asked, lowering his camera.

Rachael kept an eye on Jesi as she escorted him to the door. As he was leaving, Jesi commented, "She's hoping Jake will like her new 'do and come running after her." Every person in the salon laughed as Jesi returned to the chair, a move that made Rachael happy.

"I hope he doesn't put those pictures on the Internet," Rachael said. She really didn't want to stir things up with Jake. She sent him a text to warn him. "Jake, some guy just got some pics of me getting my hair done. They'll probably end up on the Internet. Trying to stir up some fake issue between us. We're okay, right? I am."

Jake returned her text immediately. "Yes, we're good. Sorry he bugged you. Send me a pic of your hair."

Not only did the photographer post the pictures, he had them on his blog before they could leave the salon. "Jake LeBlanc's ex . . . still in love with Jake? Or is something else going on? You decide . . . Rachael LeBlanc, according to one of her friends, is getting her hair bleached and back-combed in an effort to get Jake back . . . will it work? Is that what turns him on?"

The pictures immediately brought comments from viewers, mostly from teenage girls. "Oh my God, listen to these tweets. This is unbelievable." Rachael knew how much Jake's fans loved him.

"No . . . she can't have him back . . . he's mine!"

"If he likes bleached hair, I can please Jake. Going to his concert tomorrow night in DC and think I'll get my hair done just like hers. He's mine now!!"

They all laughed at the comments and at the pictures, but Rachael had no idea how much of an impact her new hairstyle would have on Jake's fans until the next night, when Jake sent a text to Rachael. Jake included a photograph he took from the stage looking out at the audience during his concert. It seemed that the posting of the photographs had gone viral and that the teenage girls all wanted to get Jake's attention. The photograph showed at least half the girls in the audience with bleached and back-combed hair, or at least wearing wigs to look like Rachael's hair.

"Rachael, look what you got started. I love it! Xoxo, Jake."

Rachael didn't respond, but she was thrilled that it seemed to be helping him. His ego had always been really big, and the new craze seemed to make it even bigger. She forwarded the text to Jesi and Nicole to let them know they had all become trendsetters.

THE NEXT DAY, Rachael had reserved their usual corner table and had tied balloons on all four chairs. The server placed a pitcher of margaritas and four glasses on the table just before they arrived. As soon as Rachael saw Aunt Mary Opal's face light up at the decorations and margaritas, she knew it was a success.

"Oh my, I love you all so much. This is the best birthday of my whole life." Aunt Mary Opal hugged each of them and the server.

Rachael had brought her photography equipment to the restaurant earlier in the day. After a couple drinks, she set up her tripod, and they posed in numerous positions, including a few with exposed tattoos, just as she had hoped.

Later that evening, after Rachael returned home, she filtered through the photographs and decided to enter some of them in a fashion magazine contest without asking permission from Jesi, Nicole, or Aunt Mary Opal. "I'll ask for forgiveness later," she thought to herself.

THIRTY-FOUR

THREE YEARS EARLIER, her husband had died, her daughters were living in other states, and Aunt Mary Opal was left on her own for the first time in her life. The day she met Sandra, a hypnotherapist, was the day Mary Opal Shook chose to stop pretending that the abuse she had lived through didn't matter. The problem was that she had no idea how to live without the threat or reality of abuse.

For Mary Opal, the therapist's office was nothing like a doctors' office. It was warm, and it created a sense of security and relaxation. Sandra's question started the process of healing her decades of living with shame. "How can I help you, Mary Opal?"

"My hairdresser told me you could help me remember some things in my past. I keep trying to remember things, but every time I see myself walking down the hallway, I get to the living room and it goes dark, like someone turned the lights off. I just want to remember."

"Are you ready to do the work?"

"Yes." Mary Opal then knew that something in her past was holding her back from being happy. Sandra motioned for her to sit in a long, black leather lounge chair. The headphones were going to flatten her newly back-combed hair, so she let them hang under her chin rather than on top of her hair. The walls were covered with brightly colored paintings that appeared to be swirls of stars.

Over the following months, her therapy sessions took Mary Opal back to reliving her mother's death during childbirth, a father who didn't want her, and her husband, who appeared to everyone outside their home to be the strong rock of the family. After months of uncovering many layers of memories, one session changed everything. "Three, two, one, open your eyes and tell me where you are."

When Mary Opal entered a state of hypnosis and opened her eyes, she had just finished her coffee when Harold had joined her and her childhood friend in the café. When it was time to leave, she recounted the stark memory. "Will you take care of the baby for a couple of hours so we can go shopping?"

The pain from her memory rushed forward. Harold had turned toward her, raised his left arm above his head, and pounded the back of his hand down onto her cheek, knocking her to the floor and causing blood to drip from her lip onto the red-and-white checkered linoleum floor. She remembered the smell of the scuffed floor and the look of terror on her friend's face. That was the last time she saw her childhood friend.

That hypnotherapy session had taken her back in time to the point when shame had clutched her spirit and had separated her from anyone who had been close to her in the past. During the session, she turned the light on to the shame she had carried all those years. In the light, the darkness disappeared from her life. From that moment, Mary Opal Shook felt a freedom she hadn't experienced in decades. After that day, life became a little lighter, and the new friends she brought close to her were younger and full of life. She tried to find her old friend, only to learn that she had passed the previous year. "I'll see her soon," she thought.

Three years after she began delving into her past, she was once again sitting in Sandra's office. When she spoke, Aunt Mary Opal's voice was so soft that Sandra had to lean in to hear all the words. "I want to close one more chapter. It seems like it's the only thing left to finish."

After all the years of unfolding layers and ridding herself of shame, the only thing that remained to uncover was why she had a deep sense of secrecy inside her when she looked at the list of addresses and descriptions of so many of the beautiful vases that lined her shelves. "Here's the list. I don't remember making it, but I know I did, because it's my handwriting. Every one of those items are in my house, and I don't remember buying them. But the addresses are all in my neighborhood. Will you help me remember? I don't want to die not knowing what this all means."

Sandra studied the list, noticing that the date at the top of the paper was around the time Mary Opal had been diagnosed with cancer in 1978. The session that day was short. "Three, two, one, tell me where you are."

The session revealed a secret that Mary Opal had hidden deep in her mind. When her husband learned of Mary Opal's cancer, he had requested a transfer and moved to Washington, DC, leaving her to go through treatment without him. It was a cruel punishment, one accentuated by his fist pounding her side, leaving her with a broken rib that delayed chemotherapy treatments. Mary Opal had been hurt and angry, but her youngest daughter was a senior in high school and she had no time to feel sorry for herself. She had joined a neighborhood group of parents to help raise money for their children's senior trip to Key West. For six months, the group met at a different parent's house each week. She was the only parent to show up without a spouse, and her anger had grown.

After waking up from the session, surprised at the memories that had come to light, Mary Opal whispered, "Sandra, I took those vases from those people's houses, didn't I? How could I have done that?"

"In 1978, no one knew anything about post-traumatic stress disorder. Today, we understand more about how people deal with trauma than we ever have. It isn't uncommon for people to do things out of character in reaction to the trauma. Our minds have an amazing way of protecting us, and sometimes it means we erase or stuff memories. Sometimes, forgetting is our best choice." Sandra was calm and collected in her explanation.

"Oh my, I need to return those things to those people," Aunt Mary Opal said.

"No, you don't," Sandra quickly shot back a response, but not so calm and collected. "That was over twenty years ago. Let's find a way to help you feel complete without exposing yourself that way."

Aunt Mary Opal processed this and held Sandra's gaze. "I don't have that kind of time," she finally said. "You have to help me figure out a way to give those things back to those people. I don't have long, and I don't want to die with anything unfinished. You told me you'd help me." Her pleading voice was as weak as her body.

Sandra offered a quick solution. "You know I can't help you, but I think I know who can."

THIRTY-FIVE

NICOLE AND JESI met at Rachael's house at 3:00 a.m. Aunt Mary Opal had called Rachael, had asked that they arrive at her house no later than 4:00 a.m., and had said that they were to drive her car to run an errand for her. "What do you think she needs us to do?" Jesi asked. "And why at four in the morning?"

Nicole joined in. "And why drive her car?"

"I don't know, but whatever it is, we're going to do it," Rachael insisted. "Are you both in?" She knew her tone was a little short.

"Of course we are," Jesi said. "I just want to know if it's one of her CIA stories, that's all."

"Does it matter if it is?" Rachael, again, was quick to answer. "She would do anything for us. Remember how she saved us in Sicily? The day we almost went to jail?" She stood up, grabbed her jacket, and started toward the front door, keys in hand. "Come on. I don't want to be late."

Other than the rumble of the old engine, the drive over

in Nicole's Cadillac was quiet. When they arrived, Aunt Mary Opal's car was backed into the driveway, right next to the door. "That's weird," Rachael said. As Nicole pulled over to the left side of the drive, Rachael noticed something out of place. "What's that? There's something on her windshield." Before the car could come to a stop, Jesi opened the back door and jumped out. Nicole parked, and they all stood in the driveway as Jesi opened an envelope with their names on the outside. They had expected to see Aunt Mary Opal. Instead, she had left them a letter.

As Rachael and Nicole looked on, Jesi opened the envelope. "What the fuck, you guys? This is unbelievable." Jesi unfolded the letter. "Okay, this is what it says. 'Please follow my instructions exactly. Deliver all of the packages tonight to the addresses on the list.'" Jesi stopped reading as they each looked inside the car to see the entire back filled with packages that were individually gift-wrapped.

Confused, Rachael took the letter out of Jesi's hands and continued reading. "Each package is labeled with a number so you know which one is to be delivered next. Make sure that you stay in order, because I have arranged the packages to make delivery effortless and quick. It is important that you place the packages on the front steps and leave quickly. Do NOT let anyone see you deliver the packages. If there happens to be someone up at that time, skip that house and take the package home with you to keep as my gift to you. They must all be delivered tonight. Thank you for delivering my 'secret admirer' gifts. Remember, this is a secret. No one must know. When you have finished, return the car and place the keys through the mailbox slot at my door. Thank you for helping. I'm just too old to play 'secret admirer' all by myself."

Rachael was still looking through the car windows at the brightly colored gift wrapping. "This is so sweet."

"Shit, y'all," Jesi said. "Something's not right." She paced in the driveway. "I feel like we're in one of those stories that Aunt Mary Opal used to tell about taking envelopes to some place where a spy meets her and takes the envelope. I don't know about this. Something feels weird."

Jesi looked back and forth from the car to the door. When Rachael saw Jesi peeking through the peephole on the door, she grabbed Jesi's arm and pulled her toward the car. "Stop it. Let's just get this done so we can go home."

All the gifts were from houses in the same neighborhood that Aunt Mary Opal had lived in for almost forty years. Rachael assumed that she just wanted to do something sweet for her neighbors. She knew that Jesi assumed the worst; she just couldn't figure out what the worst was.

The delivery was quicker than Rachael had expected. Only one house didn't get a delivery because the lights were on and they could see someone through the window. They decided that Nicole would take home whatever was in the box. Exhausted and still confused about the "secret admirer" story, they drove back to Rachael's and parted ways.

THIRTY-SIX

THE NEXT MORNING, Rachael got a call from Nicole, who told her she'd set out at 6:00 a.m. to see if she could deliver the last package to the house where the man was seen through the window. Groggily, Rachael listened to Nicole's account.

"It was a cool morning, so I didn't put the top down," Nicole said. "I put the package on the step, but just as I was getting back into my car, a woman out on a morning run greeted me with, 'Good morning, nice car.' I got myself home as fast as possible."

"Wait! You what?" Rachael loudly said.

"I just wanted to make sure all of the gifts went to the right people, and I didn't feel right keeping something that she intended for someone else," Nicole said, defensively.

"Well, it's done," Rachael said. "I don't understand what's going on, but there's nothing we can do about it now. What's done is done. I have to go back to sleep. Call me later, okay?"

~

THE NEXT MORNING, Rachael started her day as she did every Sunday, playing Sarah Brightman as loud as she could while swimming laps in the pool. She considered that time to be her church service. While she was just finishing her last lap, she heard Jesi and Nicole yelling at her. She stopped swimming and looked up in time to see Nicole turning off the power to the sound system. She could clearly hear Jesi screaming. "Get out of the pool! Did you see the news?"

"What the hell, you guys? Did someone die or something?" Rachael always swam in the nude, so when she got out of the pool, she was aware that Jesi and Nicole were staring at her as she dried off. Her back-combed hair was soaking wet but was still as white as Aunt Mary Opal's, with the exception of her natural roots.

"Turn the news on, Rachael," Nicole said. "You have to see it for yourself." Nicole opened the door to the cabana, turned on the screen, and waited.

Rachael cued the television to 11Alive News. "A bizarre set of events has prompted the Atlanta Police Department to begin an investigation this morning," the anchor was saying. "Join us at 11Alive for the full story of the case of the stolen treasures, all returned."

"Oh my God. Oh my God," Rachael felt shocked and scared. "What the hell is going on?" She rushed to shut the door to the cabana so her neighbors couldn't hear the report. She knew they loved it when she played Sarah Brightman on Sundays and that they were often sitting in their backyard, smoking a joint.

"There's more, Rachael," Jesi said. "Guess who went back and got caught by some woman walking her dog?"

Jesi pointed at Nicole.

Rachael turned to see Nicole's nervous look on her face. "I'm sorry. I'm really sorry. I was just trying to make sure everyone got the gifts. I was just trying to help."

"I told you something was up," Jesi said. "Why can't y'all listen to me when I say something's fucked up?" She sat on the edge of the daybed.

The newscast started again and the room was quiet.

Anchor: "A bizarre set of events for one neighborhood in Atlanta. It seems that items that were taken from homes in the Maple Hills subdivision in 1989 have all been returned to the addresses where they were stolen from. The police want to know who stole the items and to whom and why they were returned. Here with us is the police chief. Chief, have you ever seen an incident like this before?"

Chief: "No, I haven't. Not in my entire career, since 1981, have I seen something so bizarre."

Anchor: "When you find out who returned the items, will you press charges?"

Chief: "We can't say at this time. We're just now looking into the issue."

Anchor: "But since they are returned, wouldn't that fix the problem?"

Chief: "No. Whoever stole the items broke the law, and it's our job to find out who, and serve justice."

Anchor: "Do you have any leads?"

Chief: "Yes, we do. We have a witness who saw someone, and we are in the process of checking that lead."

Anchor: "Thank you, Chief. We look forward to more from you as we move into this week."

Rachael turned to the others. "Did anyone call Aunt Mary Opal?"

"She didn't answer," Nicole said.

"Here's the thing," Rachael said to Nicole. "Your car is easy to find, and when they find your car, the woman will recognize you. Look at your hair, white and back-combed. It's not like you can pretend it wasn't you." Rachael could hardly believe this was happening. "Did she see you with the package?"

Nicole wrung her hands. "No. She came around the corner as I was getting back in my car."

"Did she see you near the house?" Rachael paced as she quizzed Nicole.

"No," Nicole said. "There's no way she saw me there. She couldn't have seen me there." Nicole was tearing up as Rachael became more agitated.

Jesi jumped to Nicole's defense. "Okay, let's keep calm. There's no reason to get upset. You didn't mean to do anything wrong."

Rachael paced back and forth. "We said we'd follow Aunt Mary Opal's instructions, and Nicole broke her promise. Now, there's no telling what's going to happen. We had stolen things in our possession. A lot of stolen things."

At that point, the live update broke in. They all froze as they watched the anchor.

Anchor: "Here is the latest on the case of the stolen treasures. We have an exclusive interview with a witness who saw the car and the people who returned the items to the homes."

"People?" Rachael blurted out.

Anchor: "We are here on Fisher Trail at the home of a neighbor. Please tell us what you saw."

Neighbor: "Well, I got up to go to the bathroom and looked out the window. There was an SUV in the neighbor's driveway, and they're not home. So I got my camera and took a picture of the car, just in case something was going on."

Rachael yelled out. "Picture? Shit!"

Anchor: "Did you see who was in the car?"

Neighbor: "That's what was strange. I couldn't see them very well, so I wouldn't be able to identify them, but it looked like three older women with white hair."

Anchor: "Did you give the photograph to the police?"

"We're dead," Nicole said. "This is awful."

Neighbor: "Yes, I did, but it was dark, so I'm not sure if it'll help."

Jesi jumped up from the daybed to pace. As she did, she bumped into Rachael and almost knocked her off her feet. She rubbed her hand through her hair. "I'm shaving my head."

Anchor: "That's all for now. We will keep you posted as we get closer to catching the white-haired women in the case of the stolen treasures, or treasures returned."

"Wait! Let's all shave our heads," Nicole said.

Rachael looked confused. "Shave? I don't know, y'all. How about we dye our hair? I'll look like a dyke if I cut all my hair off."

"Rachael, give me a break," Jesi said. "There's nothing you can do that would make you look like a dyke. You're not. You're straight." Jesi laughed, and they all seem to lighten up a little.

"Okay, I'll do it too," Rachael said. "I have electric clippers." Rachael ran back into the house and retrieved the clippers she had always used to cut Jake's hair. She removed the guard to allow the blades to cut their hair shorter, and they took turns shaving each other's heads, leaving less than a half an inch of hair on each of their heads. Nicole swept up the hair and used a brush to knock the hair from each of their shoulders.

"I need a drink," Nicole said. "Do you have any Bloody Mary mix, Rachael?" Just as the words came out of Nicole's mouth, she seemed to realize what she was saying.

Rachael burst into laughter. "Bloody Mary? You mean Bloody Aunt Mary Opal?" They laughed as the tension in the room eased, and they nearly missed the next news update.

The only witness couldn't recognize who was in the car, and the photograph was too dark and blurry. The police announced that the statute of limitations had come and gone, and they also said that since none of the items were worth enough to constitute a felony offense, they would not continue with the investigation.

Nicole and Jesi jumped for joy, but Rachael was inflamed. "That's just great," she sarcastically said. "We couldn't wait five minutes to see what happened? We had to cut all the hair off our heads and then find out that there's not even an issue?" She dropped to her knees, covered her face with her hands, and started laughing uncontrollably. "I feel like we all just got off of a roller coaster with Aunt Mary Opal driving!" Rachael stood up and headed to the door. "I have to get back in the pool." As she walked out the door of the cabana, she dropped her clothes, turned on the music, and dove into the water. She noticed that the flow of the water over her head felt much more intense with such little hair.

Jesi and Nicole shed their clothes and joined her.

Treading water, Jesi said, "I tried to call Aunt Mary

Opal again. Do you think she's just ignoring us? What is going on, y'all? Those things were stolen. I don't think I can ignore that. We need to get to the truth. No secrets. And I mean it."

"I agree," Nicole said. "I think there are too many secrets. And that was serious. We could be in jail." Nicole stepped out of the pool, wrapped a towel around herself, and poured each of them another Bloody Mary.

As the day wore on, they lounged around the pool and took turns calling Aunt Mary Opal, but they never got an answer. Rachael presented a plan. "If we don't hear back from her by tomorrow morning, let's all go over there and not leave 'til she answers the door. In the meantime, I'm starving. Are y'all okay with Louisiana food?"

After they all agreed, Rachael ordered a Louisiana seafood boil from Chef Jules, who owned the restaurant right around the corner. He didn't usually deliver, but he and Rachael had become friends, and hopefully more. After thirty minutes, Rachael greeted Chef Jules at the side gate. "Hey, thanks for bringing us dinner. We're starving."

"No problem," he said. Rachael was surprised that he was looking away shyly until she remembered her shaved head and that she was wearing only a beach towel that barely covered her torso. When he rounded the corner with the food, he must have spotted Jesi and Nicole in the pool, naked and embracing, both with shaved heads.

"Oh God, I'm sorry," he said, as he tucked his head down even further. "Um, I thought, I mean . . ." Jules looked back and forth at all of them with their shaved heads, each adorned with the same tattoo above their left breast.

Rachael's heart sank a little. She'd made handsome Chef Jules feel foolish. And now he thought Rachael was a lesbian, in a relationship with both of the women in the pool.

Still, the look on his face was priceless, and Jesi had to speak up. Arms around Nicole, she shouted, "Sorry Chef, it's just that I'm crazy about this woman. I didn't mean for you to walk in on us. And Rachael's not gay, even though she has a dyke haircut." As Jesi fell back in the pool, she pulled Nicole back underwater with her.

Rachael's face turned bright red. As she watched the shock on Chef Jules's face, she blurted, "I'm not a lesbian."

"Well, that made my day!" he said. "Dinner's on me." He smiled and winked at Rachael as he turned to leave with a skip in his step.

As soon as Chef Jules was gone, Rachael ran to the pool and jumped in, almost right on top of Jesi. When she came up for air, she whispered, "I think he likes me."

The day had started out with incredible stress, but it turned out to be a day full of sunshine, laughter, and joy. Nicole, sitting on one of the corner seats and wearing a big smile, said, "Hey y'all, this is exactly what Aunt Mary Opal told us to have. Remember? Have fun, it's the best thing to have."

They donned pool robes and sat around the table for a feast of Louisiana shrimp, potatoes, corn, sausage, and garlic. It wasn't unusual for Aunt Mary Opal to take time returning their calls, so they agreed to give her some time before they confronted her about the gifts.

THIRTY-SEVEN

ON MONDAY MORNING, Aunt Mary Opal woke at 5:35 a.m. She had spent all day Sunday in pain, and that morning was no different. It was worse than it had ever been. Her affairs were in order, and hiding her pain from the people she loved the most she knew would be impossible. Tears flowed down her face until her alarm chimed at 6:00 a.m. She knew it was time if she intended to leave the world with dignity.

No one but her attorney knew the changes she made to her will only two months earlier. When her last will and testament would be read, she was pretty certain that her daughters would be upset to know she had left one-third of her estate in a trust for Rachael, Jesi, and Nicole. She loved them dearly, and she wanted to help make their lives just a little easier. While money wasn't the key to happiness, it sure did help.

Dee and Aunt Mary Opal had gone over the details many times. Aunt Mary Opal was to arrive at the library, find the book *With Love & Light* by Jamie Butler, an Atlanta author, and place it on the return table. When

Dee saw the book, she would know to arrive at Aunt Mary Opal's house promptly at eleven that night.

Aunt Mary Opal called a cab with enough time to arrive at the just as it opened. The sun had risen high in the sky, making the air hot and humid. The cabdriver, a man she had called many times in the past, showed up and helped her into the back seat. It seemed like it took forever to get to the library, even though it was only about a mile down the road. He waited in the car for Aunt Mary Opal's return.

She slowly walked down the aisle to find the book they had discussed, but the book was not on the shelf. Not being able to follow the plan created in her stress and fear. Even though Aunt Mary Opal was normally a calm person, she was anything but calm that day. She walked to Dee's desk and angrily announced, with her voice raised, that the book she was looking for had been misfiled. "I need the book by Jamie Butler, *With Love & Light*, and I need it today."

Dee gasped and held her breath when she looked up to see Aunt Mary Opal, who was obviously in distress. She stood and took her arm to escort her away from the desk. "It's okay. I understand what you're asking for. Did you drive here alone?"

"No, the cabdriver is waiting on me. But you said that I need to put the book on the return desk." Aunt Mary Opal was in tears.

Dee stopped and placed her hands on Aunt Mary Opal's face. "It's okay. I will see you tonight at eleven. Do you need anything from me right now?"

"Just for you to be there. I'm ready."

As Dee helped Aunt Mary Opal into the cab, the driver looked at Dee with concern in his eyes. When the door was closed, he said to Dee, "I've never seen her like this. Should I take her to the hospital?" The driver had driven Aunt Mary Opal to her destinations many times over the previous six months and had seen the progression of her weakness, but never like that.

"I don't think so," Dee said. "Home is good. I will call her later to see if she's better. Thank you for being so kind." Dee made her way back into the library as the cab left the parking lot.

Aunt Mary Opal had called Rachael to cancel dinner plans with the three other women. She knew that they wanted to discuss what had taken place with the "secret admirer" gifts, but she concluded that that was just one secret she would never share. "I just think I'm going to curl up with a good book tonight. Please call Jesi and Nicole for me."

Her house was quiet, so she walked into the family room to the stereo console and played Dean Martin, turning up the sound so she would be able to hear the music all the way back in her bedroom. When she started to feel a little better, she spent part of the day making sure the house was clean and the rest looking through photographs that spanned her entire life. As the evening stretched on, Aunt Mary Opal sat at the kitchen table and poured herself a Jack on the rocks. Her stomach was upset, so she only took a few sips to help her swallow the pain medication she had been instructed to take. The feel of the glass in her hands brought back many memories of sitting at the kitchen table.

It seemed as if she had been sitting there for hours, even though it was just under an hour when the phone rang. The answering machine picked up the message, and Aunt Mary Opal heard Nicole's voice. "Hey, Aunt

Mary Opal, we've been trying to catch up with you. Please call when you get this message, okay? I'm putting my casserole in the refrigerator and will bring it to you tomorrow. I hope you get some rest. I love you." There was a pause, as if Nicole had something else to say. Aunt Mary Opal listened through the silence, expecting to hear her voice again. But there was the click of the phone hanging up.

As Aunt Mary Opal sat listening to Elvis Presley's "Hawaiian Wedding Song," her thoughts were carried to her wedding day in Washington, DC, and to the funeral of her husband. She never spoke of her feelings about losing her husband except during the head-to-head group meditation with her friends. "What do I miss most about my husband? Dancing. I love to dance. Sometimes I pretend I'm dancing with him." During the night that she shared with Jesi what she missed about Harold, Jesi had leaped to her feet and turned on the stereo. Benny Goodman's "Stompin' At The Savoy" had been the first song to play. Song after song, Jesi danced with Aunt Mary Opal. When she wasn't dancing with Jesi, she danced with Rachael or Nicole. That evening had been pure magic. They had taken turns dancing with each other, but about halfway through the evening, it was hard to pry Nicole and Jesi apart. At one point, Aunt Mary Opal and Rachael sat down on the sofa and watched them as they held each other even closer while dancing to Frank Sinatra's "My One And Only Love."

Aunt Mary Opal spoke out loud, as if it were still that night and as if Rachael were still sitting next to her while they watched Nicole and Jesi. "It's funny how amazing it is to see two people in love," she said. But it wasn't that night. She was alone, except for her memories.

As she remembered dancing with her friends, she seemed to be pain-free. "It must be the pain medication making me a little dizzy." She began wishing time would move faster, that the grandfather clock would strike eleven, and that the doorbell would ring.

When the doorbell did ring, it wasn't at the time she had expected. "Oh my, she's early." Aunt Mary Opal turned the music down as she made her way through the family room to the door. "I'm coming," she called out. It may have been her surprise at Dee's early arrival or the pain that had increased, but regardless, she didn't peek through the peephole as she usually would have done. Rachael, her clothing soaked, was standing in the rain at nearly 9:00 p.m.

Aunt Mary Opal's shock was so complete that holding in her emotions was not a choice. She fell forward and wrapped her arms around Rachael's waist as she burst into the emotional outpouring she had hoped would go with her to her grave.

Rachael lowered her head and enveloped Aunt Mary Opal, blocking her from the rain and holding her up. It was as if Aunt Mary Opal couldn't stand. Using one arm to hold her up and the other to close the door behind them, Rachael slowly and carefully moved them into the kitchen. The only words spoken were Aunt Mary Opal's. "I'm sorry, I'm so sorry."

When they were both settled into their chairs at the table, Rachael asked, "What is it, Aunt Mary Opal? What are you sorry about?"

"I should have told you. I wanted you to help me, but I was afraid you'd tell me no."

"Help you with what?" Rachael asked, confused. "You know I'd do anything for you."

The clock struck nine, and Aunt Mary Opal didn't want to wait another two hours before she was at peace. "I can't go on. It's the pain. I know you've seen me hurting. I need to end it. I was going to do it myself tonight, but I can't get the things up from the basement. Please forgive me, but I have to ask you to help me."

Aunt Mary Opal had guessed right. Rachael had noticed the signs of the pain that were evident on her face. Very likely, Rachael had recognized them as the same signs she saw when her mother was so ill.

"Is it cancer?"

"Yes. But you knew that, didn't you?"

"Yes, I did. I'll help you, Aunt Mary Opal. I don't want you to be alone. What do I need to do?" Aunt Mary Opal watched as Rachael's compassion and strength combined into a powerful resolve.

Aunt Mary Opal reached into the pocket of her pink sweater and handed her a key. "Everything's in the storeroom downstairs. I put a purple sticky note on every piece. Just bring them into my bedroom."

Rachael closed her hand tightly over the key and started to speak. Aunt Mary Opal's wrinkled hand covered Rachael's mouth as she shook her head for Rachael not to talk. "Rachael, if you don't help me, I could make a mistake. I need your help. When I'm gone, just leave everything so when they find me, they'll know I did this by myself. Just drive away. I don't want anyone to suspect that you helped."

All the equipment was brought up from the basement, where it had been stored in the storeroom for the past year. They both took great care to follow directions, making certain that the plastic tent covered Aunt Mary Opal, with no leaks, as she lay in her bed. Her hands were secured to make sure that she couldn't move the helium supply from her face before she fell into a deep sleep. They stared at each other through the wrinkled transparent plastic. Aunt Mary Opal's eyes lit up as the helium filled the tent, pushing the wrinkles flat in the plastic and making it so she could see Rachael's face clearly.

Rachael looked carefully at Aunt Mary Opal and thought how beautiful she was in her soft pink cardigan sweater and white pearl necklace. Her hair was perfectly back-combed. "I love you, Aunt Mary Opal." Tears flowed down Rachael's face.

Just before Aunt Mary Opal's eyes closed for the last time, she whispered, "I love you, too. Please tell the girls I love them."

The room went quiet, with the exception of the hiss from the helium tank pumping into the plastic tent. Within a short time, Aunt Mary Opal was out of pain forever, her pulse stopped.

THIRTY-EIGHT

As ARRANGED, Dee arrived at Aunt Mary Opal's house at 11:00 p.m. sharp. She backed the car up to the side door and rang the doorbell. The sound of Frank Sinatra was pounding through the wall. When Aunt Mary Opal didn't open the door, Dee used the key she had been given and let herself into the house. "Aunt Mary Opal?" No answer. Dee turned down the music and called out again, slowly making her way into the kitchen. "Aunt Mary Opal, it's Dee."

Still no answer. "This is weird." Dee continued to call out her name as she walked past the kitchen table. Two of the chairs were pushed away from the table, but there was only one glass of what looked like bourbon. "Aunt Mary Opal, I'm here."

When Dee reached the bedroom, she realized that Aunt Mary Opal had taken her own life, without help. She pulled up a small antique chair from the corner and sat in prayer for a few minutes before checking for a pulse. Aunt Mary Opal was gone. Dee carefully removed the plastic tent and the wrist restraints. After she put the chair back into the corner, she reached down to pick up the helium tanks and was confused at their weight. Dee turned the valve on one of the tanks. Hissing started as soon as she turned the valve. "Oh my God, someone was here and turned off the valves. I have to get out of here."

Dee moved into high gear and loaded up everything into the back of her SUV. When she left the house, it was raining again. She thought that the rain would ensure that there would be very little traffic. Shortly after she pulled out of the driveway and was on the road, an antique white Cadillac rounded the corner rather quickly, and it didn't stop or slow down. As she turned the corner, she looked back to see where the car had gone. It had turned into Aunt Mary Opal's driveway.

"Who was that? Did they see me?"

THIRTY-NINE

RACHAEL HAD BARELY FALLEN asleep when her phone rang. It was Nicole, who was screaming frantically. "Rachael, we're headed to Aunt Mary Opal's. Jesi just woke up from a deep sleep with a feeling that she needs us."

"I'm on my way." Rachael leaped up from the bed in disbelief.

"No, we're almost to your house," Nicole said. "We'll pick you up."

Rachael was scared of what was about to happen. She knew she had to act surprised when they got there and saw that Aunt Mary Opal was gone.

The white Cadillac pulled fast into the driveway, and Rachael jumped into the backseat. "What's going on, Jesi?" Rachael asked, trying not to show her surprise that Jesi felt that something wrong had happened.

"I don't know, Rachael," Jesi said. "I just woke up in a panic. It was like Aunt Mary Opal was tapping me on my shoulder or something. Come on, Nicole! Drive faster!"

When they turned onto Aunt Mary Opal's street at a faster-than-safe speed, they nearly ran into a dark SUV. Nicole swerved and just missed the other vehicle. Jesi had not seen the SUV from the front seat because she had been turned toward the back seat, talking to Rachael. Rachael was the only one who had a good look at the front of the SUV. Jesi saw the back.

Rachael turned to watch the SUV disappear around the corner. "Did that car come out of Aunt Mary Opal's driveway?" She had a sick feeling in her stomach.

Nicole pulled into the driveway. "I don't know," she said. "I think so. I was just trying not to hit it. My windshield wipers aren't worth shit, and I couldn't see it very well."

As Nicole struggled to unlock the door, Rachael panicked. "Hurry up, Nicole!" Nicole burst into tears and handed the house key to Rachael, who opened the door quietly.

The kitchen light was turned off. Jesi grabbed them both and stopped them from moving forward. "She never turns off the light in the kitchen at night," she said. "I don't like this."

Rachael knew that she hadn't turned off the kitchen light. She had also left the music on loud.

Jesi held her hands up in the air and halted the others in the kitchen. "Now, stop for a second. We don't all need to sneak in there and scare her to death. Nicole, call her name so she knows we're here."

"Me? Why me? You call her. You're the one that got us over here, as if there's some sort of horrible thing happening. Now you want me to be the one who wakes her up. No way. You do it."

Rachael remained quiet. She had no idea what their

reaction would be when they saw Aunt Mary Opal lying in the clear plastic tent. All she knew is that it would be one secret that she would never share with anyone, ever. She followed Nicole as they walked past the sunroom where the rainwater had once again seeped into the house and had puddled around one of Aunt Mary Opal's antique rugs. The rug was soaked.

They carefully and quietly made their way down the hallway, past the family pictures, and to the bedroom, where Nicole softly called out her name. "Aunt Mary Opal? It's Nicole. Are you awake?" There was no answer. "Aunt Mary Opal?" She leaned forward and peeked into the bedroom. Aunt Mary Opal was lying on her bed, with pillows propping her up slightly. There was a small bedside lamp that created a warm glow of light over a Bible that rested on a soft, pink, hand-stitched cloth that matched her sweater. As Nicole crept closer, Jesi quietly entered the room behind her.

"Is she awake?" Jesi whispered.

Rachael stayed back and shivered inside while trying to remain calm outside, ready for an emotional reaction to the plastic tent and helium tanks. When there was no such reaction, she peeked into the bedroom and gasped. "Where is the plastic tent? The helium? What the hell is going on?"

Jesi and Nicole stood arm-in-arm and looked down at Aunt Mary Opal for a long moment, until Jesi finally reached out and touched her arm. She was still, completely still, and she was not breathing. Jesi stepped back and stood in the corner with her hands covering her mouth as she began to cry. "Do y'all smell it?"

"What?" Nicole said, looking confused.

"The incense. Do you smell it?"

Nicole and Rachael, who both remembered Jesi's stories from the past, glanced at each other and shook their heads no.

Jesi said that they needed to perform CPR. As she reached out to move Aunt Mary Opal to the floor, Nicole stepped in between Jesi and the bed. "No," Nicole said. "She doesn't want you to do that. Stop."

Rachael was shocked and further confused.

"What are you talking about, Nicole? Move!" Jesi said. "Maybe we can save her." She put pressure on Nicole's right arm to move her out of her way.

"No, Jesi. Stop it!" Nicole's voice was raised. She pushed back again, placing her body between Jesi and Aunt Mary Opal.

"Nicole, you stop it!" Jesi screamed. "No! She can't go! I need her! No! We have to save her!"

Nicole wrapped her arms around Jesi and pulled her close. She soothed Jesi and reached out to Rachael, waving her in. "This is what she wanted," Nicole said. "Sit down. I want to talk to you, and it's not going to be easy for me. So you just have to listen. Okay?" No response. Rachael was in shock. "Okay?" Nicole made both of them answer her so she knew she had their attention.

They all three sat on the floor next to the bed where Aunt Mary Opal lay.

"God, it's hot in here," Jesi said. "My stomach feels upset. I have to lie down."

"Me too," Rachael said. Confusion filled her head. "Who was here? Who was in that SUV?" she wondered to herself.

They lay on the floor and ended up head-to-head. Nicole told the entire story about Aunt Mary Opal's cancer and what was inside the locked storeroom. Even though she had told Jesi about Aunt Mary Opal's cancer and her plans, she had not told her all the details.

"I had always thought that when Aunt Mary Opal was ready, I would be the person to help her," Nicole said.

"Nicole, if she was going to use the helium, then where is it?" Jesi asked.

Rachael's head was spinning. "She planned this," she thought to herself. "But how did she know I would just stop in? Oh my God, she didn't. That person in the SUV was supposed to help her." She then snapped out of it and joined the conversation, trying to cover up what she had done. "Yeah, Nicole," she chimed in. "What's going on? Where is it?" She glanced back and forth between Jesi, Nicole, and Aunt Mary Opal. "She must have just died in her sleep."

Nicole stood up and headed toward the hallway. "I'm going to the storeroom."

Rachael followed, but she was well aware that the equipment was not in the storeroom.

"But we can't," Jesi said. "It's always locked." She grabbed Nicole's arm.

"I'll break down the door if I have to," said Nicole, who was the first person out of the room and down the stairs.

They all reached the door to the storeroom and stopped cold, scared to find out whether it was still locked. Rachael, knowing that she had not locked the storeroom, reached out and slowly turned the knob.

Nicole flipped on the light. "I'm scared," she said. But there was no sign of helium or of anything else that could have been used in Aunt Mary Opal's passing. The room was completely empty, with the exception of boxes of files.

Jesi broke the silence. "This is freaking me out. It's like that news story that was on about a year ago. There was a group of people who were helping terminally ill people die, and they used helium, just like you said, Nicole. I'm creeped out right now."

"This is so fucked up," Rachael said, backing out of the room.

"No Rachael, it's true," Nicole said. "The FBI or someone did a sting on them. They showed how this guy went undercover and acted like he was dying of cancer, and when the other guy got there, he walked him through the whole thing. The guy said that when he was dead, they would take all the equipment away and that there would be no traces of the helium in the body so no one would ever know that it was anything other than his cancer. But it was really an undercover cop, or FBI, or whatever."

Rachael had begun crying uncontrollably. "Do you think it was them who came here? Do you think that's who I saw in the driveway?"

"No, it can't be," Jesi said. "Those guys got busted. I think they're all in prison right now." She stopped for a moment and turned to Nicole, who had been sitting on a box, just listening to them talk. "What happened, Nicole? What happened here?"

Nicole hesitated, and with a confused look on her face, said, "I really don't know. She told me that she was going to do this on her own, but if she did, then the equipment would still be there. But it's gone, and we saw someone leaving. I didn't even notice anything about the car. Rachael, tell us what you saw."

"I don't even know. It was a dark SUV, like half the cars on the road. I think it was a woman, but I don't know."

As she paced, Jesi joined in. "It was raining, and your stupid windshield wipers don't keep the windshield clear. I couldn't see who was driving even if it was daylight while raining. I don't know how you drive that damn car."

"Okay, I get it about my car," Nicole said, turning her head away and holding up her right hand for Jesi to stop talking. She heard about the car from Jesi every time they traveled in it.

Rachael had stopped crying and, in her mind, was trying to recall if someone might have seen her. The last thing in the world she needed was to be caught helping someone with assisted suicide. "Both of you just stop it right now," she said. "Let's just decide what we need to do next. What do we do? Call the doctor? What do we do now?"

"Let's call the police," Jesi blurted out.

"Police?" Nicole yelled. "What are you talking about, Jesi?" Her voice was raised, and she joined Jesi in pacing, but with her hands in the air. "We are not calling the police. We're calling an ambulance. They'll come over and handle it. I don't know what happened or if that person who left did what we think they did, but I do know one thing: Aunt Mary Opal was in so much pain that she wanted out. If she lived in Oregon, she wouldn't have had to stress out about it. It's called death with dignity. That's what she wanted, and it looks like that's what she got. So don't either of you think for a minute that any of us are going to make a scene out of this. Besides, if it's true, then there's no sign of helium. Her doctor will probably do exactly what Aunt Mary Opal said she would."

"What did you say?" Rachael asked, confused. "Did you say 'she'? Her doctor, did you say 'she'?"

"Yes. Aunt Mary Opal said she had talked to her doctor and that she told her there would be no sign of the helium." Nicole stared back at Rachael.

"Aunt Mary Opal's doctor is a he, not a she," Rachael said. "What is going on?"

The three of them headed back upstairs to the living room.

"My stomach's upset again," Jesi said. "It's so hot in here." She lay down on the floor, exactly where she always was during head-to-head meditation. "I don't think we should call the police. I don't think Aunt Mary Opal would want that."

Rachael walked into the hallway and lowered the temperature on the thermostat to 69 from 80. As usual, it was always one for all and all for one. They all three ended up head-to-head on the floor. Rachael picked up a pillow from the sofa and placed it where Aunt Mary Opal's head would normally have been. "Let's just think for a minute. WWAMOD?" Any time that they couldn't agree on something, they said "WWAMOD?" and their solutions came to them faster and easier.

That night was no different, as the solution came fast and easy. Jesi and Nicole had no idea who would have helped Aunt Mary Opal, and Rachael had no idea how the helium and equipment got out of the house. They all understood that the helium, if it was used, wouldn't even show up in her body. Aunt Mary Opal wanted out of pain, and she was, for good. They agreed to call the ambulance, and they agreed that Jesi would handle it because she wouldn't stutter on the phone.

Instead, Jesi couldn't even find the words. "911? Yes, I, um, I mean, I, um." Rachael took the phone out of Jesi's hand as Jesi slid down into Aunt Mary Opal's favorite chair and doubled over, crying.

"I'm sorry. She can't talk because our friend just died," Rachael said, handling the 911 operator with ease, answering the questions, and giving the information calmly and quickly. After she hung up the phone, she announced, "Now I think we need to call her doctor— him, not her. We don't even know who 'her' is." Her voice was sarcastic and pointed.

Rachael also made that call. "Is this Dr. Baker's answering service? I'm a friend of one of his patients: Aunt, I mean Mary Opal Shook. We came to the house to find that she has passed in her sleep. Yes, we called an ambulance. No, I'm not her daughter, just a friend." After she hung up, she started to cry and sat down on the sofa across from Jesi. "The answering service is going to let him know. We did the right thing by calling the ambulance."

It was twenty minutes before the ambulance drove into the driveway with its lights still flashing and lighting up the entire end of the street. The neighbors peeked out from the window next door. Rachael thought it was strange to see the neighbor, a retired general, looking back over at Aunt Mary Opal's house, and she hoped that he hadn't seen her there earlier.

The medical team came into the house and went

about their business as if her passing was merely routine. Nicole let them know that they had called her oncologist. It seemed as if they easily made the assumption that the cause of death was cancer. Rachael watched as one of the EMT's picked up the bottle of pain pills that rested on the edge of the dresser and showed it to her associate.

The ambulance and Aunt Mary Opal were gone within forty minutes. Rachael called one of Aunt Mary Opal's daughters, who seemed to be a bit detached. The daughter was going to inform the rest of the family, and Rachael assured her that they would secure the house and make sure that the hospital had her contact information. Rachael had never understood the distance between Aunt Mary Opal and her kids. She had learned early in their friendship not to talk about it. That was not the only off-limits issue; there were plenty of secrets. It was easy to make up stories about the dominatrix storeroom, but when Nicole, Jesi, and Rachael tried to make up stories about why Aunt Mary Opal's kids were so distant, they all got mad at her kids. They all knew to let those relationships be what they were.

Exhausted and confused, Rachael said, "I need a drink." She walked into the sunroom to get the Jack Daniel's, but Nicole stopped her.

"Here's the Jack. It's on the kitchen counter. Look, Aunt Mary Opal was drinking a Jack." Nicole pointed to the glass in front of Aunt Mary Opal's chair that was pulled out from the table. Jesi noticed that the chair Rachael always sat in was also pulled out from the table. Rachael was aware of Jesi as she glanced at the chair and back at her with a questioning look on her face.

The room was silent. Rachael filled the glasses with ice, and Nicole poured as Jesi reached over and retrieved the jalapeño cheese straws off the shelf and the Cheetos from the cabinet where Aunt Mary Opal always kept them.

No one spoke for a few minutes.

"What do we do now?" Jesi asked. "I feel so empty." Jesi put her head down on the table and covered her face.

"I don't know." Nicole's voice was empty of emotion. "How could I let her die alone?"

Jesi corrected her. "She wasn't alone, Nicole. Someone was here. It just wasn't us."

Nicole looked hurt. "Why? I thought she wanted me to be with her. Who was it? I don't understand what just happened. I'm so tired."

Rachael listened and shifted the conversation. She raised her glass close to the one on the table, and they all touch their glasses to Aunt Mary Opal's. "Okay, let's toast to Aunt Mary Opal. I think that's what she would want us to do. I think that's why she left her drink here. Whew!" Rachael sang out Aunt Mary Opal's cheer as Nicole and Jesi followed suit and said, "Whew!" Whew! To Aunt Mary Opal, our leader, our friend!"

They stood in a circle with their arms around each other. "Let's go, y'all," Nicole said, walking away from the kitchen table. "I'll come back tomorrow and clean up the kitchen."

"I don't think that's a good idea," Rachael said. "I'm cleaning it up right now. All we need is for it to look like we sat here with Aunt Mary Opal drinking right before she died. Call it a conspiracy theory if you want, but all we know is that someone helped Aunt Mary Opal tonight, and it wasn't us." She washed the glasses and placed them all back in the cabinet, while Jesi returned the Jack to the sunroom.

As they all walked toward the door, Rachael turned to Jesi and said, "Leave the kitchen light on." They shared glances at each other, not saying a word, and left the house with the kitchen light still on.

FORTY

AUNT MARY OPAL WAS CREMATED, and the funeral was scheduled for a month after she passed. The week before the funeral, Rachael scheduled all three of them at the hair salon for bleaching touch-ups and back-combs even though their hair was still a little shorter than necessary for a proper back-comb. Their hair appointments were on a Thursday, and the funeral was on a rainy Saturday morning. Rachael had purchased three clear plastic rain covers to cover their hair. That was a good thing, because when they arrived at the church, they were surprised at how many people packed the service. Aunt Mary Opal would never have wanted them to show up at the funeral with drooping back-combed hairstyles.

As they entered the chapel, it felt as if the entire congregation turned around to see them walk to their seats. They heard a few laughs and a couple of people gasp, and there were even a couple of elderly women who frowned in disapproval. It didn't matter. They each held their heads up high and made their way to the front, where they had been asked to sit with the family. When

Aunt Mary Opal's daughters saw them, Rachael noticed
that each of the daughters seemed to smile in complete
agreement that their mother would approve of their
back-combed hair. Later, one of Aunt Mary Opal's
daughters told Rachael that seeing them show up with
their hair back-combed and bleached made them feel as
if their mother were somehow still alive.

A COUPLE of days after Aunt Mary Opal's funeral,
someone from her family called and asked Nicole,
Rachael, and Jesi to join the family at their attorney's
office. Upon entering, Rachael noticed that a slight scent
of cigars and mold lingered in the office. The room was
small, and there was barely enough room to seat Aunt
Mary Opal's three daughters, Rachael, Nicole, Jesi, the
attorney, and his assistant. The attorney was an older
gentleman with thick white hair and a large, protruding
belly.

Jesi whispered as she pointed at him. "That's the
man, the one who was at her house."

"Ladies, as you know, we are here to read through
the last will and testament for Mrs. Mary Opal Shook. I
prepared this newest document two months ago, at her
request. It was signed and witnessed by my staff and
notarized by me." The attorney gestured to himself to
indicate that he had been the notary, as if he needed to
make a specific point that he was in charge.

Jesi broke in. "Why do we have to be here?"

"Jesi, correct?" The attorney seemed to be aware of
who each of the women were, and Rachael wondered
how he knew. "Aunt Mary Opal showed me photos of

you. Rachael will be the sweet one, Nicole will be the intelligent one, and Jesi will be the impatient one." He looked up to meet Jesi's eyes. "As to why we're here, I'll get to that in good time." He then proceeded to read the last will and testament of Mary Opal Shook. The attorney spoke in a slow, Southern drawl that made Rachael think that the entire experience seemed to be an extended moment in a Southern drama. He read for more than ten minutes, as everyone else in the room sat in stunned silence.

Aunt Mary Opal was apparently much wealthier than any of the three women had known. She left one-third of her estate—$1.5 million—to Rachael, Jesi, and Nicole. She had it placed in a trust fund and had set ground rules about how they could use the money. All three would have to agree on any money spent, and the money could not be given to charity.

"She knew that if she didn't make that a stipulation, you all might decide to give the money away," the attorney said. "She was clear that the money was for her friends to do things for themselves."

The last rule for the use of the money in the trust was that they had to have weekly ladies light luncheons as the official meetings to manage the money in the trust. Her only other request was that they use it to create a more joyful life for each of themselves. Her last words were: "Have fun, it's the best thing to have. One for all, all for one."

"There you have it," he said. "Those are her wishes, and that is exactly how we will carry forward with the allocation of funds."

Aunt Mary Opal's daughters stood up in unison. "We knew what it said," the eldest spoke softly to Rachael,

Nicole, and Jesi. "Mom told us how much she loves each of you, and God knows how much we all appreciated you being there for her. None of us were." The three daughters turned and left the room. The entire meeting seemed surreal to Rachael.

"What just happened?" Nicole stared directly into the attorney's eyes. "What's happening? I don't understand." She began to cry uncontrollably.

The attorney handed Nicole a box of tissue and leaned back in his chair, which creaked so loudly that it seemed as if it would break. "Ladies, Mary Opal loved you three so much that she considered leaving her entire estate to you," the attorney began. "But after many long conversations and a couple bottles of Jack Daniel's, well, let's just say she came to terms with a few issues regarding her daughters. There is just one other thing." He opened his desk drawer and pulled out a soft pink envelope with Aunt Mary Opal's handwriting. It read, *To Rachael, Jesi, & Nicole.*

"Ladies, Mary Opal wants you to open this letter thirty-five days after the night she died. That makes it four days from today. I can keep it here if you think it will be too tempting, but if you can keep it closed until that day, then I'll give it to you now. What'll it be?" He peered over his glasses and waited for one of them to answer.

Rachael reached out for the letter. "We'll wait. It's only four days from now."

"And another thing," he said. "She wants you to open it at 6:00 p.m. while drinking margaritas at your favorite Mexican restaurant. She said you'd know what I'm talking about."

FORTY-ONE

As Aunt Mary Opal had requested, they met at Pancho's. While the restaurant was a little rustic, the chips and margaritas were the best in town, and it was an easy drive home after a couple of margaritas.

As they were seated, Rachael noticed that their server placed four margaritas—not three—on the table. As she positioned the fourth one at Aunt Mary Opal's place, the server said, "This one's on the house."

"A toast to Aunt Mary Opal," Rachael said, lifting her glass. "We miss you."

The three of them clinked their glasses to the one on the table.

"This is so weird," Jesi said. "I just feel like she's going to walk up any minute and sit down with us." Jesi shook her head. Nicole reached over and held Jesi's hand. Rachael followed her lead, holding her hand as well.

"Okay, who should open it?" Nicole asked. "Rock, paper, scissors." Nicole motioned, as if already playing the game, by hitting her fist onto her outstretched flat hand.

"Oh, good grief," Jesi said. "Not everything has to be a competition. I'll read it."

Rachael burst into laughter. "Yeah, you? You mean like when you were supposed to call the ambulance because you would be cool, calm, and collected? You couldn't even remember your own name." Rachael and Nicole laughed.

"You're right, I don't think I can read it," Jesi said. "I'd probably just get snot all over it." She grinned, knowing that would get a reaction.

"Oh, Jesi, shut up!" Rachael said, covering her mouth as if she was going to gag, but she couldn't help but laugh. They were all a little nervous. Their lives had changed so drastically in the previous thirty-five days, and they weren't quite sure what the letter would be about or why she had directed them to meet at Pancho's.

Nicole reached in her pocket and pulled out a quarter. "Here we go, Rachael. Heads or tails?"

Rachael was a little scared to read the letter, so she figured the coin toss gave her a fifty-fifty chance of not having to read. Nicole flipped the quarter high into the air and caught it. She landed it on the back of her forearm as Rachael called out "Heads."

Nicole peeked at the quarter, hid it from Jesi and Rachael, and yelled out "Heads!"

"Oh no, I think we should do two out of three," Rachael said.

"Just kidding," Nicole said, picking up the pink envelope. "It was tails. I'll read it."

"A thousand times I've watched you two play that game," Jesi said to Nicole. "And almost every time, I am certain you make up the answer just to make Rachael happy."

Nicole smiled at Jesi but ignored her comment. "Okay, here goes." As she opened the envelope, sand poured out onto the table.

Rachael recognized it as sand from the jar on Aunt Mary Opal's kitchen counter, which she had collected from the Valley of the Temples in Sicily. They all three sat quietly, tears welling up in their eyes, as Nicole began to read.

To my dear friends, Rachael, Jesi and Nicole:

First, let me tell you that the love you shared with me made my life worth living. Without you, I would have lived out my last days alone. Thank you.

If I know each of you as well as I think, you are now sitting at our favorite table in the corner at Pancho's, you're drinking margaritas, and there is a margarita sitting in front of my chair. If for some reason you didn't buy me a drink, then Jesi, please reprimand Nicole and Rachael for me.

There are so many things I want to share with you, and if I could have things my way, I would be there with you. Please know that the only reason I left when I did is that the pain in my body from the cancer had become too much to manage and living with dignity would not be possible. I know some people believe that taking my life would keep me from going to heaven, but I don't believe that God would want me to live with the pain. I hope that as you read this letter, I am with him, and that he drinks margaritas also.

Nicole continued reading, but not without bursts of alternating tears, laughter, grief, and expressions of adoration from each of them. Their server quietly placed a box of tissues on the table.

Rachael, my dear sweet friend, you taught me to trust myself at a time when I desperately needed to know that my own feelings and opinions were not only justified, but were from good intentions.

We share the need to cater to the needs of our husbands above our own needs. When you made the decision to leave Jake, you did so from love, and you were bold and brave to do so. Rachael, I honor you for following your heart.

By now, I will have met your mother and will have told her about the beautiful flowers you planted at my doorway. I will have shared with your mother the constant and clear loyalty you gave not to just me, but also to Nicole and Jesi. She will have told me stories of you as a precious child and of your unwavering devotion during her illness.

Rachael, you were and continue to be my hero. My gift to you is freedom, freedom to know that loving yourself is the best way to love others.

Nicole stopped reading as Rachael jumped up from the table and rushed out of the restaurant in tears. Jesi followed her but stopped at the door, watching, as Rachael paced across the parking lot. Nicole placed the letter facedown on the table so she wouldn't read ahead of Rachael and Jesi. Once they were all seated again, Nicole began reading again.

Nicole and Jesi, remember the day that you joined Rachael and me in our head-to-head group meditation? Actually, the truth was that Rachael was trying to protect my secret, and in doing so, we simply made up the whole thing. That's how loyal Rachael is. I had fallen because the pain had taken over my body. She promised not to tell anyone, but you both came back upstairs from the basement so quickly. I will never know why in the world she decided to throw herself on the floor the way she did and land with her head touching my head. But, as we all know, good follows good, and you both followed Rachael like chicks following the mother hen, with total and complete trust. Once we began our meditations, I looked forward to them, and I always knew that Rachael would keep our secret.

"Fuck, I knew it!" Jesi burst into laughter, even though tears streamed down her cheeks. "I knew something wasn't right. There weren't any articles on head-to-head group meditation. I searched online for days."

Rachael took in a deep breath and pushed her lungs empty. "She made me promise. You know how she was with secrets. But I didn't know what was wrong. I didn't know she had cancer. She just told me that she was getting old and and that she tripped." Rachael stopped laughing and began going over in her mind the times she saw Aunt Mary Opal in pain and her last words, "I love you, too." For a moment, she felt guilty that she hadn't pushed Aunt Mary Opal to tell her the truth, but she quickly put the guilt aside, remembering how much Aunt Mary Opal loved secrets and how important it was that she lived life fully. They toasted again to Aunt Mary Opal. The laughter felt good.

Nicole ordered another round of margaritas and picked up the letter again. "Okay, ready?" They nodded their heads.

Jesi, you are my free spirit who has come to know that true freedom only comes through love. I want you to know that I saw you the day you followed me. I watched you from inside the dark oncologist's office. I saw your pain and your concern, but mostly I saw your commitment to loving and caring for me.

Nicole stopped reading and put the letter on the table. "You knew. You knew she was sick, and you didn't tell me." She stared at Jesi, waiting on a response.

"I couldn't tell you," Jesi said. "It was just a secret. I wasn't even supposed to know. I'm sorry."

"It's okay." Nicole began reading again.

I apologize for not allowing you to help me, and I hope you have forgiven me for not being ready to share my circumstance. From the moment that I watched you from that dark office, I never, ever questioned my safety, and I never felt alone again. I felt so much comfort in knowing that you are my friend. Thank you for constantly nurturing me.

Jesi, when you were lying in the hospital after the horrible run-in with the police, I sat with you and prayed for your healing. You don't remember what happened, and I haven't shared it with anyone. A sweet smell filled the room. It reminded me of the scent you described at your Noni's bedside and with your brother as he passed. Within a short time, all of the machines began screaming and the nurses came running to you. I backed up to the glass wall to get out of their way, and I began praying. You had died, Jesi. Those wonderful nurses saved you, and as soon as they brought you back, that sweet scent was gone. You opened your eyes and looked directly into mine. You said, "Antony said to tell you that he's waiting for you."

Jesi, by now, I will have met Antony, and I will have told him of how beautiful and free you are in your spirit. I will have told your Noni that her generosity and protection allowed you the freedom to seek and find love. Noni will have told me of how you protected Antony from harm when he was just a small boy.

Jesi, I want you to always carry with you the knowledge that Noni, Antony, and now, I, have surrounded you with our love and protection. We are watching you always.

Jesi, keep questioning things when it feels as if something isn't right, but commit to trusting yourself and your choices. That is the only way for you to keep love close to you. My gift to you is the freedom to commit to receiving love as intensely as you give it.

Jesi had wrapped her arms tightly around herself.

When she was able to stop crying, she unfolded her arms and reached out to Nicole and Rachael. They all held hands in silence. Jesi looked back and forth at Nicole and Rachael. "Thank you for loving me. I do love you both, and I do feel safe with you."

Nicole offered a little humor to lift the tension. "You better. I got hit by a police car trying to make you safe."

Rachael burst into a loud laugh and accidentally spit out chips. "It's true. I watched the whole damn thing." They all sat back and relaxed a bit.

Jesi turned her gaze to two women seated in a booth on the other side of the restaurant. "Hey, y'all, so what's their story?" She motioned to the two women, an African American woman who was wearing running tights and shoes and a taller white woman in a white coat that made her look like she was a doctor or a lab tech. The tag on her jacket was too small to read. They were each drinking margaritas, but a third drink sat on the table.

"I think they're waiting on another woman and they're going to have a three-way," Jesi said, grinning at Nicole and waiting for a reaction.

"Really, Jesi?" Nicole said. "You always think it's a three-way thing. Get over yourself. I think they're waiting for one of their mothers to get here, and they're going to come out to her."

They turned their gaze to Rachael. She kept her eyes on the two women across the restaurant, taking them in, and she focused on the margarita on their own table that sat at Aunt Mary Opal's usual place. "Funny . . ." was all she said. "Let's get back to the letter."

Rachael caught a glance between Nicole and Jesi, but neither questioned her. Nicole picked up the letter but then handed it to Rachael. "Would you take over?"

she said softly. Rachael saw that the next section was addressed to Nicole.

My sweet, sweet Nicole, I know you must be hurt that I didn't call you to help me. Please forgive me. There was a reason that I didn't want you to be with me at the end.

Nicole covered her face with her hands and leaned over crying. Rachael stopped reading and Jesi moved in closer, placing her hand on Nicole's knee. Only when she recovered did Rachael continue to read.

You see, my dear, I know that we shared a special secret, and you know what I am talking about. I am here in heaven now, where I belong. You are with Jesi and Rachael, where you belong.

Nicole, I watched you heal from the painful emotional abuse you endured. In some ways, it's easier to heal from being harmed physically. At least I was able to see my bruises turn from dark red back to the color of my skin. You had to learn to trust yourself enough to allow real love into your life. Learning to love yourself enough that you only allow love in is your purpose in life. The day you fell into my arms is the day that you became surrounded with love, devotion, and joy. Their names are Jesi, Rachael, and Aunt Mary Opal.

You have understood the importance of giving your whole life, sometimes being generous even when it emptied your spirit. Of all the people I have known in my long life, you, Nicole, have reached for and achieved success in everything you have attempted, and never did you do so if it would cause harm to others. Nicole, always trust your integrity. You live from truth. You live from truth so much that it was very difficult for you to cover up our secret. Remember that a little secret is healthy for the soul.

Rachael stopped reading. "Oh God, the secrets."

Nicole, you are a leader, and you can't change that about yourself. What you can do is never waver from truth, from generosity, or from integrity and love. When you lead with caring confidence, you are supported and loved. If you are met with anything other than love, devotion, and joy, do not hesitate to push whatever or whomever away immediately. You can only do that if you trust yourself. If someone inflicts pain or speaks to you harshly, that is their action, not yours. Love is always fulfilling. You make right choices because you come from generosity. Nicole, be generous from yourself only when you are overflowing so that you are never again left so empty that you can't see your value. Nicole, my gift to you is the freedom to live in the present moment. Let the past go. Look around you right now. You are loved.

Rachael and Jesi looked on as Nicole took long breaths and slightly shook her head up and down. She looked up and smiled, even as the tears freely flowed down her cheeks. Her face was confident, yet peaceful.

Rachael, Jesi, and Nicole, you are the gifts I wanted my whole life. Thank you.

This shall be the last thing that I want to say to each of you: Rremember to have fun . . . it's the best thing to have.

With all my love, always,

Aunt Mary Opal

"Wow," Jesi said. "I miss her so much right now." Jesi reached over and touched her glass to the one sitting on the table.

"I'm worn out," Rachael said. "I think I need to go home and go to bed." She started gathering her things as Jesi and Nicole agreed that they were exhausted as well.

Before they could get out of their chairs, they heard a woman's voice from across the room—it sounded exactly like Aunt Mary Opal's. "Whew!" They quickly glanced at each other in confusion and moved their stares, searching for the woman who had made that sound. She was nowhere. The front door was closing, and the two women who had been sitting in the booth were gone. They all rose up from their seats in time to see the woman in the running tights dance a jig in a circle, just like Aunt Mary Opal.

Rachael stopped breathing for a moment. "Do you think Aunt Mary Opal told them to be here at the same time we would be here?"

Nicole raised her voice. "Do you think that's the woman we saw leaving Aunt Mary Opal's house the night she died?"

"Shit, y'all," Jesi said. "They just got into an SUV that looks like the one from that night. Do you think they were with Aunt Mary Opal when she died?" Jesi started to wind up with mistrust. "I feel like we are all living some sort of CIA fantasy thing that she had going on. This is freaking me out!"

After they left the restaurant and as Nicole and Jesi sat in the car, Rachael used a cover story of needing to use the bathroom as an excuse to run back inside. She found out from the server that Aunt Mary Opal had been friends with the women who sat in the booth. They had been meeting there every other week at 6:00 p.m. for dinner and margaritas. One was a librarian, the other an oncologist. Rachael quickly filled with resolve. "If I didn't learn anything from Aunt Mary Opal, I learned that some things are best kept secrets, and that piece of information will stay just my little secret."

THE END

ABOUT THE AUTHOR

Shea R. Embry, a resident of Southwest Atlanta, is a woman of a certain age with a varied, and sometimes adventure-filled, background. Even as a young girl, Shea craved the ability to share stories, acting out every scene from a movie as her mother watched on.

Most of Shea's career was in the real estate industry, giving her a wide array of personalities to pull from. She has incorporated much of her life experiences into her writing, using her own style of artistic privilege to expand on her adventures.

Her main goal, as she writes, is to uplift her characters out of perceived or actual pain to states of transformational joy.

Transitional Fiction is her genre, incorporating stories that appeal to readers of Southern gothic, women's Southern dysfunction, and LGBT.

Visit her online at http://backcombandtattoo.com

ACKNOWLEDGMENTS

With sincere thanks to the following:

WYLLENE OPAL SHOOK, my mom, who always told me I can do anything I want. "You can go through walls if you have to."

LAURA VAUGHN, a light-filled friend who, by simply calling me "Famous Shea-mous", always reminds me that there are no limits in life.

CAROLYN FLYNN, my editor, was kind, encouraging, and detailed as she helped me get through my own lack of confidence as a first-time author.

A special thank you to: Bobby Ann, Nora, Jhonny and Boy Bobby, Todd, Richard, Trish, Kym and Herb, Nicole and John, Journey, Russ and Paula, Brandi & David, Shelly and Joe, KN Literary Arts, Nikki Van De Car, Michael Lucker, Writers Retreat Workshop, Hay House Writer's Workshop, and Amy Pursifull.

After a late Friday night of sharing bourbon and laughter, the last thing Jesi expected to see in her front yard, as the sun peeked through the passing clouds, was a stranger who would unknowingly change her life forever. Wearing an oversized black t-shirt with the arms cut out and a slit down the front from the collar to her chest, Jesi poured her coffee and stood in front of the large picture window that overlooked the front yard. The sun highlighted her tightly cut, muscular, olive-colored arms. Jesi's dark wavy hair, still messy from her night's sleep, was tucked behind her ears and her bangs drooped across her forehead.

Before she could even take her first sip of coffee she noticed movement in the yard near the curb. Startled to see what, at first, appeared to be a bag of trash, she nearly spit out the hot coffee, but instead swallowed, immediately regretting her choice as the coffee burned all the way down her throat.

When the bag moved two feet to the right, Jesi realized that perhaps it was a bag lady, not a bag of trash. It was a woman who was crouched down with her face less than a foot from the grass.

The sun was just peeking through to the lawn. The newly laid sod glistened with raindrops hanging onto their last existence before their eventual evaporation.

Without taking her eyes off the woman in the yard, Jesi moved her bangs aside and yelled, "Nicole, are you up? Come down here."

Nicole squeaked out a response. "I'm awake, but I think that last bourbon soaked up all the moisture out of my mouth. I need some water." Jesi glanced back over her shoulder in time to see Nicole, holding onto the staircase railing, carefully take one step at a time. Her dark red curly hair was matted up on the back of her head, pushing it all forward making it appear, to Jesi, as if she had teased her hair into a large bright red afro. Jesi held in a giggle as she watched Nicole pull her black Ralph Lauren silk pajamas, which had twisted around her waist, out of her crotch and back into place.

When Jesi turned her attention back to the woman in the yard she giggled at the sight.

"What are you laughing at? It better not be me," Nicole mumbled.

Jesi couldn't take her eyes off the woman in the yard. Her laughter billowed up. "Come here. You have to see this."

Nicole gulped down an entire glass of water and filled her coffee cup with coffee, cream and sugar. Standing side-by-side, Jesi and Nicole watched in silence for a moment. "Who is that?" Nicole asked.

"I don't know."

"What's she doing?" Nicole still had not taken a sip of her coffee. The woman held her complete attention.

"I don't know. But I think she's pulling weeds." Jesi's giggle returned.

"How long has she been there?" Nicole was not giggling.

Jesi's giggle turned to laughter. "I don't know."

Nicole shook her head back and forth turning back toward the kitchen. "God, I can't handle anything new right now, not with this hangover. Please make it go away. I'm going to fix breakfast."

Jesi's hangover was at least equal to Nicole's, so a distraction that allowed her to stay in one place was perfectly acceptable to her. She watched the woman focus on one weed at a time, sometimes twisting and pulling, sometimes pulling straight up, and other times using both hands to gather, twist and turn. All of the weeds were placed in a pocket on the front of the woman's worn apron.

As Jesi stood drinking her coffee and watching the woman in the yard, the house filled with the aroma of bacon and eggs. "Come on," Nicole yelled from the kitchen. "rbeakfast is ready. Let's eat on the back deck. I don't want to see what's going on in the front yard."

Jesi pulled herself away from watching the woman. The 1940 home was nothing like the architect had intended. After Nicole and Jesi purchased the home, their friend Rachael had designed and renovated the interior in a style that was more like an open loft than a single family home. The walls that once separated the entry, dining room, and kitchen were gone. Instead the open floor-plan created a view from the front door extending through the dining room and kitchen to overlook the formally manicured back yard.

The storm that had blown through in the early hours

had pushed the chairs on the back deck aside and had left a thin sheet of water on the marble table. After Nicole wiped the water away, Jesi slid the tan wicker chairs in place and covered them both with large beach towels. Just as they were finishing breakfast, Jesi's cell phone rang. "I've got to get that. It's probably Rachael, we're going to play racket ball later." As Jesi ran to the kitchen to answer the phone she glanced out the front window to see the woman still pulling weeds. Without looking to see who was calling, she answered, "Hey Rachael."

It was not Rachael and the voice on the other end of the phone was harsh.

"Jesi, did you know there is a woman in your front yard?" It was George, their neighbor who had moved onto the street just before Nicole and Jesi.

Surprised to hear George's voice, Jesi rolled her eyes and mouthed to Nicole, *It's Gladys Kravitz.* "Yes George. I do know there's a woman in our yard." Nicole could tell from the look on her face that a call from a nosy neighbor was the last thing Jesi wanted to hear on a Saturday morning. Nicole motioned to Jesi to hang up the phone, but instead Jesi decided to challenge him. "So, what about it?"

George pushed. "She looks like a bag lady and our neighborhood does not—"

Jesi interrupted before he could finish his sentence. "Listen George, New Orleans has a pie lady, a bead lady and a duck lady. Us, we have a weed lady. And there is no rule that says we can't have a weed lady." Her voice was raised with a sharp tone. At that she wished George a good day and hung up the phone.

Jesi turned in time to see the look of shock and

disbelief fade from Nicole's face and transform into a full on belly laugh. "We have a weed lady and George hates it?"

Still wound up from George trying to interfere with what happened on her property, Jesi ignored the laughter and found no humor in the circumstance. "Will you make our weed lady a plate of breakfast?" As Nicole started to object to Jesi's request, Jesi flashed her dark brown eyes and pleaded. "Please, please, please. It'll really make George mad and you know how happy that will make me."

Jesi knew that if she pleaded, Nicole would not be able to resist her. So it was not surprise when Nicole shook her head and smiled as she squeaked out a muffled word of agreement and headed toward the kitchen. Before Nicole could start cooking she glanced through the window at the front yard. The sun was beating down and the weed lady was gone. "She's gone."

Jesi had picked up the dishes and was just entering the kitchen. "What? What do you mean gone?"

Nicole motioned to the front window. "I mean she's gone. Our weed lady is gone."

Jesi carefully placed the dirty dishes on the white marble counter and rushed to the living room window. No weed lady. She opened up the front door and stepped onto the front porch stepping into a puddle of water that splashed up soaking the bottom of her sweat pants. The weed lady was nowhere, vanished. "Fuck. I bet George did that. I'm calling him. He had no right."

Just as Jesi picked up the phone it rang. Again, she answered and yelled into the phone without looking to see who was calling, "Damnit George, did you tell our weed lady to leave?"

Out from the phone came a loud high pitched laughter, it was Rachael, "What has George done now?" Rachael's laughter was loud enough to put a wide smile on Nicole's face. Jesi, on the other hand, was still not seeing even an ounce of humor in the situation.

"George called and put his nose in our business again. It's none of his fucking business if we have a weed lady." Jesi's seriousness was too much for Nicole and Rachael to hold back the laughter. When the laughter didn't stop Jesi finally lightened up and joined in just before Rachael yelled through the phone. "Jesi, I'm coming over. Make sure y'all are dressed."

The back door to Jesi and Nicole's house was standing open with the anticipation that Rachael would be running through the gate that separated their backyards.

As Rachael turned the corner into the house, she yelled, "What the hell Jesi? Did you say you have a weed lady? Like a reefer lady?" Jesi grinned at the sight of Rachael wearing a short white robe that failed to cover her tattoos and bright yellow clogs, and holding tall green coffee mug.

Nicole pushed her fluffy red hair back from her face, "She said a weed lady, like pulling weeds."

After Jesi and Nicole shared their entire morning events, Rachael put her coffee cup down on the counter and headed toward the front door. "Come on y'all, show me where she was pulling weeds."

Jesi rushed in front of Rachael toward the door. "I'll show you."

Nicole had been using the swiffer to clean up the water that had dripped from Jesi's sweat pants and grass from Rachael's clogs. She leaned the swifter up against the stairs and ran to keep up with them.

As the three of them stood side-by-side observing about ten square feet of grass that clearly had no weeds, Nicole and Jesi in their pajamas and Rachael only wearing her white robe, a sarcastic voice from across the street rang in. "So your weed lady didn't stay long." It was George with his brindle-colored Cairn Terrier mix named Zippy.

Just before Jesi started to verbally assault George, she felt Nicole's arm wrap around keeping her from turning around. She watched the wide-eyed exchange of looks between Nicole and Rachael. Rachael turned to George. "Hey George. Yeah, the weed lady's at my house now. We share her. I could ask if she'd work for you." Rachael wrinkled her nose as she looked back across the street at George's yard, "but I'm pretty sure her schedule is full." George huffed as he pulled Zippy's rhinestone studded pink leash and continued down the hill.

As soon as George was out of earshot Jesi leaned into Rachael, "Oh, that was good. I think it really pissed him off."

Nicole focused them back on the yard. "She did a good job. I guess it's not hurting anything."

"What did she look like?" Rachael asked.

Jesi motioned for them to go back into the house when she saw George and Zippy walking back up the hill, seemingly trying to get ahead of the dark sky and oncoming rain. "We couldn't see her," Jesi whispered. "She had on a raincoat and apron. She filled up her pockets with weeds. I think she should've thrown them in George's yard." All three tucked their heads down trying to hide their laughter.

As the front door closed, Jesi hid behind the draperies in the living room and peeked outside to see George standing over the newly-weeded patch of grass. Jesi couldn't help but think that she had just scored a victory over George, and wondered if they would ever see the weed lady again.

She was aware that Nicole and Rachael, both standing in the dining room, watched her as she concentrated on the front yard and became lost in her thoughts. Rachael broke the silence. "Hey, let's all get together this evening for meditation. I think we could all use it."

Nicole agreed. "Sounds good, but no bourbon."

Jesi, with a frozen gaze out the front window, quietly responded, "Okay, I'm in."

It had started to sprinkle as Rachael walked toward the back door to go home. She winked at Nicole. "Great, I'll bring wine instead." Right after Rachael walked out the back door, she ran back in and yelled, "Jesi, I'll pick you up in an hour. Get ready to lose at racquetball. And I want my house shoes back."

Jesi looked down at her feet and the house shoes Rachael had left the night before. "You get ready to lose. And I'll return your house shoes when I find them." She overheard Nicole and Rachael's laughter coming from the kitchen and then the back door close.